the wedding date bargain

MIRA LYN KELLY

sourcebooks
casablanca

Published by Sourcebooks Casablanca, an imprint of Sourcebooks, Inc.
P.O. Box 4410, Naperville, Illinois 60567-4410
(630) 961-3900
Fax: (630) 961-2168
www.sourcebooks.com

Printed and bound in Canada.
MBP 10 9 8 7 6 5 4 3 2 1

For Brit and Caroline.

Congratulations on your Happily Ever After!

Chapter 1

No matter what happened next, Max Brandt was *not* going to punch his best friend in the face.

No way. There were rules about that sort of thing, and Max was a by-the-book, rule-following kind of guy.

Rule number one: *There is a time and place for everything*.

And they were in a church, for fuck's sake. *The church*, by Chicago standards. A Gothic badass, sporting a pipe organ straight out of *The Wizard of Oz*. His upbringing may well have been on par with that of wolves, but a brawl beneath the vaulted ceilings and stained glass of Holy Name Cathedral was not gonna happen.

Not even when, two pew lengths and seven rows down, the best friend in question, Sean Wyse, was leaning in to the woman beside him and whipping out what was invariably some practiced line. Normally the polished bull Sean spewed to the press and female population at large didn't faze Max. But today? The guy's mouth was dangerously close to that glossy fall of chestnut waves, and suddenly the seams of Max's tux were straining as his molars ground together in a series of threatening pops.

If it came down to it, he'd haul Sean out to North State Street.

But it wouldn't.

Max was about ninety-three percent sure of that, because of rule number two: *Friends don't hit friends*.

Max hadn't roughed up a buddy since the tenth grade, when Danny Radovick made the unfortunate mistake of commenting on Max's little sister's *assets*. It had been a lesson for both of them. Danny gained a deep and abiding understanding of the value of keeping his eyes off Molly and his trap shut about her in general. And Max discovered his little sister had shit taste in guys, because she'd been pissed at him for months over ruining her shot at Danny.

Whatever. He stood by his actions.

But now, what kind of best man would he be if he showed up for the main event with matching sets of bloody knuckles and a split lip?

'Course, that might be a best-case scenario. With about fifty boys in blue already scattered throughout the first fifteen rows of pews to watch one of their own join in holy matrimony with the daughter of one of Chicago's political elite, he probably ought to consider rule number three: *Cops don't start fights. They stop them*.

Max wasn't about to spend his partner's wedding day in jail for beating the piss out of Sean just because the guy happened to have brought the one woman Max had trouble following his own rules around.

Sarah Cole. Christ, what was she doing here?

And what the hell was she doing with Sean Wyse when one week earlier Max had been within a stone's throw of getting her into *his* bed?

"I thought Sean was bringing Valerie."

Max quickly looked to Jase Foster, who'd somehow come up beside him without Max noticing. A couple of inches taller than Max's six foot three and with a build that was nothing to scoff at, Jase wasn't exactly known for his stealth, and Max hadn't even realized the guy was there. Perfect. So in addition to the bro-code violations in progress, Max was also losing his edge. A catastrophe for both his professional and personal lives.

Refocusing on Sean and Sarah, he crossed his arms over his chest. "He was until a couple weeks ago. I didn't think he was bringing anyone."

How did Sarah even know the guy? Max loved Sean like a brother, but seriously… Wyse made *him* look like a prude, which considering Max's vast and varied history with the fairer sex was saying something.

Jase scrubbed at the back of his head, a speculative look in his eyes. "With the press covering this wedding, no way would Sean bring someone he wasn't at least semi-seriously considering."

If that was the case, Sarah wouldn't have the first fucking clue about Sean's more colorful side. But Max knew, and no way was he cool with it. He loved the guy, couldn't ask for a better friend, but when it came to women—no. No girl he cared about was getting in with Sean.

"Think the new girl's already been vetted by his parents?" Jase asked.

Max was more concerned about Sean's plummeting chance of survival as he rested his hand on the small of Sarah's back. Because he knew that slick half smile his friend was wearing. Recognized the cut of his eyes. The guy was "on," probably making some joke that nudged the bounds of propriety but stayed within the lines.

And three, two, one. There it was. That bubble of laughter, pretty and light.

The sound caught Max square in the chest, busting open the vault where he'd kept the memory of it tucked away, along with the feel of her hair between his fingers, and the taste of her lips. The way she'd shuddered in his arms that one time—

Shit. There were probably rules about thoughts like those in a church too, but since Max was less than a hairsbreadth from doing physical violence to a guy he loved like a brother, he'd cut himself some slack to focus on the bigger issues.

Like stopping Sean from putting one more finger on Sarah, before Max couldn't stop himself from putting his fist into Sean's face.

"Nice laugh," Jase added, straightening his tie and then scanning the church, no doubt looking for Emily, his bride of one month. "This one seems livelier than Sean's usual fare."

Max was saved from needing to comment when Jase's face lit up like he'd just hit the Lotto.

"Hey, Em's over talking with my boss." Jase gave Max a knuckle bump and headed off toward his new wife. "Catch up with you after the wedding. Be safe up there."

"Yeah, you too," Max said, still focused on Sean and Sarah.

From across the distance, Sean straightened, a furrow digging between his brows. Probably sensing the impending threat to his as-yet-unbroken, pretty-boy nose. He looked left past one massive marble column supporting the ceiling, then right.

Right here. Max nodded. *Hey, guy*.

Sean visibly relaxed, but then he must have looked a

little closer, because those eyebrows he swore were just naturally that neat started reaching for the sky.

Sean pointed Sarah toward a woman she greeted warmly and started snaking his way up the aisle to Max.

"Everything okay, man?" Sean asked, having the good sense to stand a couple of feet off. "Could swear you were giving me that perp-assaulting-an-old-lady look there for a minute."

Yeah, he was being an asshole, Max thought. Time to take it down a notch.

Going for casual, he jutted his chin. "So you and Sarah, huh?"

"Sarah?" Sean's eyes dropped to Max's fist, and he took another step back. "Okay, I'm definitely missing something here."

Shaking out his hand, Max studied the ceiling for a second and blew out a slow breath. Because this was nuts.

But damned if he could stop.

"How long you been seeing her?" It was too much to hope this was a first date. They seemed too comfortable together. She'd laughed too easily, and with the way Sean had touched her—the way she hadn't really reacted when he did—there was some familiarity there.

"You guys serious?" Max's knuckles cracked, and Sean blanched.

"What the hell, Max?" Sean half croaked, his hands coming up between them.

The truth was that Max didn't know what was wrong with him, except that he needed an answer, like yesterday.

Sean backed up again. Only then the damnedest thing happened. Instead of the guy pissing himself, or going to his knees and begging for his life while offering up every no-big-deal-at-all detail there was to be had, the fucker chose that minute to remember they were friends.

And he started to laugh.

"Holy shit, Max," he coughed out, muttering a quick apology skyward before grinning back at him. "Dude, you scared the Chri—"

Again he pulled a sheepish face. Then wiping the grin from his mouth, he stepped closer. "Max, how do you know Sarah anyway? She's only been in Chicago for a week, and she said she was single. Besides, best I can tell, the longest relationship you've had in the past few years was that overnight with Kelly Monroe when she got herself drunk enough that you stayed just to make sure she was okay."

Sean wasn't wrong. Max didn't have any claim on Sarah. Never had, and those few hours before she disappeared the week before certainly hadn't earned him one.

Which made what he was doing all the worse.

Because Sean wasn't just a friend; he was Max's *best* friend, and had been for years before Sarah's smile had even had a chance to clobber him.

"It isn't like that," Max started, not as interested in explaining his own history with Sarah as he was in hearing about Sean's present with her. Then in his periphery, he caught the blur of an incoming bridesmaid, one hand clutching a pinch of shimmery slate skirt, the other flapping wildly at him.

"Max!" Avery grabbed his arm, urging him away from the guests still streaming into the cathedral.

Sean crossed his arms, waiting a polite distance away and not looking the least bit intimidated. Typical.

Turning his attention to Tess's maid of honor, Max

frowned, taking in her flushed face and panicked eyes. "What's going on?"

"It's Tess. She and CJ had a fight. Something stupid about him sneaking into her place last night for…you know."

Yeah, after being partners on the force for the last three years, Max knew exactly why CJ would sneak into Tess's parents' place the night before their wedding. Not like the guy was a monk.

"So they fought." This was pretty much an hourly occurrence and had been from as far back as high school, the way CJ told it. If they'd managed to make it through their wedding day without a major blowup, Max might have worried something was wrong. "What's the problem?"

Avery pushed to her toes and whispered, "She left!"

Christ.

Chapter 2

One week earlier

MAX RAN A HAND OVER HIS MOUTH, STARING UP AT THE pressed copper plates of Belfast's ceiling as he struggled for patience. There were certain things no man should be forced to endure.

"Fives, Max. Are we clear on that?" Molly Brandt asked, her head bowed over the stack of bills she was counting out on the bar in front of him. Blue eyes sparkling with mirth, she peered up at him from under a curtain of white blond streaked with teal. "Tens are better, but absolutely no singles. Trust me, you don't want to be that guy."

His baby sister lecturing him on the etiquette of tipping strippers topped the list. Man, he needed to get out of there. "Got it."

He reached for the money, but Molly splayed her hands over the piles, delivering another pointed look.

"And no touching. Not only is it frowned upon by the roided-out muscle protecting the girls, but guys who try to cop a feel are just gross."

This was what he got for asking her to break some bills before meeting up with the boys for CJ's bachelor party.

"Not my first rodeo, Mol," he assured her, earning a neatly raised brow that left him squirming where he stood. Because again, baby sisters and strippers were topics Max liked to keep as far away from each other as possible. Not an easy feat with Molly, who'd been up in his business for as far back as he could remember and showed no signs of ever wanting to leave.

Sean Wyse sidled up to the bar, still dressed in an immaculate suit, the single open button at his neck and a barely loosened tie being the only evidence he'd clocked out from the Wyse Hotel for the day. Nodding to Molly, Sean hooked the seat beside Max with a shoe that probably cost more than the monthly payment on Max's bike. "Yeah, dude, definitely no touching in the club. When the girls want to do more than dance, they give you their number or let you know where to meet them."

Molly stopped counting to meet Max's eyes for a beat before shaking her head with a laugh and handing over his cash. For as clean cut as Sean appeared, the guy had a wild side he hadn't quite given up yet.

"Who wants some rubbers?" Brody bellowed over Ed Sheeran's "Thinking Out Loud" as he emerged from the back hall behind the bar. Brody owned Belfast and was a friend who went back as far with Max as Sean, to those early days when they'd shared a quad freshman year. Their fourth, Jase, was probably still at work, or possibly sexting his new wife, Emily. Or begging her to let him get her pregnant.

"A little personal, Brod," Sean chimed in, fighting for the straight face he wouldn't be able to keep. "But I'm covered, thanks."

Grinning wide, Brody twirled a shoe box on the tip of one finger like a basketball and fell in beside Molly. His big-ass arms looked like slabs of beef beneath his black silk shirt as he dumped what had to be a hundred novelty condoms over the bar between them.

"Ordered too many of these last month for Lincoln's bachelor party. Happy you're taking them."

Molly cocked a hip against the counter, fingering through the assortment. "It's like guy confetti. Ooh, can I keep this one?" She laughed, holding up the foil rectangle with a little cartoon of Darth Vader captioned with *I will not be your father*.

It was clever, but seeing Molly that close to all those condoms was giving Max heartburn. Swatting it out of her hand, he growled, "They're for the party."

Another pointed look. "Worried there won't be enough, with all the women throwing themselves at you?"

Max inwardly groaned.

He had a reputation for being something of a player, but the truth was, the game was getting old. He dug women. Got off on finding out how many different ways he could make them moan. But this dance he'd been doing—keeping the conversation going for the sake of a connection deep enough to enhance the sex, while making sure he stayed well shy of anything that smacked of more than one night? Lately, he'd started to feel like he was going through the motions. Like maybe he'd rather just skip the dance all together.

Still, not exactly the kind of revelation a guy shared with his sister or buddies over a pile of rubbers. So he swept the spread back into the box and offered up a grin. "You know it."

—◦◦◦—

"Is this an intervention?" Sarah Cole asked her oldest friend and roommate of less than two hours, peering down at her lemon-drop martini before surveying the popular bar surrounding them. "I thought we were celebrating the start of my vacation and move back to Chicago, not forcing me to take a hard look at the blatant shortcomings of my life."

A mop of sandy-blond curls brushed against Piper Jordan's soft jaw as she took a swallow of her pink raspberry cosmo and shook her head. "See, right there. That's what I'm talking about. Only you would *dare* refer to a two-month stretch of forty-hour workweeks as a vacation. Do you have any idea how much it hurts me? There's something deeply wrong with that kind of thinking. It's like a disease."

If Piper had any idea what Sarah's workload had been like in San Francisco, or what would be expected of her once she got to New York, her friend would realize this two-month stint at the Chicago Wyse Hotel *was* going to be like a vacation.

"A disease with symptoms that include *success*? *Meaty paychecks*? And a little stamp that says *Next stop, New York*? Is that the kind of disease you're talking about?" Sarah teased, helping herself to another sip of what truly was an exceptional cocktail. Smacking her lips in approval, she set the drink back on her napkin. "Honestly, I know I work too much. My personal life has...fallen behind."

"It's been *stagnant*, rotting on the vine ever since Cory and his epic showing of scumbucketry," Piper corrected with a raised brow before taking another slurpy sip.

"You're just being dramatic now."

"So you do realize it's been four years, right?" Piper rolled the stem of her glass between her fingers, her eyes squinting as they met Sarah's. "Four years of letting life pass you by. Look, I know Cory did a number on you. And after, you felt like you had something to prove. But you've done it."

Piper reached for Sarah's hand and squeezed. "You know how proud I am of you, but it's time to put a little love into the life beyond your career. You need to have some fun."

Letting her words sink in, Piper angled toward the bartender and asked for another round.

Sarah shook her head, because as well intentioned as her friend was, she was totally off base. Sarah had a life, and she loved it. She thrived on the challenges of her career. Heck, she'd chosen this path, worked her ass off, and was joyfully reaping the benefits of all that hard work, focus, and determination. They were moving her to the *Manhattan* office, for crying out loud.

Sarah opened her mouth, but Piper cut her off by handing her the freshly delivered drink. "You deserve a life."

Accepting the cocktail, Sarah clinked her glass with Piper's. "I'm not unhappy."

"When was the last time you went on a date?" Piper pressed, her eyes sharpening like she was going in for the kill.

"It's been a while," Sarah hedged, not sure if she could really count that brief, painfully awkward and ultimately fruitless encounter she'd had eleven months ago as an actual date. Before that, she couldn't even say.

"I'm sure it has. And how about that *other issue*?" Piper asked, with a pointed glance toward Sarah's lap. "Any progress on that front?"

"Hey, eyes up here, madam," Sarah whispered, shifting uneasily.

"How is that even possible, Sarah?" Piper demanded, her expression falling somewhere between disbelief, pity, and disgust.

"I'm getting around to it. I've just been busy. It's not as easy as you'd think, okay?"

"Mmm-hmm. Right, well, maybe you can make it a priority during your *vacation* then." Piper's focus drifted past Sarah to the far end of the bar where another round of hoots and laughter sounded from the rowdy group celebrating there. "Since you'll have all this free time and everything."

The thought had crossed Sarah's mind. Things were going to be nuts once she got to New York. And even if they weren't, she wouldn't mind checking this box while she was still half a country away. Then by the time she arrived, she'd be just another girl ready to get on with her normal, albeit wildly successful life.

Downing a long swallow, she met Piper's expectant smile. "I don't disagree."

Before Piper could respond, a couple of guys from the bachelor party descended on them amid a flurry of thrown elbows, yanked shirt necks, and panted beer breath, coming to a stop with one last exchange of boyish shoving. Which was funny, because they had to be at least as old as she was, and she was pretty sure someone had mentioned them being cops.

"Hey, girls, our buddy's getting married," the shorter

one with the blond brush cut and dimples explained. "And we're out showing him a good time tonight."

Piper had picked up her phone and was texting when the taller one with the good hair cut in.

"Yeah, but it's a total sausage-fest over there. Any chance you two lovely ladies would join our party for a round of shots to even things out?"

Dimples snorted into his hand and then shouldered past his friend. "And before you say no because Jimmy here sounds like a perv, I assure you, we're all good guys. Except Jimmy. Who kind of is a perv—"

"Dude." Jimmy threw his hands over his chest like he'd been shot, earning a laugh from both Sarah and Piper. The guys were goofs. Just buzzed enough to be silly and flirty and entertaining—without coming across as obnoxious or pushy.

Not that she'd join their party either way.

Dimples shrugged. "Just telling it like it is."

Jimmy was shaking his head, laughing as he rounded on his buddy, demanding examples, which the other man lobbed back without so much as a breath of hesitation.

Sarah's phone vibrated on the bar next to her hand, and she glanced down at the incoming message from Piper.

> I'm betting someone at this party could have
> your little problem resolved in a jiff.

Alarmed, Sarah glanced up at her friend, whose thumbs were moving in a blur.

Another vibration of her phone.

> Unless you're still waiting for love.

The guys seemed to remember their goal and turned back, Jimmy running a hand over his styled hair, while Dimples nodded in that *C'mon, you know you want to* way.

Even as cute as these two were, Sarah really didn't want to. She didn't know them. Sure they might be cops, but the idea of throwing back drinks with a group of guys she didn't know from Adam? It didn't seem safe or smart.

A quick end to her virginity wasn't *that* high a priority.

She turned to Piper, but her friend's focus had shifted to some point over Sarah's shoulder. Her eyes were wide, her lips parted in what could only be described as awed appreciation.

"Jesus, you two, enough with the recruiting." A deep rumbling voice, edged with amusement and authority, sounded from just behind Sarah, freezing her in place.

She knew that voice.

Even eight years later, her heart skipped a beat and her skin started to tingle at the sound. No. There was no way it was him. It couldn't be. Sure, these were cops and this was Chicago—but still, what were the odds?

Slowly turning in her seat, she felt the air leak from her lungs as her gaze tripped over a set of powerfully broad shoulders and the tall, muscular frame supporting them; stumbled up to the solid, squared-off jaw and not-quite-straight nose she'd once run the tip of her finger down; and then finally landed on that mouth, currently set in the same off-kilter grin that had played peekaboo in her dreams for years after they'd said good-bye.

Max Brandt.

He was wearing dark-wash jeans with a thick, black

belt and a tucked-in, light-blue, button-down shirt that
was open at the collar. He hadn't noticed her yet. Not
that he'd recognize her even if he had, but those slate-
gray eyes of his were fixed on Jimmy and Dimples,
who he'd grabbed by one shoulder each, as they swore
up and down that the *girls had asked* if they could join
the party.

The laugh bubbling up within Sarah's chest had little
to do with the guys clowning around and everything to
do with her utter delight at seeing the unrepentant bad
boy who had become her most unexpected friend all
those years ago. And almost more than that.

How many times had she thought about him, wished
she'd made a different choice, and wondered what her
life would have looked like if she had?

Her phone vibrated against the bar again, snapping
her attention back from the intersection of Memory
Lane and What Might Have Been Way.

Close your mouth :-) PS, I love you.

Sarah snapped her jaw shut, but not before Max's
eyes came up.

"Holy shit, Sarah?" he asked, his brows furrowing
like he couldn't quite believe it was her. Like he hoped
it might be.

Nervously tucking a bit of hair behind her ear, she
grinned up at him. "Wasn't sure you'd remember me."

Max bowed his head, giving it a slow shake before
bringing his eyes back up to hers. "Think I'd know you
anywhere."

Distantly, she registered her phone sounding again,

but where she'd normally start to itch if she didn't have
the message checked within a half a second, right then
she couldn't imagine looking away from the man in
front of her. Not yet.

Not with that smile stretching wider every second.
Oh, that *smile*.

She'd broken every rule for that smile. Or at least
she'd been willing to.

Her phone suddenly appeared in front of her, and
Sarah had to blink to recognize that Piper was holding it
with the text she'd just sent displayed.

> Anything this guy asks, the answer is YES! We
> might have that little problem handled tonight
> after all.

Max hadn't been laying down some line about knowing
Sarah anywhere—though that was what it sounded like,
even to his own ears. With any other woman, it would
have been one.

Damn, she was still so pretty it hurt just a little to
look at her.

Her hair was longer now, those loose, dark waves
falling well past her shoulders, and her features weren't
quite as soft as they'd been at twenty, but the gentle
hollows and defined edges the years had added looked
good on her. Almost as good as that smile—the one that
had hit him like a freight train the first time he saw it,
and had him working like a fool to earn it as often as he
could for those two months after.

Her friend smiled widely at him and whipped Sarah's

phone off the bar beside her, shoving it in Sarah's face so she would see the text that had been lighting it up, he guessed.

Shit, he hoped she wasn't going to have to take off already.

"Sorry." Sarah laughed, a flush creeping onto her cheeks as she gently wrestled the phone free. "Max, this is my friend Piper Morgan. Piper, this is Max Brandt."

Piper did a double take, her hand snapping out to grip Sarah's upper arm, like maybe she'd heard his name before. A guy could hope.

"Shut the front door!" she gasped, that head of blond curls working back and forth like it was on a spindle as she looked at one of them and then the other. "This is *Safewalk stud*?"

A breath punched out his chest on a laugh. Based on the way Sarah closed her eyes in what he hoped wasn't too much embarrassment, he was guessing she hadn't coined the moniker.

"Damn, Sarah." He grinned. "And here I thought you'd liked me for my mind."

The corner of that pretty mouth twitched, and she turned her head in an abbreviated shake before meeting his eyes again.

She glowered at Piper in that adoring way girls had that threatened murder and a hug at the same time. Man, she was cute. "I swear I didn't call you Safewalk stud."

Figured. But that blush was priceless, and from day one he hadn't been able to resist teasing her just a little to get a piece of it. "No, no, I see how it was. All those nights after the library closed, and I was fool enough to think you were just taking advantage of our security program. But it was the muscle, huh?"

Sarah's head fell back in a pretty laugh. "The muscle? Max!"

Eight years ago, she'd have swatted his arm and looked away, like she was above his silly nonsense even though he knew she loved it. And in that moment, he could almost *feel* the back of her hand making contact with his bicep. But *this Sarah* hadn't touched him once. Not a hug, handshake, or physical contact of any kind.

Which was weird, because women were always touching him. More than he liked even, though mostly he let it go. But now, he was kicking himself for not just grabbing her into a hug when he realized who she was.

When she met his eyes again, Sarah let out a long sigh, waving her hand in mock defeat. "It's true. It *was* about the muscle. The late nights at the library were all a ruse. In fact, I'd plotted to wash all the Safewalk volunteers' T-shirts in hot water—so they'd shrink up and give me more of what I was really after."

Piper snorted from her seat. "Were you going to leave out the fabric softener too?" Looking from her friend back to Max, she rolled her eyes. "Her devious plots need a little work."

Maybe, but Max hadn't noticed anything beyond the playful glint in Sarah's eyes and the invisible tug he was feeling in the middle of his chest, begging him to get closer. It was nuts. She was just a girl. But as quickly as the thought crossed his mind, he recognized it for the lie it was.

Sarah wasn't—had never been—just another girl in the crowd. Not that first night he'd volunteered to escort her home from the library after it closed, and not that last night when everything changed. When she'd become more than a good deed, more than résumé material, more than a friend even. When he'd finally gotten a taste of the temptation that had been slowly driving him out of his mind since the day he met her. When he'd done the hardest thing he'd ever had to do and said good-bye.

It had been the right thing. There had been things she wanted for herself, things she deserved, that she wouldn't have been able to have with him. But now after all these years, here she was again, and he wasn't ready to let her go so quickly.

Clearing his throat, he nodded back to the party behind him. "I know Jimmy and Al already asked, but it would be great if you girls wanted to join us a while." A roar of laughter sounded behind him, signaling his reprieve was nearly over. He had to get back. "Maybe give us a chance to catch up some?"

Sarah looked undecided, which didn't really surprise him. But man, he wanted her to say yes. He wanted to find out how all those life plans she'd been making had panned out. Hear about what she was up to and how she'd been.

Figure out what to make of Sarah Cole being back.

He knew what the guy he'd been would have wanted, but Max wasn't the same man.

Piper took another sip of her drink and then cocked her head. "The man asked you a question, Sarah. What's your answer?"

Uh-huh, maybe that question was asking more than the words alone would suggest, but Max didn't care, because after a stiff breath when he'd been sure Sarah was about to decline, she hopped off her stool and said, "Yes."

Chapter 3

ONE LITTLE YES, AND PIPER WAS ACTING LIKE SARAH HAD signed a blood contract with the devil. Her friend wouldn't be getting her hopes up if she knew how things had ended between them back in school, but what happened with Max was one confession Sarah hadn't been able to bring herself to make.

No way would Max be helping her out with her little problem. He'd had the chance eight years ago—*and passed*. So, been there. Done that. Not up for another rejection.

"This isn't what you think." Sarah warned her friend in the thankfully clean and artfully decorated ladies' room. "Just settle down."

Piper wasn't convinced. Dancing her way into the first open stall, she closed the door and promptly started talking through it. "Pay attention, Sarah. It's totally what I'm thinking. Didn't you see how he was looking at you?"

Sarah crossed her arms, listening to the woman she trusted more than anyone. "I don't know. He's a player. He's wired to look at everyone like that. He'd look at your grandmother like that."

"No way. This is our guy! I can *feel* it." The toilet flushed, and Piper bounced out of the stall and went to the sink to clean up. "He looks like he'd be *good*, too."

That was what the rumor had been.

"We're just talking."

Eyeing Sarah through the mirror while they were touching up their lip gloss, Piper smiled. "Yeah, sure. And PS, I remember how you used to talk about him. You totally skimped on the details, because 'crazy hot,' while accurate, barely skims the surface with that guy." She tucked her lips together, evening out a fresh coat of gloss before elaborating. "I mean, those eyelashes! I'd kill for lashes that thick and long, but seeing them in the mix with that chiseled jaw and sexy mouth? Gotta admit, I'm a little swoony."

Join the club. "Yeah, he still looks good."

Dropping the gloss back in her purse, Piper added, "I'll get home on my own." Sarah opened her mouth to protest, but Piper held up a hand. "No arguments."

Back in the bar, the music was louder, and the crowd had increased to the point that weaving their way through the patrons took some time. When they arrived at the sectioned-off private party, Sarah's feet stayed rooted where they were, causing Piper to bump into her from behind.

This was bedlam.

A man was standing on a table and dancing between three women, two on one side and one on the other. He was wearing a white T-shirt covered in Sharpie marker, and his face was sporting a rash of overlapping lipstick kisses in various shades.

This was obviously the groom-to-be, based on the plushy ball and chain attached to his ankle and the felt top hat he was using to catch what looked like condoms being thrown by men and women alike from around the room.

"Maybe this was a mistake," Sarah said over her

shoulder, looking back in time to see an older man with rosy cheeks and a well-fed middle hoist himself up on a chair and start air grinding to the music.

Piper stepped to her side, standing close so their shoulders pressed together.

"Bite your tongue. I wanna watch."

"Yeah, but from the safety of where?" The guys were rowdy. Sure they didn't seem like they were going to hurt themselves or anyone else, but moderation definitely wasn't the theme of the night.

Piper elbowed her. "I'm guessing anywhere. Looks like your Safewalk stud is still volunteering to keep people out of trouble."

Sure enough, Max was rounding the table, amusement and concern warring in his eyes as he got ahold of the older man's sleeve and waved him toward one of the booths bordering the area. Whatever he said, the guy took it well, throwing his head back for the kind of laugh that couldn't be faked. And then he was walking to the half-full booth of guys.

Max looked up, catching Sarah's eye, and started over to where she and Piper were hovering at the edge of the room.

Piper leaned closer. "Vacation time, right?"

Right.

"Hey, girls, sorry you had to see that," Max said with a grin. "CJ's dad is a party kind of guy, even when it *isn't* his kid getting hitched. But tonight? Hell, I'm keepin' my eye on that one."

"So you're like the chaperone or something?" Piper asked with one of those pitying smiles she did so well pulling at her lips.

"Or something. I'm the best man. Which means the buck stops with me, and someone's got to keep these guys out of too much trouble." Max nodded toward the party. "Let's go," he said to Sarah. "I wanna hear what all has changed with you, and even better, what's still the same."

Sarah hesitated, but then Max flashed her a smile so criminally sexy that she couldn't believe one of these cops didn't slap a pair of cuffs on him. It was the kind of smile that screamed trouble…and this time, it didn't take any of Piper's reminders for her to agree.

For a guy who had what was widely understood to be serious game when it came to women, Max sure wasn't showing it tonight. Starting with inviting Sarah to join them for a bachelor party with a bunch of guys he knew were planning to cut loose in a way you didn't want good girls around. But damn, he'd wanted to talk to her, and one look was enough to scramble his brain to the point that something as simple as asking if she'd wanted to grab a cup of coffee the next day was beyond him. All he'd been able to think was he didn't want her to fucking leave.

He couldn't even blame the booze, since he was rocking a two light-beer limit just to make sure no one ended up getting thrown in the clink for drunk and disorderly. Not that he thought these guys actually would, but considering the shit that went down every time Jase Foster got called up to be best man, he wasn't about to take the chance.

Max had enough of a reputation without that following him around too. But more, tonight was important, meaningful, and he wanted to make sure that when it was over, everyone could look back with a smile and zero regrets.

Everyone except for him, he thought, watching Sarah and Piper dancing with CJ's dad, Carl, to Janelle Monáe's "Yoga," which was both hilarious and deeply disturbing. The girls were having fun, based on the laughter he'd caught when Carl and his gang of cronies descended on them. Unfortunately, that had been about when Max found himself tied up with Mickey, who he'd been tasked with not allowing to call his ex, and CJ, who'd been making teary-eyed, overemotional toasts to Max on and off for the last forty minutes. Plus, he'd been trying to hold off the inevitable. The trip to the gentlemen's club.

There was no getting out of being in charge, not with this crowd. But he'd thought there'd be more time before they needed to leave. Unfortunately, the natives—or rather, the rookies—were getting restless, and Max still hadn't had a chance to really talk to Sarah.

Her eyes were crinkled with laughter as Carl undulated to the song like his joints weren't already five years past their warranty. Max should probably crush a couple of ibuprofen and slip them into Carl's beer. Even if the old guy was shamelessly hitting on Max's girl.

The thought stopped him in his tracks, because Sarah wasn't his girl. Not even close.

She wasn't even his friend really, though he'd always consider her one.

She was just the woman he'd *mostly* known better about. An older version of the girl who'd gotten to him in a way he hadn't seen coming. She was the harsh reminder of why the rules he lived by were important—and how bad it sucked when he tried to ignore one. But even with that fuck ton of clarification, he was pretty damn sure what he wanted was to make her *his girl*.

The reasons he hadn't been able to back in college didn't apply anymore. They were both adults now. With enough life experience to land them on even ground. So maybe this was their chance. Their window for something short and sweet. Max wasn't built for more than that, and more importantly, Sarah was only going to be in town for two months before transferring to New York. He still wasn't one hundred percent sure what her job was. She'd tried to tell him, but then Carl had started doing a thankfully short-lived striptease. Needless to say, the crowd had gone wild, so Max hadn't caught all of what she'd been saying. Apparently, she'd been in San Francisco and was being promoted to a position in New York, but for one reason or another, it required some time in Chicago between.

Max stumbled forward as someone knocked into him from behind. Turning, he found Jimmy swaying where he stood. The guy was going to be feeling this tomorrow.

"Max, the girls. The *titties*," he pleaded, a lecherous grin on his face.

Jesus. "Yeah, in a while. Hang tight, man," Max said, edging closer to where Sarah was still dancing with the senior sect.

Enough was enough. Moving into the fray, Max caught her hand and nodded toward the far end of the room. Carl and the guys let out a few heartfelt cries of protest, but Sarah laughed, thanking them for the dances and flashing that killer smile like she had no idea the damage it could do.

"Hey, sorry I've been tied up," Max said, leading her toward the back of the room where they were out of the way, but he could still keep an eye on things. "Having fun though?"

"I am," she assured him, pushing her hair back from her face. It was slightly sweaty, and a few of the dark strands had begun to curl in front of her ears, but that little bit of messed up looked awfully good on her. "And don't worry about being busy. Carl's been filling me in on all your accomplishments. Sounds like you're a real hero."

"Carl's a good guy, but whatever he told you, uh, you want to take with a large grain of salt."

Despite the fact that he already had a kid of his own, Carl had taken on a sort of paternal role in Max's life. He'd been partnered with Max's dad back in the early days, and for whatever reason, even after Max's old man got kicked off the force and later did the rest of the human population a favor and succumbed to a stroke, Carl had kept up with Max. He'd looked out for him when he was a kid, making sure things weren't getting too bad at home, that Max had what he needed, and when Max joined the force, he took him under his wing. They didn't get any better than Carl. But sometimes the old softy got carried away trying to make sure Max scored the kind of happily ever after Carl wanted for him.

"So it's safe to assume you didn't *actually* stop the kidnapping of a poor orphaned girl today by pursuing her abductors on foot and then leaping an opening draw-bridge across the river?"

Max coughed into his hand. "Not so much."

"Or take down four armed assailants, bare-handed, to prevent the mugging of a sweet old lady."

He shook his head and wiped the smile from his face.

"Yeah, I kind of figured he was trying to lay the groundwork for you when he told me you'd taken a bullet for a little boy and everything."

Max shifted uncomfortably.

"Carl must like you a lot to be working that kind of hard sell."

"Carl needs a hobby," Max muttered, with a glance back at CJ, who was still table dancing.

"How about you?" she asked, peering up at him. "What do you need?"

Max grinned because if his ears hadn't deceived him, his favorite good girl had just thrown him a line. One she looked like she might be choking on, based on the way her features froze and how she slowly started turning away.

The pink burning up her neck and cheeks was about the prettiest thing he'd ever seen.

"That didn't come out the way I meant it," she sputtered, her eyes fixed on some point high above him.

Maybe not, but he liked the way it landed one hell of a lot. Even without much chance to talk, Max knew this woman in front of him already. And he still felt the connection he'd been tangled up in those last few months of school.

Catching her hand in his, he pulled her a single step closer. Felt the hard thud of his heart when she let him. And the harder thud when she met his eyes. "What I need is to hear what you've been up to since the last time I saw you."

—◦—

"Engaged, huh?" Max might have heard something about it. He looked back over his shoulder to see the guys acting like this was the first time they'd been let out of the zoo. Cringing, he asked, "This doesn't bother you, does it? Being at a bachelor party? Getting ready for a wedding?"

Sarah waved him off with a face he thought was sincere. "Not at all. First, it's been four years since I ended things with Cory—"

"Whoa." Max held up a hand to interrupt her. "I've got a really sweet kid I volunteer with named Cory. Any chance we can refer to your ex by something that won't leave me glowering at my man every time I see him?"

Her laugh was soft as she asked, "Like what?"

"I'm thinking 'that douche you used to date' but maybe just 'that douche' for short. Keep it simple."

Sarah's mouth dropped open, her brows rising in surprise.

"I get you've probably had time to deal with your feelings about what went down with this guy, but for me? It's still fresh." While Max was definitely working for Sarah's smile, it didn't make what he was saying any less true. He couldn't believe any schmo lucky enough to get a ring on this girl's finger could be dumb enough to dick around on her while it was there. How could he not realize what he had, how precious it was? Or how many other guys would have done just about anything to have it for themselves? Yeah, it pissed him off good.

"I completely understand. You need some time to process before you'll be able to let it go, huh?"

Max shrugged, then looking more serious asked, "You've let it go?"

Sarah nodded, those big brown eyes meeting his. "Four years is a long time. Longer than we were together. And the truth is, as mad as I was about what happened, I realized pretty quickly that a part of me was more than a little relieved when the relationship ended."

"Very mature of you," Max offered, thinking about the one time in his life when he'd been in that position, and how very far from mature he'd been in handling it.

"What's with the face?" he asked with a laugh, because clearly something hadn't sat right with Sarah.

"Ugh, the whole maturity thing. If I could go back and do it again—and I'm talking all the way back to school, not just 'that douche,' though he was definitely a part of it—I'd try to be less mature about everything and just live it up a little. There's a part of me that feels like I missed out some, you know?" Sarah cocked her head and peered up at the ceiling.

"You were pretty serious about school." He could remember trying to talk her into coming to a few parties, half admiring her focus and dedication, and half wanting to corrupt her. "There are worse things to be. You can trust me on that."

Her quiet smile pulled at that squishy place deep in his chest restricted to Budweiser Super Bowl commercials and viral Facebook videos of disabled kids finishing their first race. But then Sarah was dismissively waving her hand between them. "I know you're right, and I shouldn't complain about it. That unfortunate case of early-onset maturity got me a lot of places. It set me up with a solid foundation for after 'that douche.'"

"You're liking the name now. I can tell." He sure liked hearing her say it.

Her grin admitted as much.

"I used that foundation to launch my career."

"Marketing manager?" he asked, still not clear.

"Essentially."

"So you're doing well."

"I am. And from what Carl tells me, so are you."

Despite whatever conflicted feelings she might have had about her well-spent youth, there was no mistaking the pride in her eyes when it came to her career. And yet, something about her segue made it clear she didn't want to get too caught up in talking about it, which he got. Shoptalk was a handy fallback for those times when you just needed to fill the airwaves. But Max wasn't killing time trying to be polite.

"Okay, so what do you say we leave the jobs out of it and get down to the gritty stuff?"

Her head cocked to the side. "Gritty, hmm? Such as?"

Leaning closer, Max leveled her with his most serious stare. "Snack foods. What's your go-to?"

Turns out his girl had a weakness for trail mix and string cheese. And her laugh still got to him the same way it had eight years ago. The conversation came easily. They talked about what she'd missed most in Chicago (the summer festivals), what she'd loved best in San Francisco (being able to drive up to Tahoe for the weekend), and what she was looking forward to in New York (everything). He gave up a few choice stories from the academy days. Stories he never told anyone, but shared with her because he wanted to hear her laugh. And the more they talked, the more the years seemed to fall away, and details about this woman standing so temptingly close came back to him.

Sarah's drink was empty, so he took it off her hands and leaned past her to set it on the empty corner of the table behind them. It wasn't a *move*, but the action brought him further into her space. She peered up at him as he was looking down. Their eyes met and—Christ.

He should have looked away. Stepped back and asked her something benign about her new apartment or whether she had any pets. Only he couldn't do it. Having Sarah's eyes locked with his, that gentle puff of air teasing across his neck... It was too much, and he gave in to what he'd been telling himself he wouldn't for the last hour. He brushed those few strands of silk from her cheek behind her ear.

Soft.

So unbelievably soft.

And then, standing so close, with the backs of his fingers still smoothing down the fall of her hair, he felt it. That small quake running through her from his touch. She blinked quickly, but didn't look away. Didn't step back or give him any of the warning signs that would make him ease off.

"Sarah." He didn't know what he was about to ask, but seeing her looking up at him like she had that last night, he had to say her name.

The distance between them closed, and Max realized that this time he hadn't been the one to do it. *Sarah*.

It was like a switch had been thrown, and that low buzz beneath his skin became a high-voltage current coursing through his veins. He went from barely skimming his fingers over her hair to sliding his hand beneath it, cupping her neck, and drawing her close. Her focus dropped to his mouth, and every fuse in his body blew at once as—

The air punched out of Max's lungs as one hundred and eighty pounds of drunk-ass landed on his back. Sarah stepped clear, those deep mahogany eyes darting away. *Damn it*. Max tried to catch her, but CJ was hanging tight, his arms in a sloppy choke hold.

Hot beer breath washed over Max's cheek. "Dude, this is the best party ever. I love you, man."

Max cranked his head around and gave his partner a grin as he took advantage of an open pressure point to get CJ to release his hold—nicely, because the night was about CJ and it would be a total dick move to get pissed at the man of the hour for getting in the way of the girl of the night. Except that wasn't what this was. Sarah could never be that. Not to him.

Once he had his windpipe back and knew CJ was still good to stand on his own feet, Max turned back to her.

"You okay?" he asked, hoping he hadn't bumped her or anything when CJ landed on him.

She was several steps away now, the distance growing as the guys started to gather around.

"I'm fine," she said with a smile, but he could see from her expression that she might be a little embarrassed by what had almost happened, which made him feel shitty. Because even all these years later, it would be nuts to think *that much* had changed. Sure, she wouldn't be saving herself for love anymore. She'd found it for a while—though damn, it bummed him out to think about a guy so unworthy taking something that meant so much to her. He stepped toward her, but then someone had his arm. It was Carl, so Max ducked his head to hear the older man.

"Time to hit the next stop, kid."

Max winced. The next stop was the gentlemen's club, and no way was he going to be able to ask Sarah to join them there. She was standing off a ways with Piper, both girls laughing.

When Sarah's head came up and their eyes met, he signaled for her to give him a minute. He got the tabs and tips squared away, while the guys started filing out for the cabs.

"Yo, Brandt," Lopez called from across the room, looking a little too amused for Max's taste. "Jimmy's in the can, and, uh, you want to come help out a sec?"

Max grimaced. He'd had a feeling about that guy. "Yeah," he replied. *Give me a minute*, he mouthed to Sarah.

That minute took closer to ten, and once Max had finally poured the rookie into a cab with Lopez, who'd agreed to get him home before meeting them back at the club, Max jogged back into the bar to find Sarah. To make some plans. Any other woman, and he might have offered to show up at her place after the club. Any other time, he would have left with her already. But not with Sarah and not tonight.

He walked through the bar but didn't see her.

She wouldn't have taken off like that unless she'd thought he was already gone when he'd been waiting on Jimmy to finish hurking his guts out. *Shit*. Max made another pass and even asked the girl who'd been handling their party if she'd check the ladies' room for him. But he already knew.

Sarah was gone.

Chapter 4

Present day

SARAH HADN'T INTENDED TO WORK THAT DAY. NOT REALLY.

Sure, going to a wedding as her boss's quasi-date wasn't exactly the day off. But despite not knowing any of the guests or even the couple getting married beyond that the bride's father went back with Sean's, it was supposed to be a social thing. A favor for both of them. Sean needed a date, and she needed...well, a life. Or at least that was what Piper seemed to think, and dang it, Sarah knew her friend was right.

Which was why she was at this wedding. To have some fun and spend a few hours functioning like a normal human being and, even if she was there with her boss, to forget about networking and just enjoy a celebration for one afternoon. She'd thought about Max and wondered how CJ's wedding was going, hugged her stomach when she thought about the way she'd left the party. What a coward she'd been. But fortunately, it didn't take long before her focus shifted back to the safety and comfort of work, and that part of her brain she couldn't turn off started making connections. The ideas were there, the scent of opportunity thick in the air, and pretty soon she was skating through those immense church doors into the breezy midsummer morning and stealing around the corner to use her phone. She'd fired off one email and was halfway through another when she heard it. The throaty rumble of a motorcycle revving its engine as it roared past.

Another guest stepped up beside her, blond hair with a teal streak blowing in the wind and her pretty face split in a delighted grin. "Now *this* is a wedding."

As Sarah turned toward the rumble just as it cut off behind her, her breath caught and she let out a stunned laugh. "I have to agree."

There at the curb half a block down, the bride climbed off the back of the bike, piles of soft tulle falling about her legs in ruffled layers as she threw her arms around the driver for a quick kiss on the cheek before turning to the waiting groom, who'd come tearing around the corner when the bike pulled up. He pushed his hair back with both hands, revealing a face etched with relief and apology. And then he pulled his bride into his arms and kissed her like the war had just ended, complete with a deep dip…and tongue.

Yikes, that was definitely tongue.

A round of applause sounded from the few pedestrians and guests lucky enough to catch the fireworks, and Sarah sighed, just as the woman beside her commented again.

"I don't know. I'm thinking these two might have just ruined me for all other weddings. And seriously, how can the rest of the day or anything else stand up to *this*."

Sarah laughed again, turning to the woman. She looked about her age and height, maybe a little taller, and was standing with her arms crossed, hip shot to the side. She was pretty and vaguely familiar, though Sarah couldn't place her. Not even when those bright-blue eyes met hers.

"Sorry for staring. I was thinking we'd met some-where," Sarah offered. "But maybe not. I'm Sarah Cole."

The girl stuck out her hand for a firm shake. "Molly. Molly Brandt. James Bond over there on the bike is my brother, Max."

Sarah blinked, holding her smile in place as her belly proceeded to pitch and dive.

Slowly, she turned to where the bride was now laughing with her head thrown back. The groom—without the lipstick-covered face, Sarah couldn't tell if it was CJ—was down on one knee on the sidewalk, professing something Sarah might have wanted to hear if her atten-tion hadn't been fully occupied by the *other* man in a tux. The one with his back to her, climbing off the bike he'd just parked in its narrow spot.

He straightened to his full height, shrugged a set of broad shoulders to adjust his tux, then pushed a hand back through the short brush of his hair.

Sarah tried to swallow past her too-dry throat and felt the slow churn deep in her belly at the sight of that familiar motion. She should have waited for him at the bar last weekend for a lot of reasons. But specifically, right now? Because this was going to be awkward.

Maybe he wouldn't see her.

A shrill whistle cut through the air, nearly sending Sarah out of her skin.

Molly pulled her fingers from her mouth and bounced a couple of times beside her. "Hey, Max!" she hollered, sticking her thumb in the air. "Nice entrance!"

And then Max was turning their way, his brows pulled together as he slipped off his mirrored aviators. Sarah might have been able to convince herself he hadn't noticed her except then, there it was. That smile she remembered all too well. The dangerous, almost aggressively sexy slant of his mouth and—

Molly coughed beside her. "Okay, that smile *definitely* isn't for me. Who are you again?"

Sarah opened her mouth, but a shaky breath was all that made it past her lips. Because Max was walking toward them, those long, powerful legs eating up the sidewalk with purposeful strides until he was right there. Impossibly handsome. Broad and imposing. Clean-shaven and wearing a tuxedo that looked like it had been made for him.

She swallowed.

He looked good.

After a quick nod of greeting to his sister, he turned to her with that brain-numbing smile going full tilt. "Sarah, long time." Oh man, she should apologize for leaving the bar. But with his sister standing there? Explaining how nervous she'd gotten wondering if maybe she could convince him to sleep with her? It didn't seem the way to go.

"Quite a show back there," she remarked instead, stunned that despite the utter chaos happening deep inside her, she'd found the words to reply. It shouldn't have surprised her though. Her years at Wyse had honed her social skills to such a sharpened edge that Sarah could have made comfortable conversation with an invading alien species. "Good to see everyone recovered from last weekend. How are you?"

"Yeah, Max," Molly chirped from beside them, reminding Sarah that the outside world hadn't faded completely away. "How are you?"

"Good, but late for a wedding, I think," he answered, nodding back to the bride and groom who were starting to walk toward the doors to the church.

One of the bridesmaids was signaling for everyone to go back inside. Sarah smiled through the butterflies batting around in her belly. "Better hurry then, unless you're planning another dramatic entrance during the ceremony."

"Nah, I've met my quota for the day." His eyes cut off to the right, and his smile slipped as Sean approached and stepped between them to set his hand at the small of her back.

"Hey, Moll. Max," he greeted them, flashing his even, white smile. "Sorry, but I need to borrow my date."

Sean knew Max? Thank God she hadn't had the guts to proposition him!

"*Your* date," Molly asked, raising one neat blond brow as she looked from Sarah to Sean and then back to her brother, who wasn't smiling as he stood with his arms crossed over his broad chest. Finally, Molly settled on Sarah, the grin on her face wide and full. "Forget what I said. This wedding's going to be plenty entertaining."

The Wyse Hotel gave good reception. No two ways about it.

Standing amid a group of cops gathered by the upstairs south bar in the two-story Grand Ballroom, Max shook his head at the passing server and her tray of offered carpaccio roses. Tasty little suckers, but his mind wasn't really on the food or drinks, or even the freshly minted married couple making the rounds with Tess's father.

Max crossed his arms, propping a shoulder against the arched balcony doorway, and watched below as Sarah chatted and charmed one guest after another.

Christ, she was pretty.

With those long, warm brown waves and her silky length of neck adorned with a single square charm resting at the hollow, she looked as smooth and polished as her absentee date. And that observation was giving Max heartburn. Because maybe he'd been asking himself the wrong question, wondering what Sarah was doing with a guy like Sean. Maybe he should have been asking how serious Sean was about her. He hadn't even wanted to consider the possibility when Jase brought it up, but Sean had been ready to settle down for years and Sarah fit the bill. She was poised and polite, beautiful with a girl-next-door look, a good woman with a "quality" family behind her.

Damn it.

Turning to the bar, Max walked over to Sean, who'd yet to swear the blood oath to stay away from Sarah that Max had been waiting for. Hell, the guy hadn't actually given up anything but a few laughs at Max's expense before his best-man responsibilities had called him away. Then after the ceremony, Sean had been tied up with hotel business, which was why Max had been keeping his distance from the only woman he wanted to talk to. Because what his best friend had to say was going to radically impact the kind of conversation Max and Sarah had after.

"So you were telling me about Sarah," Max prompted, leaning back against the bar.

Sean accepted his drink with thanks and a folded bill

for the bartender, then took a leisurely sip before meeting Max's eyes. "I was wondering how long it would take for you to circle back around."

Asshole. He was enjoying this. Just like Max would be if the tables were turned.

"Might be smarter to wonder how long it's going to take me to get Molly to post that St. Paddy's Day picture of you from junior year. You know the one. You were bent over the bridge puking out your nose with your pants low enough to show off the shamrock tattoo? Amazing how you can still totally see your face though."

All amusement left Sean's eyes, and he downed half his drink in one swallow. "*Temporary* tattoo. And easy, killer. Sarah has been working marketing out of San Francisco Wyse the last three years, which is how I met her."

"She said she was only in Chicago a few months."

"Yeah, but I'll get her to stay."

Something hard and painful lodged in Max's throat. Because if Sean had brought Sarah halfway across the country, the guy had intentions. Intentions Max would have been privy to if he hadn't been such a little bitch about staying out of Sean's romantic affairs. Yeah, the recreational stuff could get a tad more colorful than Max was into, and the flat-out wife hunt was mind-numbingly boring. But still. If he'd been paying attention, maybe he would have known about Sarah from the start. He could have steered Sean away. Or tried to.

"So she's here for you?"

Sean was scanning the crowd, offering a nod and truncated wave here and there. Casual, like he hadn't noticed that Max was wrestling with some seriously primitive shit while waiting on his answer.

"Got her moved in on Monday."

The vein at Max's temple was threatening to pop. "She's *living* with you?"

How the fuck was that even possible? She'd said Piper was her roommate the Friday before.

Sean's face screwed up and he let out a short laugh, doing a double take when he saw Max's face. "What? No, man. Her new job isn't opening up in New York until September first, so she's here filling in while we have a couple of people out on leave. It's not glamorous, but we need a hand and she's got the time and doesn't need any training. She started this week."

The vise around Max's chest loosened, and he had to look away as he sucked in a full breath.

"Your turn. What, did you let her talk you out of a ticket or meet her at the gym? Who's Sarah to you, 'cause I've been racking my brain trying to figure it out and I've got nothing."

Max walked up to the rail and looked over at the sea of guests. "You remember that girl from the library senior year? The one from Safewalk?"

Sean nodded, raising his glass to his lips.

"She's *that Sarah*."

The bourbon his buddy had presumably been aiming to swallow came rushing back on a cough that couldn't have felt good, based on the resulting watery eyes and garbled swearing.

Then wiping his nose with a cocktail napkin, Sean gaped at him. "Shut the fuck up."

Max cleared his throat and adjusted his stance, at

which point Sean must have remembered they weren't kicked back in his apartment or Belfast and pulled it together. That was the kind of slip Sean Wyse just didn't make. His jaw disengaged from the floor, the nearly perfect posture corrected itself, and with one smoothing stroke of his hand, every golden strand fell in line and that perpetually photogenic smile was back in place. "Talk."

Yeah, what could he really say? "I ran into her last weekend at the bachelor party. We were hitting it off like we used to"—and also not quite like they used to— "but she left before I could get her number."

"So here's the deal," Sean began in a measured tone, straightening his tie. "This isn't a real date. With things on hold with Valerie, I needed someone to bring, and Sarah was looking for something to do. Though in the name of full disclosure, I'd been thinking about making it a real date or maybe even... But it doesn't matter. I won't. I haven't gotten any vibes off her, and honestly, the way she's dedicated to her career, I don't think she'd risk screwing it up, even if I offered her a five-karat diamond and a prenup guaranteeing her half my interest in the chain."

Sean looked at Max and then leaned over the rail, no doubt finding Sarah before returning a skeptical look. "Damn, man. No wonder you were looking at me like you wanted to tear my arms off and beat me with them. *That Sarah?*" he asked, like he couldn't quite believe it.

Join the club.

Another shake of his head, and Sean added, "So I guess she didn't get married after all, huh."

Max cracked his neck. "Guess not."

———

Sarah stepped back from the gleaming vanity in the first-floor ladies' room and recapped her lipstick, marveling at how free women could be with their secrets within this public yet sacred space. So far she'd learned that one of the bridesmaids was fooling around with two different guys, both of whom were at the wedding; that three years ago, the bride's mother had offered her daughter a Mercedes if she'd break things off with CJ; and that the blond in the second stall was totally going to "do" the best man.

Max.

Good luck finding the guy. With dinner service complete, Sarah still hadn't caught more than a fleeting glimpse of those broad shoulders and that thick dark hair disappearing into the crowd. Which she probably deserved after the way she'd left the bar, but it was frustrating the heck out of her nonetheless, because during the ceremony—which had been lovely, according to everyone who'd been able to keep their eyes on the nuptials themselves—the best man had managed the impossible and finally, unequivocally distracted her from all thoughts of work.

Too bad he'd done it while she was sitting in the middle of Holy Name Cathedral with her boss beside her in the pew as she prayed lightning wouldn't strike her down for wondering if Max Brandt was still the bad boy he'd been in school. For hoping he might be. For wanting to believe he wouldn't still be hung up on trying to protect her from herself.

Leaving the chattering wedding guests in their

presumed cone of silence, Sarah returned to the party. Feeling at loose ends, she'd already checked in with the various bartenders, the orchestra, and the head server to see if there was anything they needed, but the Wyse team was running like a well-oiled machine. So she did what she'd come to do and snagged a flute of champagne from a passing tray with the intent of hitting the terrace for some fresh air and conversation.

She turned and smacked into a brick wall.

Or at least a man built like one. Breath rushing out as champagne spilled down her cream silk blouse, Sarah closed her eyes for one bracing second. Because that fast, she knew. She recognized the low current sizzling over her skin at the points where two strong hands were wrapped around her upper arms, and the punch of breath above her head.

Max.

Squinting one eye open, and then the other, she followed the trail of studs up the center of the tuxedo shirt two inches in front of her face, past the not-quite-neat tie to the olive skin of his neck, the solid jaw, and the hard set of a mouth she knew from experience could be so incredibly soft. Not now though.

"I'm sorry," she gasped, mortified by her clumsiness and certain beyond a shadow of a doubt that she'd just doused whatever spark of hope there might have been for her fantasy to become reality.

Damage control time.

She took a step back, or tried to, but—

"Oomph… Um, Max?" she asked, finding herself pulled forward again. Harder. Closer.

His hands were locked around the bare skin of her

upper arms, his chest firm and solid and strong against her own. The air in her lungs leaked out as she finally met Max's eyes.

"Sarah, wait." His voice was so deep. "Let me give you my jacket," he said, releasing her arms to shrug out of it. "Just don't step back until I do."

She gasped as the cool air touched all the places where her blouse clung wet to her skin, and a downward glance confirmed the damage was about as bad as it could get.

"Oh no," she murmured, feeling the heat of embarrassment build as she stared at the wide swath of clinging transparent silk and the distinctive lace outline of her demi-cup bra, which wasn't nearly thick enough to do anything but draw more attention to what was beneath. Her hands crossed over her chest, and she shot a panicked look around them, wondering how big an audience she'd had for this little show.

Max quickly swung his jacket around her shoulders and pulled it closed in front.

"My hero," she whispered on a quiet laugh, and this time, when Sarah looked into his face, those stormy eyes she remembered so well were looking back at her.

Her stomach dipped and the air felt thin, because of *those eyes*. There was something about the way he looked at her that scattered her thoughts and sent her heart into overdrive. Always had.

"Yeah, I'm taking my position as best man seriously," he said gruffly. "Making sure no one competes with the bride for attention on her big day." Then rubbing the back of his neck in a way Sarah couldn't help but notice pulled the wet fabric of his shirt taut around his bicep, he squinted at her, that half-cocked smile doing things it really shouldn't. "At the risk of this sounding like a line, what do you say we get out of here and find someplace private?"

Chapter 5

"NOT EXACTLY HOW I PLANNED TO GET YOU ALONE," MAX stated, his low, rumbling voice sending chills skating over Sarah's skin. "Think you'll be able to use a blow-dryer or something to save your top?"

"Um, something." She kept a few things in her office, though she couldn't recall exactly what they were. Her head was spinning, because not only was she swimming in Max's jacket, breathing in the clean Irish Spring scent of him, but he'd rested his hand at the small of her back as they left the reception and headed toward the staff elevator at the far end of the hall. And that subtle touch? It felt so good.

Too good.

Which meant with every step that passed, the tension between them—or maybe just within her—was building. The pressure strangling whatever rational thoughts she had left until finally they were standing at the elevators alone. Nothing to do but wait for the car to arrive.

She couldn't take it anymore.

"Max, thank you for this. But you're the best man. You don't have to come with me. I'll get fixed up and bring your jacket back down. Go enjoy the party."

The corner of his hard mouth softened as he adjusted his crossed arms over his chest. "Trying to get rid of me, Sarah?"

She was. Which was crazy, considering she could

practically feel the singe marks on her eternal soul for what she'd been thinking back in that church. But he made her so nervous that she could barely breathe.

Shaking her head, she smiled at him. "I just don't want you to miss the reception because of me."

The elevator chimed, and the doors slid silently open. Max extended his arm and then followed her in. "I was on my way to talk to you. So looks to me like I'm getting exactly what I was after."

She laughed. "Champagne spilled down your shirt?"

Another cut of those eyes. "Pretty sure the bulk of it went down *your* shirt, and as guilty as I feel about it, that was probably the highlight of my year." Max returned to watching the floors pass on the numbered panel, but she couldn't miss the twitch of his mouth. "I'm not proud."

Suddenly, that nervous tension building within her eased.

Because this was just Max. Not like he'd been that last night back in school, but Max like he'd been all the nights that had come before. Flirting and teasing the smiles and laughter out of her as they walked from the library back to her dorm.

Pulling the lapels of the jacket tighter, she leaned into the corner of the car. "The other night. I'm sorry I took off without saying good-bye."

There, she'd said it. Broached the subject she couldn't ignore.

Max nodded, letting a beat pass before asking, "So why did you?"

"You made me nervous," she admitted. Only that wasn't quite the truth. Max turned to her, and she sighed.

"Or rather, the way I was thinking about you made me nervous. So I guess, *I* made me nervous. It wasn't anything you did."

"Nervous, huh?" He cocked his head to the side, a playful glint in his eyes. "I suppose a gentleman wouldn't press for details about what exactly you were thinking."

Time for a change of subject, because no way was she giving that up. "So aside from tonight's wet tuxedo-shirt contest victory, what have you been up to this week, Max?"

A dimple winked at her from his cheek, and her heart skipped a beat.

"Not much," he answered easily, letting her off the hook. "You know, keeping the streets safe, sanding floors, and thinking about a certain girl who got away."

Her head came up in surprise. Not about the girl getting away. That was just classic flirty Max. But… "Sanding floors?"

Eyes lighting up, Max grinned. "Yeah, guess I didn't tell you the other night. I do some rehabbing as an investment on the side. This is my third house, brownstone in Lakeview."

"Like flipping houses?" she asked, delighted. "I vaguely remember you mentioning a plan that involved real estate."

The elevator came to a stop, and they stepped out on her floor, Max's hand at her back again. "Yeah, the plan has matured some. Originally, I was thinking about getting a two-flat, living on one floor and renting the other. Moving up from there. But a few years ago, a buddy from the force was selling his place. It needed… Hell, it needed everything. But he knew I liked to work with my hands and asked if I wanted to take a look. That was three properties ago."

"Wow, Max, impressive. And you do the work yourself?"

"Mostly. Sometimes I've gotta hire in. Sometimes one of the guys'll come over and help out. But usually it's just me and some tunes and this vision I've got about what the place will look like when I'm done."

She could see him doing it. Could see what a good balance that kind of work would make against what he did on the force.

"This one's mine," she said when they reached her office. She passed her key card over the sensor and then flipped on the lights, illuminating her temporary home away from temporary home. The office was modern and clean, large enough to accommodate a sleek conference table in black wood topped with blue glass to match her desk and the shelving unit at the back wall with a small, built-in closet at the side. Heading over to it, she left Max standing sentinel at the door. Arms crossed, feet planted wide. Looking every bit the officer, and very, very good.

"So tell me more about your life," she said, casting a critical eye at the spare blouse and peach cocktail dress hanging within. Neither was quite right, but the dress was the lesser evil by a long shot. She paused, dress in hand, still wrapped in Max's jacket. "Based on the number of times I've heard your name mentioned today— breathlessly and with obvious intent—I'm guessing you're still as popular as ever with the females?"

"I don't know what you heard," Max started, his hands coming up like he was about to launch into some kind of denial or explanation. "But I don't have any plans with anyone."

"Keeping your options open?" she teased. But the look on Max's face said she'd hit the nail on the head. Waving off whatever response he had, she steered the conversation back on track. "So I know you aren't married, but eight years is a long time. Ever get close?"

For a moment, Max just looked at her, then leaning a shoulder into the doorframe, he cocked his head. "Once. I even bought a ring."

A ring. She'd been expecting him to laugh. Swear up and down he'd never be fool enough to fall for all that love-and-forever business. But once, that was exactly what he'd done.

"What happened?" she asked, all teasing aside.

"We were young," Max replied, the corner of his mouth kicking up as he handed her the explanation she'd given herself so many times.

That half smile pulled at her own and she relaxed, sitting back against the edge of her desk. "I can relate to that."

"I bet you can. Long story short, I was better off for it." He cast another one of those devastating grins, the kind that had probably dropped more panties than she'd owned in her lifetime. "I'm not the marrying kind."

"Think you may have told me that once," she said quietly, regretting the words before they'd even left her mouth. Because then she was thinking back to that last night, the one she'd replayed too many times over the years.

Even now, she could hear the rain hitting the windows and feel the wet strands of Max's hair between her fingers. Taste the storm they'd run through on his lips. Remember how the soaked fabric of her dress pulled tight when his hands fisted at her hips and their kiss turned desperate—

"Guess I did," Max said, his gruff voice cutting into her thoughts and not a second too soon, because that memory always left her just a little aching and bruised.

Tonight, it wouldn't. "Yes, well, turns out I wasn't the marrying kind either."

Then clearing her throat, she pushed up from the desk and waved toward the sodden mess plastered to Max's chest.

"Take off your shirt and let's get on with it. I don't think I've ever been this wet."

Max's lips twitched again, and Sarah felt a slow burn crawling up her neck as she realized just what she'd said. She sucked in a quick breath, and her eyes shot to Max's. "That came out wrong."

One thick, dark brow rose, tugging the corner of his mouth along for the ride. "It came out like you want me naked, fast."

Yeah, but she definitely hadn't meant to say that. Shaking her head, she stuck out her palm. "You're bad. Hurry up."

"So bossy, Sarah," he taunted, the glint of amusement and low rumble of his voice working through her as his fingers worked the buttons and studs of his shirt free. "Not gonna lie. It kinda works for me."

She was not going to melt into a puddle right there in her office because Max was flirting with her while revealing a swath of warm, mouthwateringly well-defined olive chest beneath the stark white of his shirt.

Shrugging one thickly muscled shoulder free and then the other, he stripped off the wet garment and handed it over. "Thanks, Sarah."

Air moved unsteadily past her lips as she strained to maintain eye contact. If she looked at his body again, there was a strong chance she would either giggle or try to touch him. Or both. So she swallowed and, in a tone she only hoped wasn't as breathless as she felt, said, "You too."

There was that smile again. Wait—

Had she just thanked him for taking off his shirt? Slapping a hand over her eyes and then dropping it to her mouth, she hustled into the bathroom with the gruff sound of Max's laughter trailing behind. "Anytime, Sarah."

—∿∿—

Max eyed the connecting bathroom door and listened to the muffled whine of a blow-dryer at work, wondering whether Sarah was still wearing his jacket. And how deeply infused it had become with that subtle perfume he'd caught when he leaned in to tease her before.

Propping a shoulder against the wall, he asked. "So you and Wyse. What's going on there?"

Sean had already confirmed this wasn't an official date, but that he had considered making it one. Max needed to know whether Sarah had been hoping things would go that way.

The blow-dryer cut off.

"Business. He's my boss. Indirectly," she clarified amid the sound of drawers opening and closing. "He needed a date, and Piper had a work thing that left me with a free day."

Max felt the tension leave his shoulders.

He should have left it at that, but hell. "You're too good for him."

More shuffling from beyond the flimsy door, and then a *thunk* followed by a beat of silence.

Max straightened. "Sarah, you okay?"

He'd already reached for the knob when it turned in his hand, and the door cracked open. Through the three-inch gap, Sarah, still wrapped in his jacket, stared up at him, agape.

"Sean. He's not— I mean, there's no way Sean Wyse is *your Sean*."

That wide-eyed look of disbelief was priceless. Almost better than the realization that not only was Sarah still wrapped up in his jacket, but based on the flawless stretch of bare legs extending from the hem, there might not be much else left beneath. Panties probably.

Her bra had to have been soaked. Maybe she'd taken it off.

Which meant beneath those tightly overlapped lapels was bare, silky, pink-tipped skin.

He was a dog for thinking it, and he might have gotten around to working up some guilt, except then those wide eyes started drifting lower until Sarah was blatantly staring at his chest and nibbling her bottom lip in that nervous way she used to have.

Feeling the balance of control shifting back in his favor, Max cleared his throat.

Sarah's eyes bounced back to his, like she'd just been caught with her hand in the cookie jar.

This could be fun.

"Not sure how he'd feel about being *my* Sean." Max

laughed, planting one arm on the doorframe in a move he knew emphasized his chest, shoulders, and biceps, and could only be described as *cheap*. But hell, how was he supposed to resist when Sarah's eyes were yo-yoing up and down?

He flexed, but just a little. "Yeah. Your boss. My buddy. One and the same."

"No. With the stolen toilet? The three women?" She leaned farther into the growing space between the door and the frame, her voice dropping to a disbelieving whisper. "*Washington State?*"

Rubbing a wide palm across his mouth, Max laughed. "Sean is going to *love* that you remember all that."

Her mouth fell open. "I, uh... I would never say anything."

"I know." She was honest and kind. And the vee where the satin lapels of his jacket overlapped was starting to deepen. "Here's the thing, Sarah."

She was looking up at him with trusting vulnerability in her eyes that made him want to wrap her in his arms and protect her, almost as much as he wanted to tangle his fingers in her hair and tip her head back to kiss her.

"Yes?"

"I try to be a good guy. But, sweetheart, seeing you standing there in my jacket and I'm pretty sure not much more? It's bringing out the bad in me. You're gonna need to close this door, or I'm going to walk through it and find out exactly what's changed since college"—his gaze dropped to her mouth—"and what hasn't."

Sarah's lips parted on a gasp Max felt in all the right places, and then the door shut in his face.

He started to walk away before he did something

stupid, but stopped dead at the sound of the knob turning behind him.

His nearly dry tuxedo shirt dangled from one finger extended through the smallest gap between door and frame.

Good girl.

———⌇———

Shoulders pressed into the closed bathroom door, chest heaving, Sarah stared at her lingerie-clad reflection in the mirror.

There was still something between them. And Max felt it.

Not the big, meaningful something she'd been looking for at twenty, but the other something. The chemical something that made the air pop and sizzle around them when they kissed and had been potent enough to keep the memory of Max Brandt from fading into nothingness over the years.

Would it still be like that?

Not if he knew that even after all this time, she was still a virgin. He'd freak out, thinking she was looking for something more than she was.

But what if he didn't know?

It was clear from his sexy threat about storming her bathroom, he didn't consider her off limits anymore. Or maybe he'd just been feeling her out, trying to gauge her receptivity to something casual, based on her response.

Ugh, and if that was the case, she couldn't have blown it more if she tried.

Dropping her forehead into her open palms, she

groaned. Then after one long, deep breath worth of wallowing, she straightened.

It wasn't too late. If she was serious about handling her *little problem* before she got to New York—and she was—she could still fix this. Turn it around by feigning some sexual savviness she hadn't earned, and letting Max hang on to a simple misconception.

A moment later, she'd donned her new dress and slipped out of the bathroom. Max was waiting for her, his eyes trailing down the length of her like a touch.

"Sorry to keep you waiting," she offered with confidence she didn't feel, breathlessness she couldn't fake, and a smile born of possibility. "Guess I got caught up thinking about everything that's changed myself. Wondering if you'd like it."

There wasn't a lot that surprised Max. Hell, in his line of work, he'd pretty much seen it all—and if he hadn't seen it, he'd heard about it from his partner or around the precinct.

But this?

Sarah all but confirming his deepest, darkest hopes and dreams about the demise of her virginity with that come-hither look on her face—*fuck*. Good-bye, blood flow to the brain. Whatever he'd been pumping through that slamming heart of his detoured south. *Down, boy*.

He shook his head and swallowed, met Sarah's eyes, and felt the hold he had on himself slip. "You're beautiful."

She smiled, looking shy again. More like the girl he'd known. "We ought to get back to the reception before they send out a search party," she said.

"We should." He took the first steps, coming up to rest his hand at the small of her back. Politely. Like a fucking gentleman. Only then the feel of her beneath his fingertips sent a jolt straight up his arm, reminding him what it had been like to have her beneath his touch. To hold her and trace the smooth line of her spine. To feel the rush of her breath against his neck. Her skin heating *for him*.

"Right," she agreed. The single word was barely a whisper. Not nearly convincing enough.

"We will." Firming his fingers against her back, he drew her closer. Slowly, because that was how he'd always touched her.

Her lips parted and her breath caught, but she didn't say no. She didn't stop him.

She just watched, her gaze shifting to his mouth as he dipped down to taste her.

One kiss. The barest teasing brush. That was all it took to make Sarah gasp, spurring his every primitive instinct to life.

Mine.

He pulled back.

Another half second of that mind-blowing, supercharged, barely there contact, and best man or not, Max would have had Sarah locked in his arms, her feet off the ground as he carried her to the couch. And no telling what would have happened to the gorgeous dress that looked like it might rip if he breathed on it too hard.

Besides, a glance down at Sarah's hand clutching his shirtfront gave him exactly what he needed. Confirmation she wanted more.

He smiled—hell, grinned—down into her flustered face. "Let's go."

Chapter 6

THE BAND WAS IN FULL SWING WHEN THEY RETURNED TO THE reception. They hadn't even made it inside before a group of guys was bellowing to Max to come over for a toast. The pressure of his fingertips at Sarah's back suggested he wanted her to join them, but she shook her head. "Go ahead. Have fun."

He searched her eyes, then apparently satisfied with what he found there, snagged her phone to text himself and then handed it back. "Not taking any chances tonight."

Maybe not, but she was.

Leaning close to her ear, he promised, "Later."

Her skin tingled, and her pulse jumped. It took everything she had to nod instead of grabbing his hands and begging him for *now*, but somehow she managed. After waiting this long, what were a few more hours?

When she found her way back to her assigned table, Sean stood with a grin. Taking in her new dress, he gave her a curious look as he held her chair.

"Lovely, but dare I ask?"

Rolling her eyes, she shook her head. "Clumsy. I spilled a glass of champagne down my dress bumping into someone." Then reminding herself Sean and Max went way back, she laughed. "Max. I bumped into Max."

When Sean still stared at her like he didn't understand, she clarified. "Your old roommate?"

Seeming to snap out of it, Sean leaned back in his

chair. "No, sorry. It's just that you have to be the least clumsy woman I know. For as long as I've known you, I would say you've never been anything but completely contained. It's funny. You seem different to me, maybe for no other reason than you're *that Sarah*."

The sip of champagne she'd just taken threatened to come back up.

"*That Sarah?*" she managed weakly, wondering what exactly Sean knew about her. How she felt about it.

Before she could spin herself into too much of a wreck, Sean leaned back in his chair and cocked his signature crooked smile at her.

"Yeah. And I'm guessing maybe knowing I'm *that Sean* has you looking at me differently too."

It was true.

Until she'd put the names together, she'd never seen Sean as anything but the most proper of bosses. She'd curbed her humor around him, keeping it well within the bounds of professionalism, and thought of his as a little stiff. When in truth? The guy *knew* how to wind down. In a major way.

She let out a quiet laugh. "Maybe a little." Though it didn't change how she felt about him professionally in the least. "So I guess I can stop worrying that you don't know how to relax."

Sean coughed into his hand, then raising his drink, flashed a wink with more mischief in it than she'd ever seen before. "Whatever you've heard, they're lies. All lies."

Shaking her head, she raised her own glass. "I hope not."

An hour later, Sean made sure she had a room for a night before leaving to meet his father and one of the politicians in attendance for a private drink. Wandering back through the party, Sarah saw Max. He was standing by the head table, phone in hand, eyes locked on her.

A text came through.

Your office. Ten minutes.

She bit her lip, resting a hand over the low churn in her stomach. This was really going to happen.

Meeting his eyes again, she offered a single nod.

Parked behind her desk, fingers neatly positioned at *asdf jkl;*, Sarah stared at the light switch to the right of the door.

Even with the illumination from the hall, she had to look ridiculous sitting there in the semidarkness of her office. At her computer. Not standing in some seductive pose backlit by the city lights streaming in from her window while she sipped champagne. Why hadn't she brought a flute with her?

This was definitely worse than the sterile fluorescent wash she'd thought would make her look cold and unapproachable. Pushing back from her desk, she flipped on the lights just as Max filled her doorway.

Jerking back, she felt her breath catch as he raised a hand and let out one of those gravelly low laughs. "Easy, just me."

"Sorry," she managed through a smile that felt dangerously close to slipping from her face. She was a wreck, and he looked like the Wikipedia graphic aid for "tuxedo fine" with his jacket slung over one shoulder, his bow tie hanging loose, and the top two studs open at his neck. "I was just—just—" She let out an anxious breath. "I was acting like a total fool, trying to decide whether I'd be setting the stage for seduction by leaving the lights off or if I'd look like some freak ready to jump out of the shadows at you."

One thick brow tucked low, then Max stepped into her office. "Let's see."

Without taking his eyes off her, he reached for the switch and turned the lights off.

Sarah's heart skipped a beat, but she was smiling, hope infusing every nervous breath, because he wasn't looking at her like she was crazy. He was looking at her like he didn't want to look away.

He flipped the lights back on, offering up another criminally sexy grin. "Hmm, lights on is way better."

She didn't know what to do with her arms. Her hands. "Why is that?"

He stepped closer, sliding his hand around the dip at her waist as he spoke into her ear. "Because it tells me I'm not just dreaming again."

Ooh, was he ever smooth with that gruff sideways confession.

Because, *again*?

The idea that she'd made it into Max's dreams was... Well, she didn't really care if it was true or not. Either way, it was a damned effective aphrodisiac, and she was already leaning into that barely there space between them. Her knees going soft. Other places going hard.

He was *good*.

He was *casual*.

Only then he was brushing a few strands of hair

behind her ear, his thick fingers so light that the touch sent chills cascading across her skin.

"Max," she whispered as his thumb coasted across the sensitive skin of her bottom lip.

"Close up shop, Sarah. If I start this again before we're in my room, I don't know if I'll be able to stop."

Her breath hitched. This was happening. Tonight.

Five minutes later, Max was sliding his key card over the sensor and stepping into his fifteenth-floor suite.

He'd kept a polite distance when they left her office, through the elevator ride, and as they walked the short distance down the hall to the room decorated in shades of slate and burnt orange. But as the door closed behind her with a distinctive *snick*, she felt that familiar sense of unease fighting for position beside her anticipation.

What was she supposed to do from there?

Walk straight through to the bedroom and start to strip?

Lie down on the bed and wait?

Were there signals and cues someone who'd done this before would know?

Was she about to make a terrible mistake?

The questions bombarding her came to an abrupt halt when Max stepped in close behind her. Smoothing his hand around her waist and across her belly, he pulled her to him so she could feel the heat of his big body from her shoulders all the way down the backs of her legs. And then the warm wash of his breath at her ear.

"We can talk, Sarah." His hand curved around her hip, gently guiding her around so she faced him, so she was looking up into the eyes that had haunted her nights for years. His other hand slid into her hair, sending delicious shivers dancing across her skin as he tipped her head back. "We can have a drink." His mouth lingered a breath above hers. So close that the absence of actual contact almost hurt. "But I can't go another minute without this."

And then that brutal space between them, the one filled with all the *what-ifs* Sarah had spent the last hour agonizing over was gone, replaced by his kiss and the potential of a night that would change her life.

His mouth moved over hers in a smooth glide, creating a soft friction that wound down to her toes and parted her lips on a quiet gasp. *The way he made her feel*. One kiss, and she was *alive*.

One kiss, and she was *hungry*.

One kiss, and it was like time had folded back on itself and they were in her apartment, drowning in the rising need between them.

Breaking away, she skimmed her palms up the hard muscles of his chest and whispered, "I don't want to talk."

Freeing the first stud from his shirt, she set it on the glass-topped console. "I don't want a drink."

A deep rumble sounded from low in Max's chest as she repeated the process and pushed his shirt open with trembling hands.

"I want you." She pressed her lips against the center of his chest, went to her toes and kissed the hollow of his neck. "I can't wait another minute, Max."

If she'd thought he would argue with her, she'd have been wrong.

The thin thread of control holding Max back snapped, and everything changed. His mouth came down on hers again, harder this time, like the hold at her waist and the grip on her hair.

Her heart skipped, nervous and excited.

He wasn't being careful.

He wasn't treating her like glass.

And it was *incredible*. Hot in a way that had her melting into him, clutching at his shoulders and hair to get more.

Arms wrapped around her, Max bowed her back as he took her, devouring her with his kiss. Consuming her.

"Max," she gasped, when her mouth was no longer enough and he'd begun working his way down her throat, pulling at the tender skin with a hint of suction that had her angling away to offer him more.

He'd found the zipper of her dress and was easing the lace over her shoulders, following the newly exposed skin with his lips, his tongue.

"You're beautiful," he rumbled, kissing into her cleavage as the neckline gaped and the heavier overlayer fell to her elbows, leaving her only in the formfitting silky slip. "I didn't think it was possible you could be more beautiful than you were in college, but you are."

"My dress," she whispered urgently. "Take it off me." She didn't want to lose this momentum.

Taking a step back, he slid the fabric down her arms and past her hips, where it pooled around her feet.

And then she was standing before him in nothing but her sheer lingerie and heels. She wanted to be confident, sexy. But suddenly she felt exposed. Nervous.

She'd wanted someone *good* her first time, but Max was *out of her league*. She wasn't going to know what to do. What if Max walked away from her disappointed? Worse, what if he walked away furious because of her lies?

"Sarah?"

Oh no, he could see it. She was tensing up.

All that warm, gooey heat was beginning to cool.

But if she let this stop, would she *ever* have the courage to try again? Deep in her heart, she knew Max was the one man she trusted above all others. Her attraction to him was off the charts—even if that attraction was currently overshadowed by anxiety and more than a pinch of guilt.

She needed to do this.

He said her name again, a question in his eyes.

Straightening her shoulders, she aimed for confidence she wasn't feeling. "Sorry, I just realized I didn't send an email I meant to get out."

Max didn't move a muscle, but even in the low light of the suite, she could see the shock in his eyes. "Email."

Oops! Okay, that was definitely the wrong thing to say.

Scrambling to regain her traction on the moment, she stepped out of the puddle of silk and lace, praying her knees would hold her, and walked over to where the living area opened into the bedroom with a half wall. She leaned back into it and cocked a knee while knitting her fingers tightly behind her.

It was the kind of provocative stance she'd seen in magazines and movies, one that pushed her bust out, while hiding the fact that she was desperately holding her own hands.

"I know, workaholic," she offered with a self-deprecating laugh. "Mystery solved as to why no boyfriend, right?"

Max's jaw bounced once, twice, as he stared at her.

"Sarah, are you nervous?"

Through three beats of her heart, she thought she might tell him. But if she did, he would stop, and she didn't think she could take it. So shaking her head, she tossed another lie onto the pile.

"I…um… Sometimes when I have too much time to think, even in moments like this, my mind wanders to work, is all." She swallowed and added an honest truth. "But I want to be with you."

The hardness left his face, and he closed the distance between them. "*So be with me.*"

He kissed her again, this kiss falling somewhere between the last two. Not a taste. Not devouring. But a measured, concentrated seduction of her mouth that left her *mindless*.

Max pulled back again, keeping the distance between them when she tried to follow him. The look he gave her was scrutinizing but brief.

"Better?"

"Yes," she answered breathlessly. And this time when she pushed to her toes, reaching for him, he met her halfway, giving her everything she was asking for. And more.

She moaned, opening wider to take his tongue, meeting it with her own.

His hands were coasting up and down her back, over her hips and up her abdomen to her breasts. She could feel Max pause. He moved to pull back, but this time she wasn't going to let him go. Pressing herself to him, she threw her arms around his neck and, kissing him with everything she had, slid her knee up the side of his leg.

That did it.

He was back, returning her kiss with the same

intensity and then upping it. His hand found the back of her thigh and slid over the bare skin until he'd cupped her hip and pulled her into exactly the kind of contact she was begging for.

He was big. Thick. Hard.

She knew that was generally considered a good thing, but she really didn't want to speculate on what it would mean for her tonight.

Don't think.

Just keep focused.

Eyes on the prize.

Pushing her fingers into his short hair, she ignored the voice in the back of her head, whispering that he was going to know. That whatever ember of affection had remained between them over the years would die the second he realized she was using him.

His arms tightened around her, and then she was whirling, her toes off the ground as Max carried her to the bed. Laying her back, he crawled on top of her. It was exactly where she wanted him to be. Only that delicious heat in her belly was gone, replaced by a guilty void.

Maybe this was a mistake.

"Sarah?" he asked, looking up from the neighborhood of her navel. She hadn't even noticed.

Arching her back, she let out a little moan and whispered, "So good."

Those thick, dark brows crashed together.

"Are you…thinking about work?"

"No. I swear." It was the truth, but it didn't matter. Because he knew something was up. "I don't really like *that*." She nodded toward her panties where she could only guess he'd been headed.

"You don't?" he asked slowly, something in the way he was looking at her making her squirm.

"Come back up here." Reaching for his head, she tried to urge him back.

He didn't budge. "What do you like, Sarah?"

She swallowed at the edge she heard in his question. "Everything else."

"Yeah?"

She nodded. Scrambled for something to say that would get them back on track. Something she'd read?

"I want you, Max. Inside me." And that might have sounded a little more convincing if her voice hadn't cracked. "Hard and fast. That's how I like it." And as terrifying as that prospect actually sounded, it was her best chance of Max *not* figuring out she'd lied to him.

He nodded, his jaw softening.

Yes.

Relief flooded through her.

Max dropped a kiss on her stomach, light and small, and then crawled up her body. His tuxedo pants were still buttoned, but his shirt hung open, showing off all those bands and layers of solid-packed muscle. He was beautiful. A work of art.

The most handsome man she'd ever seen, and it was taking everything she had not to cringe away as he stopped above her. Slowly he lowered his head, turning so the next kiss he dropped was at her earlobe.

Then, quietly, he said, "Sarah, I really wanna be wrong about this, but I'm about ninety-five percent sure *you don't know what you like*."

Her breath froze in her lungs, her muscles involuntarily locking where they were.

Max retreated just far enough so he could meet her eyes. With a harsh breath, his head dropped. "How the *hell* are you still a virgin?"

Chapter 7

MAX WASN'T SURE WHAT HE WAS EXPECTING NEXT. A LAUGH, a denial so effortlessly convincing that *hard and fast* would be back on the table in the next thirty seconds. Short of that, an apology or tearful explanation, maybe? Certainly not the grumbled "Well, shit" rolling off Sarah's sweet little tongue with the practiced ease of a roughneck. But that was what he got.

Her entire body slumped into the bed as she gave up the ruse, and she stuck out her bottom lip to blow a few dark strands from her eyes before meeting his. "Okay, fine. I'm still a virgin. Big deal."

Big deal? When it was stated in that cool, business-like tone, Max could almost believe it wasn't. Maybe having her beneath him in this big bed after telling himself it would never happen was enough to make him *want* to believe it. But no way could he turn a blind eye to all the evidence suggesting otherwise.

"I'm thinking actually it kind of is." A big enough deal that through twenty-eight years, a fiancé, and he didn't want to think about how many opportunities, she still hadn't done it.

But whatever the reason, he should probably get off her. Much as it pained him, he started backing down her body, trying not to look at the bounty laid out— somewhat stiffly—beneath him.

Only then Sarah's brows pulled together, and she

squirmed—totally not helping—until she had her arms between them, her fingers curling around the open sides of his shirt. "Wait, Max, please."

It was the last word that got him. Had him stalling where he was, even when he knew beyond a shadow of a doubt that he should keep moving. Her warm brown eyes were searching his, soft and sweet. Vulnerable.

"Could you just do it anyway?" she asked with the kind of hopeful smile he'd seen when a kid was asking for ice cream after dinner.

"No!" He laughed, backing off the bed in earnest. Or at least he tried to, but Sarah followed him up, her fingers still gripping his shirt, so they were both on their knees.

"Come on, Max. It would be so quick," she pleaded.

"Oh, would it?" He should have been insulted, but hell, coming from Sarah, it was just comical.

"Yes! Just in and out. And you can be done."

He'd thought he saw vulnerability in her gaze, but clearly he'd been wrong. Because now that he wasn't a hairsbreadth away from heaven, the light was better and there was no missing the turning wheels behind those big, brown eyes. The calculation.

The utter lack of experience.

Apparently knowing he wasn't going to give it up was just the aphrodisiac she'd needed, because suddenly Sarah was all confidence again.

"Just looking for a one-pump chump, huh?" he asked, peeling her fingers free of his shirt and then dropping a kiss on her still-closed fist.

"Exactly!"

Christ. This had to end. He had the feeling if he didn't

cut her off, pretty soon she'd be promising to lie there quietly so he could get it over with.

Pass.

Those few well-tended fantasies he'd held on to over the past eight years were already shot to hell, which was a damn shame considering his relationship with them had outlived any other he'd attempted, real or imagined. Max rubbed a palm across his face, then met Sarah's eyes with a single, definitive shake of his head.

She sat back on her knees and let out a quiet, defeated sigh that got to him more than any of her offers or cajoling. He'd heard it before, and it reminded him of the last time they were together. She'd been asking him for the same thing then, and like now, the casual element that would have been his expectation with any other woman, any other night, hit him like a blow. Because for some unfathomable reason, he'd always thought Sarah was offering him more. *And he always wanted it.* But apparently he wasn't the kind of guy she wanted *more* with.

He wouldn't forget it again. And he wouldn't hold it against her either. After all, he'd been the one who made sure she saw him the way she did.

Stripping his shirt off, he held it out. "Put this on. We're going to talk, and no way is it happening with you sitting there in your bra and panties." *Lacy* bra and *economically* cut panties in what had only a few minutes before become his favorite shade of pink.

One mahogany brow pulled into a slow, calculating arch. "Why's that?" she asked, fingering the fabric of his shirt as she searched his eyes for weakness. "Not sure you can hold out against a little lace and a lot of skin?"

Jesus, who was this woman, and what had she done to that too-sweet, too-agreeable girl whose easy acceptance of his last dictate had been the harbinger of the worst years of his life?

"Trust me, Sarah. I'm sure." But seeing her nearly bare would make it hurt a hell of a lot more.

"Fine," she huffed, sticking her arms into the over-large shirt. Letting the fabric gape, she leaned back against the headboard, fingers linked over her belly, legs outstretched in front of her and crossed at the ankles. "If this makes you more comfortable."

"It does." Not. Even. A. Little. Bit.

And that knowing upward curl of Sarah's lips wasn't helping in the least. He'd entered dangerous territory, and there wasn't any backup for a situation like this.

"Look, I'm sorry, Max," Sarah started, her bare feet shifting together. "I don't know what I was thinking." She peered at the ceiling and blew out another laugh. "Okay, I did. I thought you would be good and maybe you wouldn't notice, and it would be no big deal to you and a huge life changer for me. But I still should have been honest with you."

He held up a hand. There were so many things wrong with what she'd said—starting with her belief that a guy who wouldn't notice she was a virgin could even have a shot at being good, and ending with the idea that anything she qualified as life changing for her could be no big deal to him.

"I'd like to think, since you trust me enough to try to trick me into being your first, you might trust me enough to tell me what's going on. Why now? Why me? Why not that douche you were engaged to?"

She raised a brow at that, then cocked her head and let out a pretty laugh. "He really was a douche."

Glad they were in agreement. But it didn't get him where he wanted to go.

"Sarah, talk to me."

He just wanted to understand. Hell, maybe he needed to.

"Look, I never intended to hold on to my 'virtue' this long," she said, uncrossing her arms only long enough to make the finger quotes. "I don't know if you remember, but waiting on marriage was never part of my plan."

He remembered. Even now, he could feel it. See it. The wind off the lake catching in her hair as she laughed over something she'd heard about him from the weekend. Something he'd only then realized he regretted. But rather than own up to it, he'd turned the conversation back to her, challenging that not everyone was waiting for marriage like she was.

It had been nuts, the way his heart had started thumping hard like he'd just finished a game of hoops, when he was just waiting on a confirmation that shouldn't have mattered to him at all, but did.

Sarah had turned to him with that screwed-up look on her face and laughed again. "I'm not waiting on *marriage*, Max. But to me, sex is meaningful, you know? It's the kind of shared intimacy I don't want with just anyone, anytime. I want it to be special and, at least the first time, I want it to be with someone I love. Kind of desperately."

He'd felt that statement down to his gut, hating the way it confirmed what he already knew. As bad as he wanted Sarah, he couldn't have her.

"You were waiting for love," he replied to the Sarah

of all these years later. The one who'd been in love at least once—because she'd taken the douche's ring and put it on her finger. "The desperate kind."

"I guess I was. Pretty sad to be sitting here with the one guy who knows that, after being just plain desperate in front of him."

"We're friends. We're allowed to lose our cool in front of each other."

She cut him a wry look from beneath those thick, dark lashes. "If you say so."

"Come on, Sarah. What happened?" He wanted to know. *Desperately*, but hypocrite that he was, he couldn't tell her that.

"In my defense, the douche seemed like a pretty good guy when we met. It was after you'd graduated—"

"I know." He'd asked about her, remembered how fucking bad it felt to hear she'd gotten serious with someone.

She paused, a questioning look in her eyes, but quickly continued. "So I was a couple of months into senior year when we started dating. He totally respected my feelings about sex and never pushed. In fact, when I finally told him I thought I was ready, that I loved him and wanted us to be together that way, it turned out he had stronger convictions on the subject than I did. He thought we should wait until we were married."

"*He* wanted to wait?" Max couldn't believe it.

"Not really. Turned out, he wasn't talking about both of us waiting. But I didn't find that out until a few months before the wedding."

A few years into dating. Jesus. No one deserved that kind of betrayal, but the idea that Sarah had suffered it? He wanted to hunt Cory down and put his fist in the guy's face. "Damn, Sarah. I'm sorry."

"After we broke up, I was so mad. Disgusted that I'd been waiting for this prick all those years—only to realize he hadn't thought I was worth waiting for at all. So I went out with the sole intent of picking up a guy and getting rid of this albatross between my legs."

"Albatross?" Max choked out, his eyes seeking that shadowy spot beneath his shirt.

"I know, way to sell it." She laughed.

Jesus, that she was having to sell it at all? Forcing his eyes back to her face, he asked, "How'd that turn out for you?"

"I realized the minute I walked into the bar I wasn't going to follow through. Cory had cost me enough time. I wasn't going to let my feelings and resentment toward him cost me what I'd been waiting all my adult life for. I wanted my first time to be special, so I decided to wait." She drummed the fingers of her hand over her arm. "And in the meantime, I figured I'd throw myself into my career. Which it turns out I do very well."

"So I hear. Sean says you're kind of a badass."

A look of pure unadulterated satisfaction lit her eyes. "Nice of him to notice."

That pang of jealousy hit him again, making him feel like a total ass. Sarah wasn't into Sean. Not that it mattered now anyway. "So how did we go from waiting for special to hoping I wouldn't notice this was your first time?"

Sarah shrugged. "Special got stale. Honestly, Max, that first year after the breakup, I was completely turned off to dating. And after that, it wasn't so much that the guys were turning me off as my career was turning me on. I was getting so much satisfaction from kicking ass and taking names. I don't know. Dating just fell off the radar. I mean, I tried it on and off, but eventually I decided it was time to just bite the bullet and say, 'Get thee behind me, virginity.' Only it never worked out. I mean, in case you haven't noticed, the whole I'm-still-a-virgin-but-I swear-it-doesn't-mean-anything conversation can be kind of a mood killer."

"I can't believe there weren't any takers." Most guys just weren't built that way.

Shooting him a nasty look that had him laughing again, Sarah crossed her arms tighter. "Of course there were takers. But by the time we'd worked through the assurances and wary looks, I just wasn't interested. I might have given up on waiting for love, and waiting for special, but I don't think it's too much to ask that I at least be a little turned on." She huffed, waving one dismissive hand his way. "So for a number of reasons, it just kept not happening. But it needs to.

"I don't want to go through what happened with Cory again. It's not like I'm ready for my happily ever after. Right now is about my career, and maybe picking up a little experience in the dating arena on the side. But eventually I will be ready to get serious again, and I'm hoping when that happens, I'll have had enough experience to know more about what I want in a man, in a relationship. To know what's important to me. What's not."

"You want to play the field a while," Max offered, cringing inside over how mistaken he'd been with her. Not that he'd thought this time he'd get to keep her. She was only in town for a couple of months, and he knew better than to try to get in the way of a woman's plans. But for while she was here?

Well, not exactly what she'd been looking for. And the more she talked, the less he could blame her.

"I want to do some *research*, so when the time is right, I'll be able to make an educated decision I can be confident about."

Because she didn't want to get hurt again. It killed him to think about the mind fuck that douche had done on her. How, as tough as she seemed, she was still so afraid of letting herself be hurt.

"The thing is, Max, it's tough to tell what kind of connection you have with someone, what you like about them and what you don't, when first *you're* worrying about the coming conversation, and then *they're* worried about what that means."

Yeah, he could imagine.

After another frustrated breath, she looked up at him. "When I ran into you at the party, and I realized there was still something between us, I thought *maybe*. Maybe we could have one night. The night we never had back in school, but I'd wondered about for I won't even tell you how long after. One night, and this obstacle that feels like it's in the way of everything would finally be gone. Only then I started thinking about having *the talk* with you, and I just couldn't. So I left. But after, I was kicking myself for letting it stop me. And anyway, that's why I decided not to say anything tonight. It wasn't right, and I'm sorry."

She was killing him. A woman like Sarah, so smart and sexy and sweet, ought to have a man loving her every night. If things had been different, it might have been him. She wouldn't be a virgin, that was for damn sure. Because while he'd had her, Max would have made sure she was coming apart with his name on her lips every chance he got.

But she hadn't wanted that from him. And what she had wanted? Well, he'd wanted more for her.

"Sarah, I get it. But I can't be the guy to help you out."

Her shoulders slumped as she quietly asked, "Can you tell me why?"

"Because I'm the guy who remembers your eyes when you told me you were waiting for love. I'm the guy who wanted that for you so bad he walked away to make sure you had a shot at it. I'm sorry, but I don't think I could live with being the guy looking into your eyes when you realized what you'd done with me meant you were never going to get it.

"You deserve more. And even with you telling me you don't need it, I still want you to have it."

Sarah sighed, a half smile on her lips.

"It's okay, Max. You're a good guy, and I don't want you to feel bad about doing what you feel is right. But I do kind of wish I could stop offering more than you want to take though." She laughed lightly, but Max's guts twisted with what she'd said. He couldn't tell her how wrong she'd been. How much he'd wanted what she was offering eight years ago. How he'd wanted more.

Crawling off the bed, she handed Max his shirt back and walked over to where her dress lay on the floor. Slipping the first layer over her head and then the second, she let the lacy fabric slide down her body.

Again, she was killing him.

She glanced over her shoulder. "A little help?"

He crossed to her and had the zipper half up, his fingers burning to spread out over that creamy expanse of skin, when she blithely stated, "I get why you said no. And it really is fine. I'll find someone else to assist with my *little problem*. There's got to be some palatable prince out there willing to help a girl out when she needs a favor. I'm ready to get this over with. And I'd like to do it before I get to New York and the rest of my life starts for real."

His hand slipped from the zipper. "Sarah—"

She turned to him, no judgment or apology in her eyes. Just honesty. "It was good to see you, Max. And while I may not have shown it, I really do appreciate the friendship."

He nodded, that knot in his gut getting worse as she slipped into her heels and then found her purse.

"Where are you going?" he asked.

A slender brow rose.

"Becoming platonic sleepover buddies with my hardest crush is a low even I won't sink to. I've got my own room. Take care, Max."

He could stop her from leaving. All it would take was a few steps, and then he could kiss the last thirty minutes out of her memory. Now that he knew she was inexperienced, he'd go slow, warm her up to his every touch before moving on. He could give her everything she wanted and—

And the door closed behind her.

"Take care, Sarah."

Chapter 8

MAX HAD BEEN SHARING SUNDAY MORNING BREAKFAST with Molly since she'd first started showing up at his lakefront dorm for weekends his freshman year. Three years younger than he was, she'd still been in high school and living at home when he left for college. He'd been nervous about leaving her without an ally in the war zone where they'd grown up, so when he'd found her sitting outside his door that first Friday evening, two weeks into school, he'd welcomed her with a sigh of relief rather than grudging reluctance.

He'd never had to worry about her getting in the way, since she'd spent most of her life trying to stay out of it. And with the alternative being weekends at home with Vick and Dana Brandt screaming at her and each other, Molly wasn't about to make any trouble. She'd been fifteen, and best of all, she'd looked it, with baby-blue eyes that seemed a little too big for her face and that gangly posture she hadn't quite grown out of. Which meant Max hadn't needed to lay anyone out for getting ideas about her, because they all knew she was way too young.

'Course by his junior year, Molly was seventeen and the story had changed. But by then she'd been practically living with him, Jase, Brody, and Sean for two years, and his mom had finally followed through on more than a decade of threats and left his dad. Despite having to throw some heavy glares around while reiterating his *little* sister's not-so-legal status, Max liked having her close enough to keep an eye on. He liked her knowing she could count on him to be there for her no matter what—and knowing she could be counted on to—

"Bow-chicka-wow-*wow*. Hey, Bro!" Molly sang out from behind the island that served as both a table and a division between the kitchen and living room in the apartment she shared with a revolving door of roommates.

"Enough with the porn music, Molly. It wasn't like that." Yeah, Molly could be counted on to make sure he felt as dirty as she thought he was on any given day of the week.

"Well, it kind of looked like that, Big Brother. Considering you stole Sean's date right out from under him." She made a show of looking all around. "And yet, I don't see her here. Which means pull up a stool and start talking. Sean was a total ween and wouldn't give me anything last night except that she's *that Sarah*."

Molly had a thing about keeping track of Max's dates, and not just because she loved giving him crap about them. The way she saw it, she needed to know who to avoid if casual turned cranky, and Max couldn't blame her. So he ponied up names, first and last, and the most pertinent details of his dating life without argument.

But this thing with Sarah? Somehow it didn't feel like it fell under that same umbrella. Or maybe he just didn't want to talk about it.

"I sure as shit didn't steal Sean's date. And what do you even know about *that Sarah*?"

"I know you spent the whole night watching every move she made from across the ballroom. I know you had the cheesiest grin I've ever seen when you came back after she spilled her drink on you, and I know you had it *B-A-D* bad for her at the end of school. I also know that last night she came with Sean, and—"

"And she left alone."

Molly snorted, staring him down. "Yeah, if you say so."

Max tried to hold out, but soon enough, those blue eyes boring into him had him squirming. "Fine. I met her in her office. But she wasn't really Sean's date."

"See, was that so hard?" Not waiting for an answer, Molly started cracking half a dozen eggs into a glass bowl, making the only breakfast he'd ever seen her make that didn't come pouring out of a box and include a toy three-quarters of the way down. "So what happened? Looked like there might be something more going on with you and *that Sarah* than there is with your typical pickups. She seemed different. Like, not the type I'd have to worry about flashing her crotch-less panties every time the wind picked up. And unless I missed it, she didn't have a bubbly girlfriend trailing along for whatever dirty business the three of you might get into."

Max's hands came up in front of her, a protest poised on his lips, but Molly just waved him off.

"Whatever. Even if she did, I don't need the details. Just make sure you use the antibacterial soap by the sink before you touch anything. My point is, Sarah looked different. You looked different." She poured some milk into the bowl with the eggs and then a generous amount of dried spices and seasoning before going at the mixture with a fork. "I got my hopes up, but today you look like roadkill. So what happened?"

He might as well tell her—she'd have it out of him

sooner or later. "Turns out we didn't have the same thing in mind when we left together."

Molly leaned onto one hand, her expression warning him about the lecture to come. "Obviously, I wasn't privy to all the exchanges leading up to your illicit meeting. But from where I was sitting, you had a look about you, like maybe you were interested in more than just your usual couple of hours of fun. So I guess I could see where she might have gotten the idea this wasn't just a two-hour thing." Molly paused. "If it even takes you that long. I don't really want to know."

Then her face screwed up, and her head wagged back and forth in indecision as she stared at the ceiling a moment before looking back at him. "Wait, maybe I do want to know. Not the gory details, because gross, but just the time thing because when I—"

"Stop right there!" Max choked out, pushing back from his stool. "Don't even think about finishing that sentence. I'm begging you, *don't make me think about it*." He shook his head, wishing he could shake the seeds of those traumatic thoughts from his mind, while Molly snickered quietly to herself.

Returning to the original thread, he clarified. "Sarah's moving to New York in two months. So believe me, I wasn't painting picket fences in my mind."

Molly half snorted, half laughed. "But that's totally funny to imagine. Right?"

"Uh-huh, sure. But I guess I thought that maybe it was more than just—"

"*No way!*" The fork clattered against the side of the bowl. "*You're* the one who wanted more than the few hours, and *she* wasn't interested?"

Max growled, rubbing his hands over his face because this conversation seriously might kill him. He couldn't tell Molly about Sarah being a virgin. His little sister was actually pretty good about respecting other people's secrets. But so was he, and this was no one's business but Sarah's.

"Let's just leave it at we were interested in different things."

For a minute, she just stood there looking at him. Then she rounded the island and wrapped her arms around his neck, pulling him down to smack a kiss on his cheek before basically shoving him away.

It was possible Molly still had a few emotional intimacy issues left over from being raised by parents who made no secret of treating her like a burden.

Reaching out, Max caught her by the shoulder and pulled her back in for another longer hug, because when it came to his tough-as-nails little sister, he was a softy who'd never really stopped seeing her as that five-year-old dirt ball looking at him with her big, blue eyes and asking him to read her a book.

"Thanks, Sis," he said. "I needed this."

She went back to whipping up her eggs, a goofy grin on her lips, as he dropped onto the stool at the far side of the counter. He meant it. This thing with Sarah had thrown him for a loop, and while talking about it with Molly wasn't going to happen, it was nice to have someone to hug him when he fucking ached with regret over a choice that he knew to the bottom of his soul he wouldn't change, even if he had it to do again.

—◆◆◆—

Monday morning, Sarah sat in her office, her stomach knotted with nerves. Not once in her career had she considered a relationship, a dalliance, even a freaking cup of coffee that had the potential to impact her career. Men from Wyse had asked her out, sure. But she'd made it clear from day one that wasn't happening. She'd never made an exception, never even thought about it.

Until Max Brandt.

What had she been thinking?

Well, she'd been thinking it was *Max*. The crush from back before she'd been trying to prove anything to anyone, most of all herself. The guy she'd always think of in the context of his relationship with her, before she thought of him in the context of his relationship with, say, *her boss*.

Her stomach roiled and she closed her eyes, grimacing.

She wasn't worried about what Sean would think about her going out with Max. Or staying in with him. Or doing whatever consenting adults might do.

But what if Max told Sean what had happened between them Saturday night? What if he told her boss she was some crazy, manipulative psycho?

What if she became a joke between them? What if she became a joke throughout the entire chain? Throughout the hotel industry?

What if she'd just killed her career with one single, stupid attempt at putting her personal life back on track?

"Stupid, stupid, *stupid*," she chided between shallow breaths.

"Damn, Sarah, I've been hard enough on myself since Saturday night," Max said from her open office door, his deep voice cutting through her self-directed disgust and making her jump. "Not sure I can handle you calling me names too."

"Max, what—" She shook her head, then smoothed back her hair as nerves and excitement tangled within her. "What are you doing here?"

He was dressed casually, his broken-in jeans striking the perfect balance between hug and hang, while his collared T-shirt offered just enough cling and stretch around the solidly packed muscles of his chest, shoulders, and arms that Sarah had to wonder how he'd made it all the way to the hotel without some woman ripping it off him. He looked that good.

And yeah, now she had a pretty good idea of how she'd managed to be so stupid. Because already, she could sense her brain cells expiring one after another.

"I wanted to see you," Max said, his gray eyes locked on her intently. "Make sure we were okay. After everything."

She closed her eyes, all the tension and worry that had been building within her since she'd left his room suddenly draining out in a rush. This man wasn't the kind to make a joke of her. He cared about her. Even after all the years, even after the stunt she'd pulled, she could still see that protective streak shining through. Heck, she could feel it.

With a shake of her head, she pushed back from her desk and walked around to him. "I appreciate it. I may have been a little anxious about how we left things myself." Taking a quick look past him, she checked that the hall was clear, then leaned against her side of the door. "I've never even come close to smudging the line between my personal life and my professional one before, and it's completely freaking me out."

Max nodded, the barest hint of a smile at the corner of his mouth. "I get that. It's pretty much the same for me with the force. I didn't really think to ask you whether it would have been a problem for you. I guess because you were Sean's date. Sort of. And I knew you first. But for what it's worth, what happens between you and me won't have any crossover to what happens between you and Sean. He and I are friends, but we're also adults and get the whole boundaries thing."

"Well, if it isn't my two favorite people in the world," came the booming voice of the last man Sarah wanted to see right then. Leaning into the hall, she winced. Sure enough, Sean was on his way toward them. "Max, you make any headway talking Sarah into staying in Chicago yet?"

Max shook his head, pinching the bridge of his nose. "Hey, man, I was on my way up to see you in a bit." His eyes shot back to Sarah's. "Just to say hi."

It would have been comical, except… Sarah stopped to consider and let the smile pushing at her lips have its way. It *was* comical. Her would-have-been hook-up standing beside her boss was her worst nightmare, but somehow she knew Max would make everything okay.

"Excellent," Sean proclaimed, beaming at them like they were his kids. "But, Max, since you've got a couple of hours before you have to be at work and I'm here now, what do you say the three of us go down and grab breakfast together?"

Sarah was about to open her mouth in protest when Sean shook his head.

"I insist."

"No can do, Sean." Max had his hand on Sean's

shoulder, giving him a squeeze that seemed friendly enough, except for the way Sean's eyes shot to Sarah and then returned to Max.

Straightening his suit jacket, Sean returned the "friendly" grip on Max's shoulder, his knuckles going white as he urged Max out the door. "Fine. I'll walk you out now. Sarah, just meet me down at the restaurant in twenty, will you?"

"Of course," she answered, not exactly relieved. "See you in a few."

Max couldn't help the smile twisting his lips as Sean— who was probably four inches shorter and thirty pounds lighter than he was—muscled him down the hall like some punk kid getting dragged to the principal's office.

Obviously, Max could have stopped. But the truth was, he liked Sean's protective streak toward Sarah, so who was he to get in the way? Especially when he'd only been trying to protect her himself.

The elevator doors opened, and instead of going up to his office, Sean took them down to the parking level. A couple of guests were riding with them, so both men remained silent until they stepped out onto the concrete ramp.

Sean turned on him, all but bristling with rage. "What the fuck is this?" he growled, the reaction intense enough for Max to take a step back, narrow his eyes on the other man, and wonder exactly what Sean's feelings for Sarah were. Because this *protective* looked like more than professional consideration. Even with a heap of friendly intent sprinkled on top.

"Back down, man," Max said in a level tone. "I was just checking in to say hi to Sarah, see how she was after this weekend. I don't know what you think was going on—"

"What I think is that you're blowing her off the way you always do. That you got whatever you were after, and now you can't be bothered to have breakfast with the girl you took off my arm on Saturday night. A girl I only let go because you seemed legit."

"Took off your arm? Let go?" Max growled. "You said you were just friends."

"We are, dickhead. Good enough friends that I don't want her heart getting traipsed over by your libido."

"Trust me, that's not what's going on here." Jesus, why was everyone assuming the worst? And why did it make the fact that Sarah wasn't interested in more than a night with him so much fucking harder to swallow? "Look, you didn't accidentally run into me at a gas station, Sean. I came to her work to check in. Something I wouldn't do if I didn't care about her. And not that it's any of your damn business, but my libido left her alone. We're just what we always have been: friends."

Sean gave him a *don't bullshit me* look, and Max put up a hand. "Friends who know better. But that's the end of the discussion, man. Sarah works for you, and this is personal."

A moment passed and then, appeased, Sean straightened his tie. "See you tonight for Jill's thing?"

So they were good. "Yeah, see you tonight."

Max texted Sarah before heading over to the station, letting her know everything was cool with Sean and that it had been good seeing her. There was a finality to it he didn't like, but the truth was Sarah wanted something Max couldn't give, something casual and no big deal. And sitting around burning through his stomach lining while he watched from the sidelines, waiting for her to find the guy who could give it to her, didn't sound awesome.

Good-bye was definitely the way to go.

———

Jill was a sweet girl who had been working at Belfast since Brody opened the place a handful of years ago. No, she wasn't the kind of friend that came over every other week with the rest of the guys. But they all cared about her.

Which explained why this hole-in-the-wall theater was pushing about ninety percent capacity for a nine forty-five Monday night performance of a play written by Jill's boyfriend. The kid was nice, but based on his last three productions, he wasn't in line to become the next Oscar Wilde.

Max scanned the faces in the crowd, recognizing about half of them. Brody had had a hand in the night's box office success. The guy had a habit of buying up tickets and then handing them out to his hordes of friends. And because Brody was asking them to go, they always did. The guy was such a teddy bear—unless you gave him a reason not to be.

Gotta love him.

Halfway down, Brody was sitting with his beefy arm slung around Molly's shoulders, talking animatedly with Jase and Emily, who were seated on Molly's other side. There were a handful of open seats on Brody's left, so Max dropped into one and reached across to ruffle Molly's hair.

"Guys, Emily, how you doing?" he asked, wincing as he realized he'd done it again when Emily rolled her eyes and laughed. He'd separated her from *the guys*. "Sorry, Em. You know I love you, but you've got too much class to be lumped in with these yahoos."

Emily raised a brow, the dark-brown eyes his buddy had turned into a marshmallow over flashing a bit of edge as she replied, "I know your game, Max. Trying to keep me the odd woman out. But I'm telling you, Jase is never going to throw me over and come back to you. Just accept it. I'm here to stay. So find yourself another pretty girl. This one's mine."

Max laughed at their ongoing joke, loving that she gave him shit.

Brody looked back and forth between them. "Yeah, about that. Word on the street is Max may have already found a pretty girl to replace Jase."

The hell?

If any of them actually knew how it had gone down with Sarah, there wouldn't be a word about it.

"Look, whatever you heard—"

Brody pushed his russet mane of overlong hair off his face and then reached into his jacket and pulled out a flask, offering it around before helping himself to a hearty swig. "I was talking with Janice this afternoon. She heard you had a pretty serious look about some woman from Saturday night."

"Brody, that was you?" Jase asked, leaning forward in his seat, an incredulous look on his face. "Man, I was trying to get Janice's attention for thirty minutes while she was on the phone, but she kept brushing me off."

Janice was Jase's long-time admin and a source of more gossip than any of them could account for.

"Lighten up, Jase," Brody chided. "She has a recipe for crème brûlée that's just this side of heaven, but when I followed her instructions, mine didn't turn out the same. She was talking me through the steps."

Jase sat back, and Max was about to jump back into the conversation to clear up the misconceptions about his *serious* status when Jase leaned back in, his eyes narrowed and his voice conspiratorially low. "So where did Janice hear it? Who the hell is she getting all her gossip from?"

Four sets of eyes rolled, and Molly just shook her head. "Let it go, Jase."

Enough of this shit.

Max leaned into the group, veeing his fingers toward his friends before bringing them back toward his eyes to ensure he had everyone's attention. This was the last time he was going to say anything about it.

"There's nothing going on with me and Sarah. We were friends years ago, and yeah, there was a time when I thought maybe there'd be something more, but that's not how it went. It just wasn't meant to be. I knew it back then, and I know it now. All that happened on Saturday was I finally got a chance to catch up with her. Yes, I care about her, but chances are I won't even see her again before she leaves for New York at the end of the summer. So whatever ideas you guys have, get over them. And for fuck's sake, stop spreading rumors. Understand?"

Instead of a round of agreement, all he got were four sets of eyes staring past him, each registering varying degrees of amusement.

He turned to look over his shoulder and jerked out of his seat.

Sean grinned at him, his hand resting lightly on his guest's shoulder. "Hey, guys, you remember Sarah?"

Sarah had been prepared for the bad theater. Sean had warned her ahead of time, assuring her in no uncertain terms that this play would be the worst she'd ever endure. So she'd looked forward to the experience with no expectations of anything more than an evening out with her pushy boss who thought she'd get a kick out of the show and was looking for company. What she hadn't been prepared for was Max seated with the rest of Sean's friends. Or her boss, one of the most intelligent, business-savvy men she knew, playing dumb when he turned to her all innocent and asked, "Didn't I mention everyone was gonna be here?" before all but shoving her into the open seat next to Max and then darting off to grab something from his car.

Fortunately, Brody, Molly, Jase, and Emily were completely welcoming, and after Max's initial murderous look at Sean, he seemed to find the situation as funny as she did. The play was every bit as bad as promised, but they all watched attentively and stood cheering at the end.

"What do you guys say we head back to Belfast?" Brody suggested, clapping one friend after another on the back as he passed. "Anyone with a ticket stub gets a drink on me."

Jill, who'd played the part of the grocery fairy, threw her arms around him and smacked a big kiss on his cheek. "Thanks, Boss."

Sean nodded at Sarah. "What do you say? It's tradition to grab a drink after the show."

Max was walking with Jase and Emily just a few steps away. Sarah wasn't going to look to him for an answer. It wouldn't be fair.

"Come on," Sean urged, flashing her a look that was shockingly mischievous and so not what she was used to from him at the office. "You told me just this morning you wanted to get out and do more in Chicago while you were here. This is your opportunity. Belfast is one of Lakeview's most popular bars. And you'll *earn* VIP status just by showing up with me."

She laughed, realizing this was a done deal. "Yeah, that sounds good. But just one drink. I've got to work tomorrow."

Sean rolled his eyes. "Yeah, right. I'm pretty sure you can handle your workload in about an hour's time. Which reminds me—I could use your help with a few other things tomorrow afternoon. If you're interested, that is."

Sarah's ears pricked up because added responsibilities were like whipped cream on her brownie. "Yeah, what are you looking for?"

"Nah, nah. How about tonight you just enjoy yourself? Come in after lunch tomorrow for work. Do something fun in the city in the morning, or don't do anything at all, but let's just have a good time tonight." She knew Sean well enough not to bother asking him if he was sure.

"It's a deal. Just give me a moment, and I'll meet you outside."

Sean nodded and headed over to where Molly was

talking with Jill's boyfriend. Sarah turned, finding Max with a single glance over by the far wall. He was a man who stood out in a crowd. And though he was talking with a couple of friends, his eyes were locked on her.

She'd agreed to go with Sean, but if that made Max uncomfortable, she'd find an excuse to get out of it.

She cut through the crowd, and Max met her halfway.

"So what'd you think of the show?" he asked, an easy smile on his face.

"I had a great time," she answered honestly, because she had. Then turning to glance behind her, making sure Sean or Molly wasn't standing too close, she added, "I didn't know you'd be here tonight."

Max shoved his hands into his jeans pockets and let out a gruff laugh. "Yeah, that makes two of us." And then meeting her eyes, he added, "But I'm glad you are. Coming to Belfast?"

"If you don't mind. But honestly, Max, I don't have to. If it makes you uncomfortable at all—"

"Don't be ridiculous. I'll give you a ride. If you don't mind the bike, that is."

Sarah's belly dipped. The bike. She loved the bike, loved the idea of wrapping her body around Max as he tore through the streets. Except—"Sean's actually waiting for me, but thanks for the offer. I'll see you there."

"Oh, right." He rubbed the back of his neck. "See you there."

Chapter 9

IT DIDN'T TAKE MORE THAN WALKING THREE FEET THROUGH the door to know why Belfast was one of Chicago's favorite watering holes. Sarah stepped through the open doorway to the left for a peek into the restaurant side of the business. It was closed now, but she could see the decor was similar to that of the main bar. Copper ceiling tiles and gleaming, warm honeyed wood contrasted with exposed brick and pipes strung with white lights throughout.

Oversize TVs were hung strategically around the space so patrons interested in seeing sporting events would be able to, without overwhelming those who weren't. The bar side was set up with a handful of high-end pool tables and darts, and a back room held a stage for live music. The space had an upbeat vibe and a welcoming ambiance, which explained how, even at near midnight on a Monday, Belfast was pulling a decent crowd.

Brody stood by the edge of the bar, closest to the door, waving her through with a burly arm and a wide grin.

"Sarah, my girl!" he greeted her warmly. "You been here before?"

She stepped up beside him, smiling as he flagged the bartender for her order.

"No, this is my first time. It's great! What's everyone

having?" she asked, wanting to join in the fun the way all these friends were accustomed to doing it. Brody's eyes lit up.

"Oh great, now you've done it," Sean said with a heavy sigh. "He's going to be showing off all night. You're on your own, lady."

Sarah's brows rose, but before she could ask Sean what he meant, Brody raised his hand, his finger out and thumb up like a gun ready to fire.

"Amber there in the yellow sweater with the frilly business around the neck is a rum and Coke; her boyfriend, Gene, likes Newcastle. Em can't get enough of the hard lemonade, and Tallia beside her is an Amstel girl."

Sarah laughed, understanding what made Sean run off. "Seriously, you know what everyone ordered?"

Brody beamed, his mouth opening again, but then Max was there, slinging an arm around his buddy's shoulders. "This is my fault, Sarah. I should've warned you before you came over. This guy loves to brag." He pulled Brody in for a one-armed hug.

Brody's hands were up in front of them, his head shaking from side to side. "It's her first time at Belfast, man. I just want to make it memorable."

This time, Sarah had a grin she couldn't contain. "Well, color me impressed."

Brody made one of those told-you-so faces at Max, who just laughed.

Then raising a brow at his buddy, Max leaned in closer and said, "I'm guessing she'd be more impressed if she had a drink." He leaned over the counter to the bartender and ordered a couple of Goose Islands for them.

Brody's big shoulders slumped, his mouth hanging

open slightly as if jealous that Max had placed her order. "Man, that's just cold."

The beers were up, and Max handed Sarah hers, clinking her glass before taking a drink.

"Come on, we're about to start a game of darts," Max said, resting his hand at the small of her back as he led the way.

Sarah laughed. "Darts? You still play?"

"You know it." Max grinned, slanting a look over at her as they walked back to the table where Molly, Sean, Jase, and Emily were set up. "Okay, but you've got to do me a favor. Don't say anything about how you play."

Sarah stopped where she was and turned to Max. "Seriously?" She crossed her arms over her chest. "I thought you were all about the rules, Max. Mr. Do-the-Right-Thing? I'm a little disappointed to see you trying to stack the deck."

At least the guy looked chagrined. He rubbed a hand over his jaw. "I know, I know. And I'm sorry. But you know how much I like to win."

She shook her head in mock disapproval. Max's brows rose expectantly, and she relented, issuing a heavy sigh. "Fine. However you want to play it."

After a barely contained fist pump, he returned his hand to her back, ushering her over to the table where everyone was waiting. "You guys don't mind if Sarah joins us for a game, right?"

When they all agreed, he met her with an earnest stare. "You've seen people play darts before." he asked, motioning toward the board with his free hand and then breaking down the basics of the game before looking around the table at his friends. "How are we doing teams?"

Emily pursed her lips and looked at her husband adoringly. A little too adoringly.

"How about you and me, honey?" she asked, nearly banking the competitive fire in her eyes enough to keep Sarah from seeing it. But in Sarah's line of work, it paid to catch details.

So Max wasn't the only one who liked to win.

"Sean, you're with me," Molly stated, flashing an impish grin back at her brother.

Sarah let out a small sigh. So that was how it was going to be.

"Oh. Well, okay." Max nodded to his friends before grinning back at Sarah. "Looks like it's you and me. Why don't you go first?"

Emily hopped off her stool, nodding in agreement. "Yeah, and remember, it's fun. Nobody takes this too seriously."

It took everything Sarah had not to roll her eyes and laugh. Yeah, right.

Stepping up to the marker on the floor, Sarah took the dart Max handed her. Tested the weight and rolled it between her fingers. Sending Max a tentative glance, she pulled a nervous face. "I just hope I hit the board."

Max coughed into his hand.

She sent the dart sailing and closed her eyes.

"Oh, you dirty snake!" Emily accused, her finger outstretched to where Sarah's dart had landed neatly in the centermost ring of the board.

Max shrugged, looking as innocent as a lifetime bad boy could possibly look. Not very.

Sarah feigned a gasp, holding her hand up in front of

her mouth like she couldn't believe what had just happened. "Wait, was that good?"

Emily cracked her knuckles and straightened to her full height, which was probably a good seven inches taller than Sarah's. She might have been intimidated, but Sarah dealt with powerhouses towering over her nearly every day.

Besides, it was clear from Emily's expression of delight that Jase's wife was practically salivating over the challenge. Friendly as it might be. Which Sarah definitely got.

She threw again. "That's called a bull's-eye, right?"

Molly dropped her head into her hands and let out a plaintive cry. "This is my karmic payback for not being nice enough to let the new girl play on my team. Dang it!"

And again. "Wow, pretty neat how they're all practically on top of each other like that, huh?"

Max grabbed the back of his chair and pulled it out to sit. "Oh wait, did I forget to mention Sarah's the one who taught me to play?" And because he was apparently a gloater of the worst kind, he mock whispered, "I wouldn't play her for cash. Just sayin'."

Sarah couldn't help laughing at the pile of floundering egos sprawled out around her. Except for Sean, of course, who'd been kind enough to keep his mouth shut about the game of darts they'd played back in San Francisco two years earlier. When she'd wiped the floor with him.

Walking back to her seat beside Max, she held her hand out for a passing five. But instead of their hands meeting and slipping apart, Max caught her fingers in his, holding until their eyes met.

Wow, that half-naughty, totally satisfied smile on his lips—mixed with the laughter in his eyes—caught her off guard. For a moment, she got that crazy roller-coaster feeling, the one that left her just a little less than in control. That reminded her of how much Max affected her and finally had her looking away, hoping he didn't catch the hot blush creeping into her cheeks.

Because tonight was about being friends—the *more than* ship having sailed Saturday night.

A fact underscored by the arrival of a blond in a pair of formfitting, strategically ripped jeans with a thick black belt that hung low on her hips, motorcycle boots, and a T-shirt so short and tight it might actually have come from the children's section.

The blond walked up to the table and exchanged animated hellos with everyone before stepping into the vee of Max's legs. Looping one well-toned arm around his neck, she leaned up to whisper something in his ear.

Sarah hopped off her seat. "Be right back, guys."

If ever there was call for a feigned trip to the ladies' room, this was it. She'd felt her mouth fall open as Max's friend practically crawled into his lap, and Sarah was not going to be that hopeless girl watching from the side of the party as the guy she wanted hooked up with someone more his speed. Not again. And definitely not with the same man.

—⁓—

As a cop whose ability to rely on his reflexes could mean the difference between life and death, Max was thinking maybe it was time for a career change. Either that or he needed to get his shit together. Because the minute Andrea had walked up to him, sliding between his legs like she belonged there, Max's ability to act fast and minimize the damage of a potentially explosive situation basically got flushed down the toilet. All he'd been able to think was *Oh shit* because Sarah was sitting two feet away.

And then she hadn't been.

Before he even had a chance to politely pass on Andrea's offer of company, Sarah had scooted off the chair she just sat down in and asked Molly where the ladies' room was. She hadn't looked upset. But hell, for whatever reason, the part of him that reacted to Sarah so differently than he did to other women wanted—no, *needed*—her to know he wasn't interested in Andrea.

Which was why he found himself following Sarah. She passed the bar and rounded the corner to the back hall where the restrooms were. But rather than going in, she stopped, leaning against the wall as she dug her phone from her purse.

"Sarah," he said, not wanting to startle her. "Hey, sorry about that with Andrea. She caught me by surprise."

Sarah grimaced. "Hope I didn't make you uncomfortable, or anyone else. But I was feeling kind of awkward there. Not because I thought that you and I… Ugh, you know what I mean."

He was pretty sure he did. Because while they'd agreed that nothing was going to happen between them, he was having one hell of a time shutting down the possessive bullshit that kept firing up every time Sean or any other guy seemed to notice Sarah was alive. So pretty much nonstop.

It didn't make sense. It wasn't rational. But there it was.

Sarah bit her lip, refocusing on her phone. "It's totally fine if you're interested in whatever Andrea was offering. More than fine. I mean, you didn't even know I was going to be here. I just showed up with Sean. So, of course…" She let out a sigh and met his eyes, that sweet sort of critical look on her face. "Okay, and now I feel like a total idiot. *Sarah, stop talking*."

Max wanted to reach for her, pull her against his chest, and hug her. Hell, he could practically feel himself burying his nose in her silky dark hair, but it probably wasn't a good idea. Having her that close, being able to smell her subtle perfume and feel the softness of her curves against him. Yeah, better not.

"No, Sarah, you're not an idiot. I am. Andrea was there before I even realized it, and I was the one feeling awkward. I didn't know how to handle it. She's a cool girl, and we're friends. We've been friends for a long time. So jumping back like she was on fire would've made everyone feel like crap. But I wasn't interested."

"Well, like I said, it would've been fine if you were. I just didn't want to watch it." She laughed in her self-deprecating way and added, "Been there, done that."

Max's brows furrowed. "What are you talking about?"

Returning her phone to her purse, she cocked her head. "I've seen you hook up with other women, Max. Back in college. That handful of parties you talked me into. I knew I wasn't your date. I knew you weren't into me. But there was that *thing* between us, that little *maybe* in the back of my mind. Anyway, when the party would wind down, and one of the girls who'd been hovering around you on and off throughout the night suddenly stuck close, hooking her fingers into your pocket, and you'd wrap your arm around her shoulders and pull her in. Whisper something in her ear that would make even a girl as bold as she was blush and smile." She shook her head. "Well, I've seen enough of that."

There was no judgment in her eyes. No hurt or accusation. Just a statement of fact from a woman who knew herself well enough and had the confidence to give him that simple truth.

Still, something deep in his gut twisted, hearing her confession. Because he remembered those parties too. He remembered inviting her, even though he knew they weren't her speed. He remembered justifying his actions by telling himself he was just trying to help her have some fun. Get out and meet a few people. He'd even told himself if she came to his parties, he could keep an eye on her, make sure she didn't get into any trouble and no one hassled her. Like he was some fucking savior, instead of the asshole trying like hell to come up with any excuse he could find to be near her.

And when she'd shown up those few times, he told himself he was doing the right thing by making sure they both knew nothing was going to happen between them. By making sure she saw exactly what kind of a dog he was when it came to women. So *she* wouldn't be tempted. Because if she had been? Hell, that was one temptation he hadn't known if he'd be able to pass up.

"Sarah," he started, not sure what to say, what not to say.

She shook her head. "I can see you're about to apologize for something, and you absolutely don't need to. I'm not upset about it. But I think it's plain to see I'm still attracted to you. And even though we both agree there's nowhere for that to go, I'd still rather not see you with someone else if I don't have to."

"You won't. And just so we're clear, I wasn't looking for anything other than a few hours of fun with my friends tonight. That's still what I want. I hope what happened with Andrea doesn't cost me one of them."

Sarah smiled brightly, turning her shoulders so the right one lined up with her chin. "Definitely not."

Damn, she was so easy. So straightforward. Well, aside from trying to trick him into taking her virginity. But he couldn't hold it against her. She'd had her reasons, and while he was fucking glad he'd figured out what was going on before doing something neither of them could take back, at least he got where she was coming from.

Now they understood each other.

"Great. Let's go kick some ass." He grinned. Because Emily was damn near impossible to beat and had a lesson in humility coming he couldn't wait to watch Sarah serve up.

By the end of the night, Sarah was pretty sure she'd either made a mortal enemy or a new best friend. On the one hand, Emily had called her every name in the book and a few Sarah was pretty sure had been made up on the spot. On the other hand—

"Ooh, come on, Sean. You *have* to find Sarah a job in Chicago," Emily pleaded, giving Sean the big eyes while clasping her hands beneath her chin. "I want to keep her!"

"Yeah, Em, I want to keep her too. Why else do you think I brought her out?" Sean asked, flashing that smooth, charming smile Sarah's way. "I'm counting on you guys for the hard sell."

Jase stood behind his wife, his hands on her shoulders. "If anyone can land the deal, this one can," he said proudly.

They were a cute couple. Both crazy tall and gorgeous. Jase had that sort of tousled Superman hair to match his broad shoulders and above-average height. Emily was runway gorgeous, with silky-soft strawberry-blond hair and the kind of long legs Sarah, coming in at a measly five foot four, had only dreamed of. And jeez, the way Jase looked at Emily when they were together—so completely in love—had given Sarah a case of the dreamy sighs.

She scooted back on her stool. "You guys are awesome, but for as much fun as I had schooling you in darts"—she looked directly at Sean—"I'd go out of my flipping mind if this job was permanent."

There just wasn't that much to do, and they both knew it. She thrived on challenge, period.

"So how long are you here again?" Molly asked, kicked back in her chair as she picked at the label on her bottle.

"Last week in August," Sarah replied. "I start in New York September first."

"Nice! That means you'll be around for all the festivals." Molly gave Brody—who'd joined them about thirty minutes before—a pointed look. "I get her for Brew to Be Wild." Then turning back to Sarah, she leaned over the table, explaining, "You get to try twenty different beers *at the zoo*, which is awesome, if you haven't been there."

"I remember the zoo, though it's definitely been a while. But what a fun idea."

"Yeah, there's no shortage of cool stuff through the summer," Max agreed, leaning into Sarah's side so his arm pressed briefly against hers. "You remember all the art fairs, neighborhood festivals, and music?"

She nodded, but the heat of that contact was distracting her with how good it felt. No one touched her like that. Work friends didn't break physical boundaries except on the smallest scale, and this full shoulder-to-elbow press, platonic as it may have been intended, was just so good.

Turning, she met Max's eyes. They were closer than she expected.

"I, uh… Yes, I remember you telling me about your favorites one night. Taste of Chicago and Blues Fest. Lollapalooza."

"Damn, how do you remember that stuff?" Max asked, smiling as he searched her eyes in a way that set the butterflies loose and made her speak before she thought.

"At the time, I think I might have been hoping you and I would go together."

Max tipped his head closer. "Yeah, I'd been thinking about that too. Only I kept telling myself it wasn't a good idea."

Right. Like she was telling herself now.

"I remember thinking the same thing." Breaking the eye contact that was starting to make her a little breathless, Sarah took a sip of her beer. "Just thinking about all those *good ideas* and *right things* and *responsible choices* makes me want to go back and throw them all out the window. Probably would have ended up having a heck of a lot more fun." And a hell of a lot less heartbreak.

Setting down her glass, Sarah realized another conversation was still taking place at the table.

"Molly, you get that I'm the boss, right?" Brody bristled, leaning back in his chair and stretching those thick arms out wide. "I ought to get to take Sarah to the zoo one with the beer tastings. Booze is my thing."

"Screw that, boss man." Molly chuckled, clearly unconcerned about the employee-employer workplace power dynamic as she flipped him off with an impish smile from where she was slumped down in her seat. "You can take her to that pole-dancing contest we saw out in St. Charles. Show off some of your mad skills."

"Jesus," Sean cut in, waving a hand between them like he wanted to wave away the mental imagery. "You realize, I'm trying to sell Sarah on staying, not send her bolting out of Illinois in terror because of you bunch of tools."

Molly laughed through her nose. "*You're* a tool."

Sean didn't need to worry. These guys were exactly what Sarah needed. They were fun and real, and made her laugh like she couldn't remember laughing in a very long time.

Twenty minutes later, things were wrapping up. The beers had been cleared, the tabs settled, and the last rounds of congratulations made to Jill and her boyfriend and the rest of the players who'd come to the bar. Sarah was getting ready to leave when Max came up and helped her with her light sweater.

"You have wonderful friends," she said, trying not to get distracted by how close he was standing or that his hands had brushed her shoulders before she turned to look at him. "Thanks for letting me spank them in darts tonight. This was just what I needed."

Max shrugged, his arms crossing over his chest. "Glad to have you on my team. And glad for the chance to hang out."

For a moment, she wondered whether he was going to ask if she'd like to do something another time. Or if she wanted a ride home. But she knew he wouldn't, and not just because he'd asked earlier and she turned him down. But because of that *thing* still lingering in the air between them. If he wanted to see her again, it wouldn't be as friends, and they both knew it.

It was for the best. She didn't need the distraction or the temptation or any of the other confusing things Max tended to be for her. And the one thing she did need? Well, he wasn't offering.

Tonight had been a freebie. Sean orchestrated it, and neither she nor Max had played a part in that. Which meant they'd been able to enjoy the time together without the expectation, anticipation, or implication of *something more*.

Their eyes met one last time, holding as she smiled. "Take care, Max."

～～～

Friday night rolled around at a snail's pace. Probably because Max hadn't been able to stop thinking about Sarah all week. On Wednesday, he'd been watching the front door of Belfast from the minute he walked in—a full hour before everyone was supposed to meet up— because a part of him was holding his damn breath that Sean was gonna show up with Sarah on his arm.

But when his buddy strolled through the door alone, Max spent the next two hours telling himself he was glad about it. That it was what he'd really wanted to happen. Just like he told himself he wasn't going to go home that night and take the edge off thinking about the taste of Sarah's kiss.

Obviously, he was a liar on both counts. And today he'd woken up feeling like crap because of the naughty—like, triple X–rated naughty—dream from the night before featuring his favorite good girl letting him teach her all about being bad.

Shit. And now he was getting hard again, just thinking about it.

Thankfully, he was in the confines of his own home instead of stuck behind the wheel of his patrol car with his temporary partner asking him if he was okay every ten minutes because of the way he kept shifting around.

Picking up the Sheetrock he'd cut the night before, Max positioned the pieces around the room where they were going to be hung. Sean had said he'd be over about now to help hang as many pieces as they could in the hour and a half before everybody else showed up to watch the fight on pay-per-view.

Sure enough, a few minutes later, Max jogged down the stairs to answer the door. Sean was there, but instead of the blue jeans and band T-shirt Max had been expecting, Sean was dressed like he was…shit, doing anything other than hanging Sheetrock.

"What's up?" Max asked, nodding at Sean's cleaner, more casual attire.

"Sorry, man," Sean said, walking past him into the

rehabbed downstairs hall. "I can help for about thirty minutes with whatever you've got, but change of plans tonight. I gotta bail."

Damn, that sucked. "No problem. Cool of you to come over anyway. Let's see what we can get done."

Sean nodded, leading the way up the stairs. After all the times he'd helped out, the guy was as familiar with the brownstone as Max.

"It's fucking weird that you don't have any furniture in this place." Sean looked around the way he always did, like he expected Max to have picked out bedroom sets and china cabinets over the last three and a half days for the handful of rooms not currently under construction.

"It's temporary," Max said, reaching the top of the stairs and waving Sean toward the front room overlooking the street. "I've got everything I need."

"What you have are a mattress shoved against one corner of the living room, a metal hanging rack, and six milk crates for your clothes. You need some furniture. You *live* here."

"I have a couch. And why would I fill this place when I'm just gonna sell it? Houses show better empty, and what the hell am I going to do with all that crap when I move into the next place and need to rip down the walls and fix the wiring and all the other shit that comes with gutting a house?"

Sean shook his head as he ducked through the plastic draping that kept the construction dust contained. "Yeah, but you live in these places for almost a year. The least you could do is give yourself a functional kitchen. And before you tell me you've got one, one pot and a drawer

full of plastic silverware don't count. And FYI, those
lawn chairs you have for your guests are fucking ridiculous. Nobody likes sitting in them."

"Yeah, yeah," Max replied, having heard it all before.
Sean was probably right, but what Max had was just so
easy. It was hassle free, and he was used to it. Maybe
one of these days he'd get around to investing in a
couple more comfortable pieces of furniture, but for
now he was good.

Sean picked up one of the sheets of drywall and held
it in place while Max grabbed his drill.

"So what've you got going on tonight?" Max asked,
digging out a few screws so they could get started. He'd
taken this room down to the bones, so it would feel good
to finish and check it off his list. Positioning the first
screw, he lined up the bit.

"Not much. Just Sarah," Sean said with a shrug. "She
needs a favor, and I said I'd help her out."

Max hadn't even realized he'd hit the power, but the
drill whirled, flying off the screw and into the drywall.
And then the drill was on the floor, and Max's hands
were wrapped in Sean's shirt as he backed the guy
who'd been like a brother to him across the room.

"No. Fucking. Way. Sean." That was the sound of his
crazy train going off the rails.

But then the element of surprise had worn off, and
Sean's feet dug in. Grabbing hold of Max's wrists, he
pushed back into the space between them.

"What the fuck, man?" he demanded through gritted teeth.

Max knew what he was doing was bullshit. Again.

But all he could see was Sarah falling back on her

bed. That spill of dark silken hair pooling over her pillow as her lips parted and her back arched.

Beneath Sean.

"A favor?" Max demanded, unable to stop himself from pushing his friend with a solid shove. "Just planning to help her out? Or have you been helping her out already?"

Sean's head turned to the side, his eyes closing for a brief second.

Was that guilt? Jesus, he'd already had her. Max's gut churned so hard he could barely breathe.

"Fuck this, Max." Sean glared at him. "I thought it was kind of cute that first day when you about lost your shit thinking I was on a date with her. Hell, I might've even encouraged it some, since it was about fucking time you stopped dicking your way through Chicago one night at a time. But do you get off your ass and do something about it? No. You tell me there's nothing between you. Right. Denial. Fine. You're slow, so I figure I'll give you another shot. Another night out with Sarah, who happens to be one hell of a girl. But you still don't do anything.

"And now here we are, four days later. Have you called her? Have you done one fucking thing, other than trying to toss me up against a wall, for what? I don't even know. No. You haven't, and I've about had it with your bipolar possessive bullshit. So back the fuck off before I put my fist in your face and have to spend the next week explaining why to your little sister."

Max let go of Sean's shirt and shook out his hand, which felt strangely numb. His heart was slamming in his chest, but he'd held on to his sanity enough to know everything Sean had said was true.

Clearing his throat, he took a step back. He tried like hell, but he still couldn't meet Sean's eyes when he asked, "So now you want her?"

"It wouldn't fucking matter if I did, because *she's not interested in me*!" Sean spit back. "In case you're too blind to see it, the only guy she's looking at is you. So what the hell is going on here?"

Now Max did meet his friend's eyes, and all he saw there was confusion.

Okay, confusion and a good amount of pissed off. "What kind of favor was she asking you for?" Max asked, forcing himself to back up a step and then another.

"Piper's out of town, and she needed help moving something," Sean grumbled, then giving Max a pointed look, added, "Not that it's any of your damned business. Right?"

What the hell was wrong with him? Sean was right. He was acting like a grade-A asshole. But the idea that Sean was going over there to help her out with that *little problem* she'd come to Max with first had been enough to send him off the deep end. Which was nuts, because she'd told him flat-out that she'd find someone else to help her with it. And he'd nodded like it was no big deal. Like that was some solid plan he supported.

Like he wasn't going to go nuclear the second he thought about it actually happening.

Sean walked back to the sheet of drywall now lying on the floor. Crouching down, he ran his thumb over the spot where Max had lost control of the drill and his mind.

"This is still useable. You want to get back to it, or should I roll up my sleeves and pound the snot out of you?"

"Sean, man, I'm sorry."

Max shook his head and reached into his pocket for a wad of bills he slapped into Sean's hand. "This is for the pizza. Forget the drywall. And the favor too. Stay here and watch the game with everyone when they show up. I gotta go."

Chapter 10

THE FRIDGE WAS GROSS. KNEELING IN FRONT OF THE OPEN door, her semiretired yoga pants not nearly enough padding to protect her knees from the scarred wood of Piper's kitchen floor, Sarah scrubbed the darkened crevices and mystery splatters in the *new* used fridge Piper had "scored" from some friends. Friends who had been willing to get the massive appliance up the stairs and into the apartment, but drew the line at crossing the kitchen to back it into the spot where the old one had been.

Sarah couldn't believe she'd had to call Sean to help, but the guy had always joked that if he could get her to Chicago, he'd help her move in himself. This counted.

The buzzer sounded from the lobby security door, and Sarah pushed to her feet. Joints aching, she rushed over to the intercom, buzzing Sean up right away. This would be nice. He was always good company, and she could use the break from thinking about Max, who'd been on her mind way too much. She'd buy a pizza and see if Sean wanted to stick around for a beer.

Walking back to the sink, she stripped off her rubber gloves before doing a quick wash up to her elbows, just in case any of the *gross* had gotten on her.

Catching a glimpse of her reflection in the window above the sink, she flinched. The messy bun, ten-year-old tank top, and dust-covered yoga pants were casual

in a way she and Sean—for as much as they got along—
didn't do. Whatever, it was too late to change or add a
little makeup, and honestly, it was just Sean.

A knock sounded, and she opened the door. "Hey,
thanks so much for—" But the rest of whatever she'd
been about to say died on her lips as she registered who
was standing in her doorway.

Not Sean.

Not unless he'd found a way to grow a few inches and
add a whole lot of muscle overnight. She dragged her
eyes up over the solid slabs of hard chest, neatly pack-
aged in an old Atari T-shirt flecked with bits of plaster
and paint, up the thick column of his neck to the jaw that
was flexing in time with her pounding heart, then up into
the eyes she'd been dreaming about for years.

"Max," she croaked, looking past him. "Is Sean with
you?"

"No."

"Then what are you doing here?"

Max scrubbed the back of his head, looking down
the hall behind him like he was thinking about turning
around and leaving. Like he wasn't sure if he should
have come. Then blowing out a harsh breath, he met
her eyes.

"I'll do it."

Her brows lifted, her lips falling open as she felt the
impact of those few words. She swallowed, stepping
back so he could come inside. After one last look for
Sean, she closed and locked the door. This was no conversation for her boss to stumble into.

"For the sake of avoiding any more awkward misun-
derstandings, when you say *you'll do it*—"

"I'll be your first," Max clarified flatly as his hands fisted at his side.

Not exactly the body language of someone gleefully anticipating the task ahead of him. In fact, if she had to put a label on it, she'd say Max looked like he was downright dreading what was to come.

But if he didn't want to, then why was he there? Was he offering her a pity f—

No. No way, no how was she going to let the man burning a hole in her fantasy file ruin everything by *grudgingly* giving it up for her. She still had her pride. Or at least a little of it.

"Look, Max, it's very generous of you to offer," she started, trying to keep the humiliation out of her tone, "but unnecessary."

She waited for him to say something. To make another flimsy offer or just fall back against the wall and let out a gusty sigh of relief. Anything so she could deal with it and move on. She would get Max out of her apartment and crawl into a nice bottle of wine to cool the burn of embarrassment. Maybe Sean would just cancel. The fridge wasn't that important. They had those Popped Rice Crisps in the cabinet. Chocolate chips too.

When nothing happened, she finally forced herself to meet Max's eyes, and what she saw in them most definitely wasn't relief.

"Max?"

"So you—you already found someone else who took… I mean, you don't need… You aren't still…" Max broke off, rubbing a hand over his face as if trying to clear something he didn't want her to see.

Ahh, now she got it. And didn't really appreciate it

either. How fast did he think she moved? It had been less than a week since he'd turned her down. And while she fully intended to get her situation resolved before moving to New York, it would be nice if she could stop thinking about Max before propositioning the next guy. Call it common courtesy.

"Umm, no."

Max's head came up with a jerk. The air he sucked in seemed to fill his frame, broaden his chest and shoulders, and straighten his spine.

"No?" he asked again, taking a step toward her.

Sarah let out a sigh and held up her hands. "If you really want to know, I'm not interested in a pity lay. While it may be hard to believe, I've still got my pride."

"Pity lay? Your pride?" Max shook his head like he didn't get it. Which really irked her, because this was one conversation Sarah didn't need to have. Her ego had taken enough of a beating as it was.

"That's right. Look, I appreciate that you don't want to leave me hanging, but I assure you, I'll be able to handle this on my own. I get that you've always been a charitable guy. But this"—arms out to her sides, she pointed inward toward her *little problem*—"*this* is my limit."

Max ran a hand over his face, wiping away his confusion and leaving what looked suspiciously like amusement in its place. His mouth started to twitch, but as far as she could tell, there wasn't one damn thing about this worth laughing at.

"No, Sarah, the reason I'm standing here grinding my molars into dust isn't because I *don't want you*. And I'm sure as hell not offering a pity lay. What's happening here is now that I've stopped telling myself I can't have you, I'm doing everything in my power to keep from just *taking you*." His eyes raked down the length of her, and his voice lowered. "Grabbing you and backing you up to the nearest wall. *Fuck*."

The nearest wall?

A wall sounded really, *really* good. Lots of potential.

"What you're seeing, Sarah," he said, taking another step toward her, "isn't reluctance. It's barely maintained *restraint*."

Her pulse skipped, and her hands came together in front of her chest. "Really? Like you're actually having to work to hold yourself back?"

"Yeah, but don't look so happy about it," he said with a pained laugh.

"No, I know." She shouldn't. But he looked *miserable*. Like it required some Herculean effort not to just *take her*. Oh jeez, that was really good stuff. "It's just that after thinking you might be forcing yourself to do it to accommodate me? Okay, I know it's stupid. But I can't help liking that you find me hard to resist."

His brows pulled together, his eyes clearing. "I've always found you hard to resist."

He said it like it was the most obvious thing in the world. Like she should know. But that wasn't the way she remembered things.

"What's changed?" she asked, needing to know before things went any further. Before she let herself believe again.

Max reached out and tucked a bit of loose hair behind her ear. "Not me wanting you. Just how I felt about whether I could actually have you. Sarah, I know you could do better. You deserve better, but if you've decided you don't want to wait—" He closed his eyes and blew out a slow breath.

"I've been losing my mind thinking about you with some other guy. I know it's shitty. I know we're not together. That you're not looking for forever in this. And neither am I." He stroked her shoulder with the backs of his knuckles, sending a tremor through her as she leaned in. "But I could do this for you. I could do this *with* you, and I could do it right."

Only then she remembered. "Wait, Sean's on his way over."

"No, he's not," he said, glancing away. But not before she caught the hint of guilt in his eyes.

That didn't look good.

She was almost afraid to ask. "What happened to him?"

"He…uh…mentioned that he was coming over here to *help you out* with something. That you needed a *favor*."

Her eyes went wide. "And you thought—"

"Yeah."

"This is what you were talking about when you said you were losing it thinking about me with someone else?"

"Pretty much."

"Sean's okay?" Please let her boss be okay!

"So far, he's gotten out of helping me hang drywall and helping you move your fridge. He's fine."

Her brows lifted. "So we're alone in my place, with no one else on their way over, and a change of heart between us." Stepping closer to Max, she rested her hand against his chest. Her body responded to the way he was watching her, and it made her bold. "Whatever shall we do now?"

The muscle in his jaw flexed, and she thought she could hear the popping of one molar against another.

"Not what you're thinking." His arms closed around her, his hands moving toward opposite poles along her back. "We should talk a minute, Sarah."

She laughed softly, because she didn't know how he figured they were going to talk when he was ducking down to run his mouth along the length of her neck, melting her brain with soft, openmouthed kisses and just the barest hint of suction against her skin.

Dropping her head to the side, she offered him more access and felt her world spin as he drew harder.

"Max," she gasped, as warmth stirred low in her center. "No more talk."

His head came up, and the heat in his eyes set her on fire. "No more talk," he replied, grabbing her by the backs of her thighs and hiking her up so that her legs wrapped around his waist as he found her mouth with his and kissed her hard.

―――――

Max backed her down the hall past one closet, Piper's room, and a bathroom before hitting pay dirt with the doorknob that led to Sarah's bedroom. Finally. Her kiss was making him crazy, and the way she was clinging to him was driving him wild. Her arms twined around his neck, holding tight, and her leg was caught up at his side where he held her with one hand beneath her thigh and the other around her back. Jesus, her mouth was sweet.

He wanted her like he couldn't remember wanting anything before.

Almost there. He braced his knee on her bed, ready

to lean her back and follow her down. He wanted to feel the give of her body beneath his, the spread of her legs as she made room for him, the rush of her breath against his cheek as he burrowed his face into her neck. Yeah, he wanted all of that, but then he saw it. The shift he felt only a second later, when everything in Sarah went from *yes, yes, yes*...to some small part of her whispering *no*.

It didn't happen with words; it was more of a physical thing. A tensing of her muscles. The fingers that had been kneading the back of his skull tightened into a ball there, and then the last, most significant tell of them all was one eye squinting open before pinching shut even tighter than before, suggesting someone was starting to freak out and didn't want him to notice.

"Don't stop," she pleaded, still clinging to him, even as her nerves gave her away with the crack of her voice.

Max pressed his forehead to hers, closing his eyes as he sucked a slow breath.

"Baby, we've got to."

Releasing her hold around his neck and waist, she sank back into the mattress with a pout. "You're a tease, Max."

Catching one of her hands in his, he interwove their fingers and pulled them up over her head.

"You're impatient."

One slender brow arched at him. "I'm a twenty-eight-year-old virgin, Max. How much more patient can I be? I'm just nervous. But I don't want to stop."

Then her other brow bounced as high as the first, as a light filled her eyes and she craned back to look where he'd placed their hands.

"Oh wait, is this a control thing?" she asked, sounding just a little too eager. Her voice dropped to a whisper, and she said, "I've read books about this, and while I admit they do it for me a little bit—I'm not going to lie—it seems a little advanced for a first time."

Max stared down into her wary but excited eyes, his brain all but shutting down from the information coming at him. Because knowing the idea of a little control play excited her? It hadn't exactly been on his agenda, but hells to the yeah, if she was up for it. Only that game was definitely reserved for the advanced class.

"You're killing me here, Sarah." Her free hand flattened over his chest in a maddening caress he could barely think past. "It's not a control thing."

"Then what's the problem?" she asked, wrapping her legs around his hips.

"The problem is, I want to give you something special. Meaningful. I want you to be ready."

Sarah's fingers were at the back of Max's T-shirt, tugging it toward his shoulders as she let out little grunts between her words. "You're still thinking…about that girl…who was waiting on a fairy tale. News flash: it blew up…in her face." She flopped back and met his eyes. "Come on, can't we just do it?"

Jesus, they were back to this? He wanted to say yes.

Right then, there wasn't any fear in her eyes. He'd backed off, so she'd started to advance. But something told him that as eager as she might be to get it over with, it would be a whole lot better if he took it another way.

"No. Sarah, listen a minute. I've got a plan. I think it might work for both of us."

"Oh yeah?" Her hands played along his ribs and down his sides. Max lifted himself up so she could press her palms against his chest the way she had before. The way he'd liked.

Only instead of flattening against his pecs, her hands moved lower. Tickling their way past his abs to the button on his fly. "Sarah," he warned, voice tight, because a part of him really wanted her to go there.

Taking the possibility off the table, he lowered his weight over her, trapping her wandering fingers where they were, barely breaching his waistband.

"No fair," she pouted in a huff.

Damn, she was cute.

Dropping his lips to hers, he kissed her and then pulled back.

"Are you listening?"

"Yes. Under protest."

"That's fine. So here's the deal. This isn't just going to be your first time. It's going to be my first—and probably only—time *being* someone's first time. I want it to be special for both of us. I don't want to be some box you check off your bucket list, Sarah. I want it to be good."

"I've heard the rumors, Max. Heck, I actually *saw* your name written on the stall wall in the ladies' bathroom at Belfast. It said 'For a good time.'"

His chin pulled back. "Did you scratch it out?"

"No. But if I go back, I could take a Sharpie with me, I guess…but what I'm getting at is that I've been hearing how *good* you are since college."

"Yeah, but a first time is different. I don't want you waiting for me teeth gritted, bracing for impact." He lowered his mouth to the shell of her ear. "I want you desperate and aching for me. Breathless. Moaning. Baby, I want you *ready* for me."

He heard her swallow, felt her breath become shallower, and saw the color rise across her skin. She looked at him, completely serious. "Okay, this isn't me pestering you to get what I want, but after that, what you just said, I think I might actually be ready *right now*. Really."

Max chuckled, and though it half killed him to do it, he backed off the bed.

Sarah pushed up on her elbows, a little scowl on those sexy lips of hers. "No dice, huh?"

Much as it pained him—and promised to pain him all through the night ahead—no. "So here's what I'm thinking. You let me take you out a few times, and we warm up to it. Together."

It would be perfect. While neither of them was looking for something serious, there was nothing better than spending time with this girl. And for once, rather than trying to stifle that chemistry or connection or whatever had been there from the start, he'd be able to foster and encourage it. Build on what was already between them to give what they were about to share at least a fraction of the meaning it deserved.

"You need to *warm up to it*?" Sarah asked, her voice squeaking just a little.

She plucked at the tank top he'd been admiring on her since she opened the door, curling her lip in distaste. "Okay, maybe I get that."

"You've got it wrong, Sarah." Leaning back over her, he braced himself on one arm and reached for her hand with the other. This wasn't something he'd normally do, but no way was he going to let doubt eat at her insecurities.

He pulled her hand to where his fly was straining from the hard-on behind it.

She gasped and met his eyes.

"For the record, physically, I'm more than capable of getting the job done. But, Sarah, for you to remember it the way I want you to, for it to be special, we *should* warm up to it. I want to romance you. I want to tease you and give you time to think and wonder about what it's going to be like between us. I want to build that slow burn inside you, so by the time we're together, you're *on fire*." He stroked her cheek. "That's what a first time should be like. Like your next breath depends on it."

"You could do that, without it getting complicated?"

"It's already complicated," he said, removing her hand from his fly, because while he definitely liked it, that wasn't really a first date activity. "Hell, I nearly punched my best friend in the face when I thought he might have been on his way over here to offer his own assist."

She blinked. "That would have been bad. He's my boss, Max."

"Yeah, but I pulled his head out of the toilet when he passed out drinking once, which trumps the boss thing."

A steady stream of air passed her lips. "I've been working for this promotion for years. Chicago is supposed to be an extended stopover. I can't afford complicated."

He knew that and was proud of her for keeping her priorities straight. No way would he risk screwing up her plans.

"How about we uncomplicate it then. Put a few ground rules in place."

A skeptical brow raised his way. "Like what, no kissing on the lips?"

He laughed. "We're talking about maintaining the semicasual component of once-in-a-lifetime special sex here, Sarah—not prostitutes protecting their hearts." He shook his head, remembering that this was how it had always been between them. Conversations made all the more entertaining by their frequent need for clarification. His girl got the craziest ideas, and damned if he didn't get a kick out of hearing them. "You give me four dates over two weeks to get us to our goal. And when it's over, you let me kiss you good-bye, and we go on as *just friends* with a wicked hot memory between us."

Sarah climbed off the bed and began to pace. No question he had her full attention now.

"Is the fourth date part of the warm-up or the day the deed gets done?"

"It's *do* day." Not a chance in hell he'd be able to wait longer than that. Already, he was regretting saying four dates instead of, say, two.

But Sarah freezing up beneath him wasn't something he ever wanted to experience again. If she knew where the lines were drawn, what they weren't moving past, she'd be able to relax and enjoy the journey, and by the time the lines went away, he sincerely hoped she'd be ready for it.

"And the good-bye kiss," she asked, her hand coming up in question. "With tongue?"

Max ran his palm over his mouth, trying not to grin. "Definitely with tongue."

Now, with all the important facts sorted out, she took one last debating breath before giving him a single nod. "Okay, so when's this first date, and what exactly does it entail?"

"I'll tell you while we move the fridge."

Chapter 11

WITH ONE LAST STROKE OF SUNFLOWER-YELLOW NAIL polish smoothed on the nail of her big toe, Piper cocked her head and cleaned up the edge with her thumbnail before returning her attention to Sarah, who was tucked into the corner of the couch in their cluttered living room.

"So let me get this straight. He showed up at the door last night after nearly beating up your boss so he could help you out with the fridge *and* your other little problem?" Piper asked, pointing to Sarah's lap, which was apparently her favorite new thing to do.

It might normally have gotten a rise out of Sarah, but with all that was happening, with the way her body had basically been on overload since Max left the night before with the promise of a date later that day, all she could focus on was the basic exchange of information. "Yes."

"Except then he doesn't actually take care of your problem at all. And informs you that the expected wait period has just been extended to two weeks."

Sarah set her glass of water down on the end table and slumped back into the couch, her chin resting on her chest. "Right. Four dates that gradually build up to the big event."

"Because he wants you really, *really* ready for it when it finally comes."

"That's the plan."

"Okay, you do know, if you actually wanted to, you could go out and have this situation handled in the next hour. Seriously, I know a guy—"

Sarah's hand was up, cutting Piper off. "Not another word, Piper. I was feeling a little waffly about the four-dates thing, but you just sold me on it. This"—she pointed down at her lap—"is not an 'I've got a guy' situation."

Her friend shrugged, a wicked look in her eyes. "But I do."

She'd regret this. Sarah knew she would, but she couldn't resist. Leaning forward so her elbows perched on her knees, she asked. "But seriously, what does that mean, you have a guy? I know you work with a lot of men down at the radio station, but does one of them have a reputation for getting off on virgins, or is there actually some guy extending an offer of sex on an as-needed basis?"

Piper stood up, amusement flashing in her eyes. "Don't worry about it, Sarah. You're all set with your date tonight, or at least you will be once you start getting ready." Offering her hand, she tugged Sarah up from the couch. "On the upside, I'm guessing it's pretty safe to say this date won't require any waxing, right?"

Sarah laughed, pulling her friend in for a hug. "I guess not."

An hour later, Sarah was dressed in a pair of cropped jeans she'd paid a ridiculous amount for but that had flattered her figure to the point where abandoning them in the store would have felt like an unconscionable crime. Her blouse was a silky, short-sleeved number with a delicate pastel brushstroke pattern and a dozen tiny mother-of-pearl buttons down the front. Walking into the kitchen, she did a little turn in the doorway for Piper, who was eating peanut butter off a spoon at the sink.

"What do you think?"

"I like it," Piper said, nodding approvingly. "It says 'I have a great ass, but you're not getting any' while ensuring he'll be wishing he could."

Piper could always be counted on for a colorful, concise review.

Scooping out another enormous glob of peanut butter, she asked, "So what are you guys doing on your date tonight anyway?"

"Dinner, I think, and then—"

"Yeah, yeah, that's great. What I'm asking is what kind of *play* you're going to get since you know he's not putting out."

Uh-huh, that. "He said we'd start slow. But beyond that, I don't really know. I don't know if we'll do anything." It probably seemed a little backward, considering Max had seen her naked once in the last week, and she'd had her legs wrapped around him at least twice. But both times they'd failed to launch, so maybe backing up a few steps wasn't the worst idea ever.

Piper was making one of those slightly disgusted faces. "Slow. Mmm-hmm. That's sweet, I guess."

Actually it was. Max said he'd wanted to give her as much of the experience she'd been cheated out of as he could.

The intercom squawked, and Sarah's heart skipped a beat. She buzzed him up and left the door open while returning to her room to fasten the buckles on her block-heeled sandals and check her makeup. She'd gone with a lighter look, glossing her lips and adding a bit of bronzer.

Mascara, liner, and a neutral palate of shadow finished her eyes. A pair of oversize hoops with a narrow band completed her look.

She was ready.

Or at least as ready as she could be.

Piper was chatting with Max by the door when she returned. He was standing in that wide-legged stance that seemed to be his natural state of rest, dressed casually in a pair of jeans and a gray, long-sleeved T-shirt that hugged and stretched over the hard, packed muscles beneath.

The *body* on this man.

"Hey, gorgeous," he said, letting his eyes roam over her from head to toe and back again.

And that appreciative look—it got to her good. Because suddenly the air felt thin, and her heart was going faster than it should.

Licking her peanut-butter spoon, Piper waved good-bye and sauntered back toward the kitchen, leaving them alone in the hall.

Max's brows pulled together as he nodded after her. "Piper know what we're doing?"

"I hope you don't mind," Sarah said with a wince. "We've been friends since the first grade, and I guess I wasn't really thinking about whether it was fair to you for me to tell her." Biting her lip, she took a step closer. "Which is completely hypocritical, because now that I'm thinking about it, I'm realizing I'd about die if you'd told anyone what we're doing. I'm sorry, Max."

Taking her hand in his, he shook his head. "Sean knows I'm taking you out. Couldn't really keep it from him after the way I've been acting, but beyond that he doesn't know anything."

Sarah looked at where their hands met, the low charge from that point of contact making her heart stutter and skip. "Thank you."

"Yeah, well, for the sake of full disclosure, whatever Sean knows, Molly knows about seventeen seconds later. And what she knows, Jase, Emily, and Brody will know about ten seconds after that. So if you feel your ears start to burn, it's because they'll be speculating pretty much nonstop about what's going on with us. Probably for about a year after you've moved to New York."

"Is that all?" she asked with a laugh.

"Honestly, could be longer."

"Well, thanks for the heads-up. And just so you know, Piper is the only person I share this sort of information with, and despite how she might come across, she's actually very discreet." Putting up a hand, she clarified, "*If* you get her to swear to secrecy up front. If you don't, well, make sure you do, is all."

Max grinned, still playing with her fingers. "Fair enough. And it doesn't bother me that she knows. Seems like this might be one of those things where it helps to have someone to talk to. So I'm glad you have her."

When he said things like that, it made Sarah glad she had *him*. This was going to be the best vacation fling of her life, and she couldn't wait to get to it.

Max took her to a tiny noodle place under the tracks. The lighting was bright and the air scented with fresh ginger and spice. As the hostess led them to a window seat in the corner, Max's hand stayed settled at the small of Sarah's back. From the time he'd picked her up, he'd maintained almost constant contact. Holding her hand, running the backs of his fingers along the line of her arm, rubbing a bit of her hair between his fingers and then taking her hand again.

So date number one must be about getting used to physical contact. That made sense in a clinical way that she would have expected to turn her off. But even knowing the logic behind those light, frequent touches, it didn't. It felt natural, easy. She'd say comfortable, except with every second he played with her fingers, weaving them between hers one way and then another, tension was building within her. A good tension, but one *comfortable* definitely didn't describe.

Not when it made her shift in her seat and her breath catch.

The dinner was amazing—fresh, light, and delicious—while the conversation came as easily between them as it always had. They talked about their careers. Their friends. Their family. Or at least Max talked about Molly and the friends and guys from the force he counted as family. He'd never given Sarah more than a few words about his parents, but what he'd said had been enough for her to understand that his home life growing up hadn't exactly been idyllic.

She told him about her first job with Wyse and how, when she met Sean, he'd seemed so uptight that she'd actually worried he might have less of a life than she did. She still couldn't quite believe her boss was the same man Max had warned her off back in college. It was crazy.

Almost as crazy as what they were doing.

"What are you thinking?" Max asked, rubbing his thumb in lazy patterns across her knuckles.

"That this is nuts. What we're doing." More of that

light friction from the rough pads of his work-worn hands. She really liked the feel of them on her. "Pretending to be out on a date when we both know what it's really about. What's coming."

Max picked up his beer with his free hand. Then after a swallow, he leaned closer, whispering conspiratorially, "You have no idea what's coming, baby. But you can be sure you're going to like it."

Shivers ran through her, leaving a path of goose bumps in their wake. Something Max hadn't missed. The cocky smile that had been driving her wild all evening dropped from his lips as his eyes turned dark, intense. "And there's nothing pretend about this date. I wouldn't have asked for it if I didn't want it. Sure, we both know you're headed to New York at the end of next month. But that doesn't mean we can't have something short and sweet for a few weeks while you're here."

"Sweet?" She wasn't sure she liked the sound of sweet. It sounded bland. Like a temptation easy to pass up for something more exotic.

"Yeah, sweet. Pretty sure nothing could make me think of being with you any other way, Sarah." Pulling her hand to his mouth, he dropped a soft kiss over her knuckle, letting his lips skim the sensitive flesh. "Think about this dinner. The chili and coconut together. Things can be hot and sweet at the same time, you know?"

The air left her lungs in a rush. The way he was looking at her wasn't sweet at all. Maybe that was all that mattered.

"Guess I'm going to find out."

Max leaned closer still, his lips spreading into that better-judgment-shattering smile she'd been falling for since that first night at the library. They were so close she could feel his breath across her cheek. "I guess you will."

Dinner ended, and they walked back to Max's car. It was still early, and Sarah's belly had started working itself into knots. Because what were they going to do next? She knew sex was off the table for two weeks. And yet they were supposed to be working toward it. So was he going to take her back to his place and start with the *warming up*—or was he just going to take her home and say good night, because the first date wasn't about getting busy?

When would he want to see her again?

What—

"What do you think about a movie?" Max asked, giving her hand a light squeeze and then pulling them to a stop about a half block down from where he'd parked.

She turned, surprised and more than a little pleased to hear their date wasn't over. "A movie sounds like fun."

Looking especially pleased with himself, Max asked, "Sounds like a first date too, right?"

How could such a powerful, imposing man, big and gruff and controlled, be so completely adorable? "Very much."

Sarah was starting to understand why Max had gotten a reputation for giving good date. The guy seemed to have thought of everything. He'd picked a movie and had the times for the next show at the AMC on Michigan. His selection was a little surprising. She would have pegged him more for a big-budget action adventure than a golden-years journey of self-discovery, but whatever. They were getting to know each other again, and this was definitely new information.

As they walked through the theater to find seats, she found herself wishing their date was just a little more real. Despite what Max had said about it, she knew the score. Anything with limits set as clearly as theirs couldn't be entirely real. But she was okay with that. She was having an amazing time with an incredible man. And when it was over, she would have New York. Still, another time, another place, two less commitment-phobic people?

Turned out, Max was a back-of-the-theater guy.

She'd never sat in the back row before, preferring a seat two-thirds back and dead center, if left to her own devices. But Max hadn't asked. Holding her hand, he'd led the way, and when they sat, he flashed her a wink that had her stalling where she sat. Because the wink plus the back row? Her jaw dropped.

"So, good reviews for this one?" she asked, fairly certain she knew the answer already.

The lights dimmed, and Max threw an arm around the back of her chair. Playing with the ends of her hair, he fired another one of those criminally hot smiles her way. "Not really."

Sarah's heart was racing, her skin tingling with antic-ipation. The film started to roll, but all she could focus on was the half-empty theater in front of them, the light tug and gentle pull of Max's fingers moving through her hair, and whether he was going to make a move or if he was waiting for her to.

What exactly was going to happen in the back of this theater?

Would she have to tell him to stop? Would she even want to?

"Nervous?" Max asked quietly. He knew. Of course he did.

"Maybe." No sense in lying when the guy had had her number from the start.

He pulled her closer, making her feel somehow sheltered. Protected. Safe. At least until he leaned in close to her ear, his smile evident in his single-word response. "Good."

Her mouth dropped open on a gasp that fell somewhere between outrage and amusement, and she turned, ready to tell him what he already knew. How bad he was. But before a word left her mouth, he was there, taking advantage of her parted lips with the press of his own.

That same hot charge surged through her, powering up every nerve, turning her on. His lips were firm and skilled, rubbing against hers first softly, then harder. Drawing with light suction, and then teasing with barely there contact until Sarah was breathless, her body on fire.

This guy could kiss.

Max cupped her cheek, then smoothed his palm beneath her hair. "So sweet," he groaned, closing the distance between them again. The hard press of his mouth against hers was heaven, almost as good as when he eased his tongue between her lips, dipping in for a taste and then curling and sliding against her. Licking and twining.

Driving her senseless.

She'd been kissed over the years. Skillfully. Tenderly. Passionately. But she'd only been kissed like this by Max. Or maybe it wasn't so much what he was doing—although seriously, sucking on her tongue almost had her ready to spontaneously combust—but more how her body responded to *him*. Like the chemistry was simply different. More potent. More addictive.

Her fingers were in the short brush of his hair; her body was twisted in her seat. With the way he was kissing her, that armrest was the only thing keeping her from climbing into his lap. She needed more, but all she was getting from Max were his hands coasting over her shoulders and arms, and occasionally making a trip down to her hips, waist, or ribs, where his fingers would flex once before he groaned against her mouth, and then return to her shoulder.

Hot and achy for his touch, she tried to maneuver her breast into his hand, but Max just chuckled under his breath, then moved his mouth to her ear. "Patience, baby. One date at a time."

She shook her head, biting her lip to keep from whimpering at the sensation of his jaw against the tender skin of her throat. "I think we're good, Max," she said, panting as quietly as she could. "We don't need to wait. I'm ready."

It wasn't exactly begging, but it was close, and with the way he'd been making love to her mouth, it was justified.

"Right here in the back row of the theater, huh?" he asked, lips curving against her ear.

Infuriating man. "You could take me home." She didn't want to wait.

He dusted kisses across her neck, then licked her earlobe. "We could. Or we could enjoy what we're doing right now and not worry about where it's going." He caught her lobe between his teeth and gently tugged, sending a hot pulse of sensation rushing between her legs. "We could make what we're doing last."

And just when she could barely stifle the needy sounds trying to get free, thanks to that light clasp, he *sucked*. "Max!"

"Trust me, Sarah. Let me make this good for you."

Pulling back, he searched her eyes, and she realized that somewhere along the way, they'd gone from her nearly climbing into his seat, to her pressed back into her own, Max leaning over the armrest into her space. She loved the look of him above her. "We've waited this long. Let me have a few more dates so I can make it right."

She blinked, her thoughts snared by what he'd just said. "*We've* waited?"

The corner of his mouth quirked up. "Yeah, Sarah. We've waited. You've been waiting for your first time, and I've been waiting for you since that last night back in school. Since before that. Do you have any idea how badly I wanted to say yes to you? How hard it was to walk away? I'd be lying if I told you I haven't thought about it over the years. Wished I could have had you and been doing the right thing too."

Her throat was tight, her heart racing. *This man*.

How could he make her feel so wanted while turning her down?

"Okay, Max. We've waited this long."

He ducked down, kissing her again. When he pulled back, it was to say, "You won't regret this."

She hoped not.

By the time the movie ended, Sarah felt like she'd made up for the general lack of lip action over the past several years all in one night. And if there were any others suffering a kissing shortage, she'd probably made up for theirs too.

They waited until the rest of the theater had cleared out before leaving, and when they walked out, it was with Max's arm wrapped around her shoulders, holding her close. Truth, without him supporting her, she wasn't sure she'd have been able to make it out of the theater on her own. Her knees had turned to Jell-O long before the ending credits started to roll.

They were quiet on the ride back to Piper's apartment, Sarah's thoughts still too scattered after the assault of that kiss. Max parked about a block down, then jumped out and rounded the car to get her door for her.

"Full-service date, I guess," she teased, loving the attention he was paying her.

Max's brow furrowed, and he looked down at the door he'd just gotten for her before asking, "Huh?"

Oh man, this guy was even more perfect than she'd thought. He wasn't even pulling moves with that gentleman bad-boy stuff. He just did it. Without even thinking.

Max walked her up to her door where he kissed the daylights out of her one last time, leaving her breathless and dazed when he pulled back and brushed his thumb across her bottom lip.

"Thank you for taking me out tonight," she whispered.

The corner of his mouth kicked up again. "My pleasure, Sarah."

She unlocked the door and let herself into the apartment. Then after locking up, she fell back against the wall and slid to the floor, a helpless smile on her face. Piper's head of blond curls popped out from her bedroom. Eyes going wide, she stepped into the hall, letting out a whoop as she bounced around.

"Oh, my precious baby hussy!" she squealed. "You did it! I'm so proud of you. Holy shit, I can't believe you scored on your first date. But from the looks of you, it must have been amazeballs. Jeez, can you even walk? Do you need an ice pack? Ooh, tell, tell, tell!"

"An ice pack?" Maybe for her mouth, because Max had seriously kissed the heck out of her. "Actually, I could probably use some lip balm."

Piper's jaw dropped. "This blown-away, one-breath-shy-of-delirium look is from *head*?"

Sarah somehow gathered the strength to snort. She pushed herself off the floor, shaking her head as she walked into the kitchen and dropped into one of the chrome-rimmed, diner-style chairs surrounding the table. "There was no head. No sex. It was just kissing." She reached down to unfasten the buckle on her sandal and added the hard-earned qualifier to that statement. "Really, really incredible, superhot, thoroughly soul-shattering kissing."

"Kissing?" Sliding into the chair across the table, Piper stared at her in blatant disbelief.

Sarah nodded, running her fingertips across her sensitive lips.

"Shut up," Piper gasped. "No way."

"Oh yeah."

Seconds passed, and then Piper stretched an arm across the table toward her. "Okay, I don't want this to sound weird or anything, but since Max is into doing favors and all that, and I have a genuine curiosity here... Do you think he'd be willing to kiss me?"

Sarah's head popped up, something ugly clawing at her chest as she thought about Max's mouth anywhere near Piper. It was nuts. She didn't have any claim on him. But still—

"And the only reason I ask is because this whole-body meltdown you've got going is completely blowing my mind. I really need to know for myself whether the kiss this guy is laying on you is that spectacular or whether you just need to get out more."

"Sorry, Piper. You're going to have to take my word on this one."

———

Getting in his car, starting the engine, and actually driving away from Sarah's place took everything Max had. Jesus, it wasn't like he hadn't known what he was getting into. He'd kissed her before. A handful of times now. Enough so, he couldn't claim ignorance about how her kisses hit him: hard and with a lasting impact.

The first time, it'd taken weeks to get past her kiss. To shut down the justifications and rationalizations, and stop getting into his car with the intent of going back to school, finding Sarah, and telling her he was wrong. That they both were. And then taking her in his arms and finishing what they'd started. Yeah, *weeks* before he could trust himself not to do something stupid, but it had taken more like a year before he stopped comparing every kiss he had to the one they'd shared.

Her kisses definitely had staying power, but after those last two aborted attempts where she'd frozen up beneath him, he'd forgotten to brace for the impact. Tonight, her kiss had nearly knocked him on his ass.

Thankfully, he'd had the foresight to take her to the movies instead of back to his place. If they'd been alone when she asked him for more, hell, he wasn't sure he had it in him to deny her. To deny either of them.

Max parked his car, lucky to find a spot within a half mile of his place. Just as well he'd had to walk, because it had given him a few more minutes to cool off before he found Molly waiting for him on the front stoop. A quick glance at his watch confirmed it was almost midnight.

"Moll, what are you doing here?" he asked, unlocking the front door as she stood up and dusted off her rear.

"What? No 'Hey, Sis, good to see you'?" She stuffed her phone and earbuds into her oversize canvas bag and followed him inside. "Hope you don't mind, but the roomie is getting some hard-core action back at my place, and even with my door closed, I feel like I know way too much about her sexual proclivities."

Max shrugged. "No problem. But didn't you stay over at Brody's place last week for the same thing?"

She shrugged like it was no big deal, only Max could see the fatigue in his sister's eyes. In addition to being a part-time manager at Belfast, she cleaned houses and did some web design, so when she went home to sleep, she really needed it.

"Yeah, I think they might be getting serious though. So maybe I'll just ride it out until whatever happens, happens."

Max shook his head and walked into the kitchen, figuring she could probably use a beer. He reached into the fridge, grabbed two, and cranked off the caps with the mount on the wall. "Another one bites the dust, huh?" His sister was a great girl, a little mouthy with a lot of attitude, but when it came to her roommates, she was respectful and accommodating. She just had shit luck. "When did this one move in?"

Molly took the beer with a weary smile and dropped onto the corner of the couch. "Three months ago. I was hoping I could get at least twelve out of her, since she wasn't stealing anything or suffering from severe anger issues or suddenly between jobs with no income. Whatever, it'll all work out."

That was Molly. Ever the optimist.

"So what had you out so late tonight? Or should I say who?" she asked with that nosy gleam in her eyes.

"Date with Sarah," he answered, knowing there was no sense in trying to keep the truth from her.

"Dude, are you in *lurve*, because a *date*? I can't remember the last time you actually owned up to a date."

It had been a while. "Jesus, Moll. Don't get ahead of yourself. Yes, Sarah is different, and this was definitely a date, complete with dinner and a movie, but relax about it. We're just having fun."

"And she knows that?" Molly pulled her legs up to sit cross-legged at one end of the couch.

"Yeah," he answered with a laugh, leaning back into his corner. "She's been pretty clear on what she's available for."

"Well, that's a bummer. Was kind of hoping she'd be the girl to shake you up a bit." She cut him a look. "You know, she reminds me a little of—"

"Don't go there." The words came out a little harsher than he'd intended, but he knew the comparison Molly was about to make, and he didn't like it.

"Yeesh, sorry, Max. I just meant they were both sort of different from the girls you generally *don't date*."

Max shifted uncomfortably. "I know. Sorry."

"No worries. I'll totally forgive you as long as you dish. You seem sorta tense maybe. What's that about?" Molly had that pushy look again. "Because now I'm thinking, dinner and a movie, and you're home *before* midnight."

"Okay, okay, that's enough." He knew what she was saying. And for the millionth time, he wondered why Molly seemed incapable of respecting traditional sibling boundaries. Little sisters weren't supposed to ask their brothers about sex.

"Come on," she cajoled. "Tell me she turned you down. I know it's not nice, and you know how much I love you. But the way you blow through women, seriously, nothing would make me happier than to hear that you got denied."

"Fine, I got denied," he said with a smirk just confident enough to leave Molly wondering.

Her brow crumpled, and she pushed her shock of colorful hair back from her face, casting him an uncertain look. He lifted his beer for a swig, still holding her eyes. The key was not to look away first. And sure enough, after a beat, Molly blew out a frustrated breath.

"Dang it, Max!" she groused. "I hate it when you do that. I hope she did turn you down, and that your balls are so blue they're about to explode."

Wish granted, at least on that last part. Not that he'd give her the satisfaction of knowing.

She crossed her arms and huffed again. Then shooting him a sidelong look, she asked, "So you're going to see her again?"

"Yep." That was the plan. "I'll give her a call in a day or two."

Molly raised a brow at him. This wasn't his usual MO, so he threw her a bone. "She's only in town for a little while. We used to be friends, and hell, I'd like to see her while I can. But Molly, for real, it's not serious."

At least it wasn't for Sarah. He'd always been in too deep with her. But he'd handle it.

Molly's hands came up in front of her as she gave her head a slow shake. "No, no, I wouldn't assume it was."

Bullshit. His sister was all about assumptions. "Molly," he warned, with the kind of threatening tone she'd been blowing off forever.

"Whatever you say."

He didn't like the look he was getting, but he knew better than to keep trying to sell her. Pushing up from the couch, his half-drunk beer in hand, he stretched out his back and shoulders. "Staying up a while?"

She shook her head. "No. I've got a ton to do tomorrow. Mind if I take the couch?"

"You could have the bed," he said, wishing that for once she'd take it. But she didn't.

"Gross. I'm afraid I'd be visited by the ghosts of hookups past."

Right. She knew he never brought women back here. Just like he knew the only reason she wouldn't take his bed was because if she did, she'd feel like she was putting him out, and then she wouldn't be comfortable coming back if she needed a place to crash. And he wanted her to always feel like she could come back.

When he had everything locked up and the lights were off, he stretched out in bed and stared at the ceiling. Sarah reminded Molly of Joan. That was what she'd been about to say when he'd cut her off. Funny, except that wasn't quite the way it worked. She had it backward.

Shit, he didn't like to think about Joan. She wasn't a terrible person, and he wasn't hung up on her. But all it took was her name and there she was, stepping out of the shadows and taunting him with his mistakes.

She'd been sweet. Pretty with dark hair, gentle eyes, and a shy smile that hadn't belonged at the party his police academy buddy's hookup had brought her along for. She'd reminded Max of Sarah, simple as that. So when they met and he felt something like the tug that had been there two years before, instead of resisting it and doing everything in his power to show this last-year nursing student he *wasn't* the kind of guy she should be with, he worked his ass off to show her he was.

Looking back, he'd been so focused on showing Joan how right he was for her that he might have ignored some fairly obvious signs that they weren't right for each other. That the girl he really wanted had moved to California with the guy she was planning to marry—yeah, he'd looked Sarah up a time or two. He'd been curious—and maybe finding a quiet girl who looked like her wasn't the answer.

But like before, recognition came too late.

When she graduated, he convinced Joan to take the job that would keep them together rather than the one on the far side of the state where her family lived. The one she'd planned to take in the town she'd planned to return to. He should have known better. Getting in the way of a woman's plans never paid off. He knew it firsthand, but after letting Sarah go, hell, he just hadn't wanted to believe it.

For a while, things between them had been good. They got along. He knew how to tease her into one of those pretty laughs that almost felt right. She mostly didn't mind when he got assigned to nights and couldn't take her out with her friends as often as she liked. She still went out, and he was glad she had people to spend her time with, especially because she wasn't enjoying the job she'd taken.

He felt guilty about making her change her life to be with him, hated that maybe he was the reason she didn't smile as much. He did everything he could to try to make it up to her in other ways, but his efforts always fell short. They weren't right together. But instead of accepting he'd made a mistake, Max thought she needed more from him.

Dumbass that he was, he bought her a ring. *Lucky fuck* that he was, she told him about the guy she'd hooked up with *before* Max had a chance to give it to her. The guy from her hometown who'd been up visiting Chicago for a weekend. Her plans only temporarily derailed, she moved back to western Illinois, and not long after that, she married the guy. Good for her.

Too bad Max hadn't left her and her plans alone in the first place.

Chapter 12

THERE WAS A REASON SARAH ALWAYS KEPT HER WORK AND personal lives separate. And Sean Wyse meeting her at the elevator first thing Monday morning, an expectant grin on his face as he asked her how her date had gone Saturday night, was it.

"Come on, Max won't tell me a fucking thing," he urged, keeping his voice quiet enough so Sarah was the only one within range to hear her boss drop the workplace f-bomb. He'd most definitely been showing her a different side of himself since he'd been outed as *that Sean*, and she didn't mind a bit.

"It was a date. Nice. What's there to tell?" she asked, passing one office after another at a racewalker's clip. Only the heels were holding her back.

Sean let out an incredulous laugh. "I want to know if my guy's made any progress toward keeping *my girl* here in Chicago. I'm banking on his irresistible charm to snare you so I can keep you for my own."

Sarah stopped where she was, turning a raised brow to her boss, who was literally rubbing his hands together. "*Keep me for your own?* Creepy much, Sean?"

"Whatever. Did he pick you up in the car or on his bike? And tell me, please, he took you someplace good. I think we both know I only have this one shot to land you, and I'm counting on Max to do it for me."

She knew Sean was joking. Mostly joking. He wanted

to see her stay in Chicago, but anyone who'd worked with her for more than ten minutes knew a *man* would never impact her career plans. At least not again. Still, it was fun to play along.

"Well, you can rest assured Max delivered an excellent date. Dinner was terrific, the private boat tour too. But the *serenade*," she stressed, delivering an Oscar-worthy sigh before going on. "That's what really blew me away. Who knew Max could sing like that. Or dance?"

Sean had stopped walking, a smacked look on his face that was killing her, but then he scowled and jogged a couple steps to catch up again. "Don't tease me. Getting my hopes up only to crush them is seriously uncool."

"Sorry, Boss," she said, reaching her office door and not meaning the apology at all.

She walked inside, setting her bag down before slipping into the chair behind her desk.

Sean dropped into the open club chair and crossed one foot over his knee as he leaned back. "Okay, seriously this time. How was the date?"

Sarah thought about telling him it was none of his business. But the truth was, Sean was her friend, even with the professional foundation behind it. And he was Max's friend too. She couldn't blame him for being curious. "It was good, Sean. Really nice. Max is a great guy, and I've always enjoyed his company. So it was nice being able to spend an evening with him."

It was an honest-ish answer. But friends or not, there were lines a girl didn't cross with her boss. And detailing how his best friend had thoroughly and completely ravaged her mouth was one of them.

"Hmm. Nice?" Steepling his fingers beneath his chin,

Sean leaned forward. "That doesn't exactly sound like a rave review."

Sarah let out an exasperated breath. "Very nice?"

"Better, but it still sounds like my man is going to have to step up his game."

Sarah started busying herself with organizing her already-neat desk, because she was thinking about Max's game. He most definitely didn't need any improvement. The way he'd kissed her, taking control of her mouth, had left her breathless and aching—

"Holy shit," Sean muttered under his breath. He was staring at her, his raised brows all but assuring something in her expression had given her thoughts away.

"Or maybe his game is just fine. Sarah, Sarah, Sarah." Yeah, there was way too much going on in that smile of his. "You have plans for lunch today?"

The sudden change of subject threw her off, and before she could think about why he might be asking, she simply told him no.

"You do now." Sean pulled out his phone and fired off a text.

"Wait? What are you doing?" she sputtered.

"Telling Molly to meet you at noon. I might not be able to strong-arm you into giving up the details, but that girl is relentless." He glanced down at his phone again, his smile satisfied. "All set. She's in." Then Sean was pushing out of his chair. "Hey, keep an eye out for some files from my office this afternoon. If you've got any spare time, I could use a hand with a few things."

Sarah nodded, her focus back where she loved it most. On work. She'd done some extra work for Sean the week before. Challenging work. Exciting work. And if he was looking for more of the same, she was all in. "You bet."

———~~~———

Max made it until 6:42 Monday night before he broke down and gave in to the need that had been eating at him since Sarah closed her door on Saturday night. Pulling his phone from the beat-up jeans he'd thrown on after work, he took the stairs two at a time to the second floor and brought up Sarah's contact info. The front room had a bay window with a built-in bench he liked for kicking back. Sitting down, he hit Send and waited three rings for what he'd been thinking way too much about.

"*Max*," she answered, her voice stirring a hundred images of the smile behind that single word.

"How was your day, Sarah?" he asked, knowing she'd had a full one, complete with a visit from his little sister and a morning stalk by Sean.

"*Entertaining* would probably cover it." He liked that she didn't sound put off. "How do you manage to date at all with these people in your life?"

He let out a gruff laugh. "Honestly, I don't do a lot of dating. Which is the only explanation I can offer for the feeding frenzy with my friends and family. You're a bit of an anomaly in terms of my romantic life."

"Hmm." She drew out the sound like a sigh. "Lucky me."

"Pretty sure I'm the lucky one." For a lot of reasons. The first being that this woman was giving him the time of day. The second that she wanted something from him that would hopefully compensate for his overenthusiastic friends' obnoxious behavior.

"Do you ever *not* have a smooth line?" she asked with a melodic laugh.

It wasn't a line. Not that she'd believe him if he told her, so instead he asked, "For real though, how bad was it?"

The canopy of leaves rustled in the wind outside his window, and as he waited for her answer, he wondered if she'd like this view as much as he did.

"Sean was in rare form. He seems to think you're the key to keeping me in Chicago. I tried to set him straight when he met me at the elevator this morning, but he was back in the afternoon trying to pimp you out again."

Max coughed. "Shit, and here I thought Molly was the one I'd be apologizing for."

"Oh, she is. Definitely." Sarah laughed. "She wanted to know if I was hiding Shangri-la between my legs."

"What?"

"Because apparently only a fabled wonder like that would be enough to keep her brother on the hook."

Jesus. He got that Molly didn't have a whole lot of experience dealing with the women he dated. But come on. Some things were just obvious.

"I'll talk to her. Ask her to back off a little." A lot. Like keep at least fifty yards between them.

"I took care of it," Sarah announced easily, a sing-song quality to her voice that sounded like gloating.

He was almost afraid to ask. "Umm, how?"

"I told her I was so excited to have a girlfriend to share all my intimate details with." He was pretty sure that was a delicate snort he heard coming through the line. "Then I explained that I hadn't been with a lot of guys, but from an anatomy standpoint—"

"Whoa, whoa, whoa. Hold on there a second, Sarah."

"And that's exactly where she stopped me too. But just to make sure she backed off, I told her I had an appointment to get waxed, and, well, suddenly, she had an emergency shift to cover at Belfast."

Max choked on his laughter, unable to reconcile the relentless sweetheart he knew and liked a hell of a lot with the demon who'd gotten the upper hand with his little sister. He might even like her more.

Rubbing the center of his chest, he leaned back into the wall. "Who are you?"

"Me? Why I'm the same girl you used to walk home from the library. Just all grown up, with a handful of years learning how to make the business world bend to my whims. Why, don't you like it?"

Max grinned. "I think I like it a hell of a lot." Then, because he couldn't help but ask, "So you're getting a wax?"

—⁓—

"It's hump day," Piper stated from where she was lying on her stomach on Sarah's bed, knees bent, her feet scissoring above her. "But I'm guessing it's too much to hope that'll be what happens with your date."

Sarah adjusted her orange bandana-style halter top and then leaned into the mirror to check her light makeup. Her hair was pinned up in a sexy, loose bun with a few tendrils hanging around her face, and plain gold studs adorned her ears. Max had said he was taking her on the perfect summer date, so she'd opted for a white eyelet skirt that flowed around her knees and a pair of canvas wedge sandals.

"This says summer date, right?" she asked, doing a little turn for Piper, who readily agreed.

"It says summer date that doesn't involve you getting any." She might still be a little sore about Sarah's flat-out refusal to let her test-drive Max's mouth, but she'd get over it.

"So can you clarify this setup for me again? He's sort of wooing you. Building the romance and anticipation, so it will be all off the charts when you finally get down and dirty. But it's just a favor. And you think it's going to be over once you get your V-card punched."

Sarah blotted her lips and then turned to lean back against the dresser. "That's what we agreed to."

"But if it's a vacation fling," Piper pouted, "why couldn't it at least go the distance of the vacation?"

Part of Sarah found some appeal in that. Especially after the way she and Max had been talking the last couple of nights, sharing long conversations that never felt old. He made her laugh. He made her feel good. And she liked it. But anything more, she didn't know. It was probably smart to keep things limited to their original arrangement, not that Max had given her the first clue he'd been thinking about extending it. But even if he had, sticking to the two weeks felt smart. Then they'd have the rest of the summer to hang out as friends if they wanted, and by the time she left for New York, there wouldn't be any sting left at all.

Max arrived on time, looking incredibly hot in a pair of cargo shorts and a polo T-shirt, and Sarah was practi-cally salivating at the sight of him when Piper casually commented she'd heard Max was quite the kisser.

"Piper!" Sarah coughed, immediately trying to usher Max out of the apartment.

To his credit, Max wasn't the least bit fazed and,

stopping with a hand against the doorframe, winked back. "I try."

It was too much. Sarah made it as far as the stairwell before doubling over with laughter.

"What?" Max demanded, his grin spreading wide as he watched her.

"*I try*," she mimicked, lowering her voice to where it cracked, and she burst out laughing again. "And here I thought you were just a natural."

Catching her by the wrist, Max reeled her back in to him and looked down into her eyes, a sexy smile playing on his lips. "I might be. But that doesn't mean I'm not giving you my best effort."

Her laughter died.

He had the most beautiful eyes.

"You with the lines." She sounded a little weak even to her own ears, and Max certainly didn't miss it. The corner of his lips curved higher as he lowered his mouth to hers and gave her a slow, sweet, lingering kiss. A confident kiss. An effortless kiss.

A toe-curling, set-her-body-on-fire kiss that ended with her back against the stairwell wall and her fingers balled in the front of his shirt—way too soon.

When she looked up at him again, she was breathless. "Now you're just showing off."

Casting her a mischievous look, he set a hand on her lower back as they started down the stairs. "Not yet, I'm not."

The warning or promise landed low in the pit of her stomach, the weight of it doing things to her body even that kiss hadn't done. All she could think was just *wow*.

Being the typical guy that he was, Max couldn't let

the kissing thing go. On the ride over to the Diversey
Driving Range, Sarah noticed him staring at her while
they were stopped at a light. When she asked what
he was thinking, he replied, "Just contemplating my
tongue-to-lips ratio." She'd swatted his arm, fighting a
giggle with everything she had as he turned back to the
road and deadpanned, "What? It matters."

At the range, it got even worse. Or maybe it got
better, since Sarah couldn't deny the fun she was having.

They picked up a bucket of balls and claimed the tees
closest to Lake Shore Drive. There were a handful of
other golfers filling a few spots farther down the row,
but for the most part, their backs were to her and Max
as they lined up to swing. Which meant it was almost
like they were isolated. Good thing, as Max was intent
on "helping her with her form," regardless of her drives
soaring long and straight down the center of the range,
while he was shanking one after another. Still he came
up behind her, wrapping that big body of his around her
so they were pressed together in the most intimate way.

He felt so good.

"So you were talking about my kissing, hmm?" he
asked again, fishing for details.

"I might have said it was *okay* after our last date."
Someone needed to take this guy down a peg or two.
Though based on the gruff laugh, warm and genuine,
it clearly wasn't going to be her. Not that she minded.

Truth, Max's cocksure attitude had always appealed
to her a little more than it should have.

"You're asking for it, Sarah."

She was. Definitely. Whatever *it* was. Before she
could ask him to clarify, he was leaning even closer.

"Here, baby, let's try a few like this," he offered, his arms bracketing hers from behind, the heat of his muscled chest and thighs soaking into her from her shoulders to her knees. They held the club together, drawing back for the backswing and then rotating through on the first of several practice swings.

Max turned his chin into her neck, nuzzling closer. His breath washed over her cheek and jaw, sending chills gliding down her arms. Making her edge ever so slightly deeper into his hold.

"That's good," he rumbled against her ear. The sound of his voice so close was intoxicating.

She tried to focus. "That swing wouldn't have even made contact with the ball."

Max's smile spread against her skin. "I couldn't care less about golf, Sarah. If I did, I'd have *you* give *me* lessons—which maybe I'll be able to convince you to do once I stop looking for excuses to get my hands all over you every minute we're together."

The lines from this guy! As if she wasn't a sure thing. As if she wasn't the one who'd all but begged him for sex. But damn, if those lines didn't work.

Max moved his hands from where she gripped her driver and settled them over her hips like he was showing her more about that swing. Only she was pretty sure traditional lessons didn't include the instructor's hands roving down and forward, flexing against the student's thighs. Just like the quiet moans she was trying to stifle when Max nuzzled closer and sucked against the skin beneath her ear probably wouldn't be deemed appropriate in an actual instructional setting either. Good thing they were just having fun.

"Max," she whispered, needing more than what they could have there at the far end of the range.

Her plea fell on deaf ears, because suddenly Max was straightening behind her and taking a step back. The rush of wind off the lake touched all the places that had been warm only seconds ago, and she ached—actually *ached*—for more of the teasing touch he'd just given her.

He was right. She'd be out of her mind with need by the time she finally convinced Max she was ready.

Max was seriously about to bust a nut. Right there. At the Diversey Driving Range.

Like he was fifteen fucking years old.

But damn, Sarah got to him. She thought he was throwing her line after line, but she had no idea. All that over-the-top mush gurgling out of his mouth every time he opened it was exactly what he'd been thinking, feeling. Sure, he tried to play it cool and return to the controlled guy he liked to be, but he kept finding himself slipping. Saying too many of the things he thought out loud.

What was really crazy? He liked it. A lot.

"Want another bucket, or should we get out of here?" Max asked when they'd gone through all the balls.

Handing over her club, Sarah pushed to her toes and whispered in his ear. "I'm ready for anything."

Max laughed, leaning in to her as he returned the clubs. "You're really good. You play a lot for work?"

"Some. But I grew up on the back side of a golf course, so I learned pretty early. But you've got potential," she offered, flashing him one of those smiles that went straight to his groin. "With practice, who knows? A year from now, maybe I'll blow back through town and you'll spank me with your long game."

Was she trying to talk dirty, or was it just him?

When a guy was trying to keep a lid on his libido, there were certain things he really shouldn't hear. References to spanking in any capacity were among them. Because then he started to think about Sarah peering back over her smooth bare shoulder at him, her hair spilling around her arms, teeth dug into her bottom lip as he—

"Or maybe I'll practice too," she said with an impish glint in her eyes, "and bring you to your knees again."

And now he was thinking about going down on his knees in front of her, pushing that pretty white skirt out of the way and licking his way up the silky length of her thigh. Pressing his mouth to where her panties were—

Sarah cleared her throat, jerking Max out of the mouthwatering fantasy that was going to have to wait for a later date.

"Sorry, what's that?" he asked, feeling like he'd just gotten busted with wood in science class, but determined to play it cool anyway.

"I was just asking what you wanted to do next. This was so much fun, but it's still early. So maybe we could go…" She waved a helpless hand as that pretty pink he'd never get used to pushed into her cheeks. Damn, he wanted to take her someplace. Piper would be at her apartment, and his house wasn't fit for Sarah. So maybe a hotel. Yeah, another big bed like the one he'd had her on that first night. Not the mattress on the floor in the corner of his living room.

But this was only date number two.

"I've got a place," he said finally, taking her hand and leading her back toward the car. It wasn't the kind of place she was thinking of, but as far as sticking to the plan went, it suited his needs to a T.

———✧———

"Oh, Max, this is amazing," Sarah breathed against his ear. Considering where his hand was, he hoped she wasn't talking about the view of the skyline from the spot he'd claimed for them on the strip of park in front of the Planetarium. "Max!"

Damn, he liked the broken, needy sound of that.

He'd brought a couple of woven blankets from the car and laid one out on the grass to sit on, while wrapping the other around them. When they first arrived, Sarah sat in the vee of his legs, leaning back into his chest as they talked about nothing and everything, the words between them easier than they ever were with the women he hooked up with.

It was strange, but as bad as he wanted to get his mouth on her again, he didn't want to give up the talk. He didn't want to sacrifice the sound of her laughter or the way she teased him. So he'd appeased himself by touching her as the conversation continued. Stroking the length of her arm, running his lips against her shoulder. Testing the softness of her skirt between his fingers before finding the smooth skin of her thigh beneath and testing the softness there as well.

It was like nothing he'd felt before.

And then she'd gone and done it, followed his lead by letting her fingertips brush over the backs of his hands as he touched her. Tracing the lightest patterns over his forearms. Letting her words trail off as she shifted just enough so they could do more than talk.

"Jesus, your mouth is making me insane, Sarah," he swore, rubbing his lips back and forth over hers as his hand smoothed over her belly, his thumb brushing her ribs just beneath her breasts. "You're so damned soft."

They were wrapped in the blanket, and while no one would doubt they were kissing, there wasn't any outward evidence of what else was happening beneath.

"Max," she half moaned as his hand pushed higher to cup the swell of her breast. It was perfect, just filling his palm with nothing to waste, her nipple peaked hard like a tight bead beneath that sexy-as-fuck halter thing she had on.

He kneaded her gently as he sucked at her lips and played with her tongue. Drowned in the wetness of her mouth.

Finding his thigh as she braced herself with an arm behind her, she squeezed, her fingers digging into his muscle as he thumbed that taut bead again and again. He drank in her whimpers and quiet cries, forcing himself to hold back when all he wanted to do was grab her hip and pull her around so she was straddling him. So he could rock into her heat and—

Christ, the fantasy just degenerated from there, with visions of panties and bandana fabric flying in all directions, pretty white skirts ripped up the front, and his cock there where he wanted it most.

How the hell was he going to make it through another date without taking her?

Chapter 13

"YOU SEEM A LITTLE OFF. EVERYTHING OKAY, SARAH?"

The question came from Sean as they rode the elevator up from the parking level.

She grimaced, hating that her DEFCON 1–level frustration was apparent to her boss. But maybe she could learn from this. "What gave me away?"

He raised a brow. "I guess it was weird seeing you drop your coffee in the parking lot."

Right, the case of the clumsies resulting from her brain being all tied up with thoughts of Max and their date the next night. The *third* date, which he wouldn't tell her anything about except that she was going to like it even more than their second date. Which she'd liked to an *oh yes, please don't stop* degree already.

Unfortunately, he had stopped. And she'd been "off" for two days since.

Sean pinched the bridge of his nose, giving her a contemplative look. "But it was the swearing that really clued me in. And then when you kicked your travel mug. Yeah, that was a Sarah I don't see every day."

Her eyes bugged. She hadn't. Only the slight throb in her toe and scuff on her shoe suggested that yeah, she had.

"I'll get it together, Sean. I'm sorry you had to see it though."

Raising a brow, he laughed. The doors opened on her

floor, and she stepped out. "Don't sweat it, Sarah. It was kind of a relief to see you were human after all. Hell, everyone has off days."

"Thanks for understanding." The doors slid closed, and she started toward her office, her body feeling like it didn't belong to her. Her breasts were swollen and sensitive, and a coil of tension was ratcheting tighter with every second that passed, bringing her closer to the next time she saw Max again.

She thought about his hand between her legs, petting her over her panties. His thumb playing with her nipples. Her next step missed the mark and her heel buckled, sending her into the wall with a thud.

She couldn't go on like this. She'd never make it.

At her office door, she dropped her purse and then hit the top of her head on the doorknob when she tried to gather up the mess. Her phone sounded with a text.

It was Max.

> Can't survive another night. Please do society a solid and agree to move our date up to tonight. Or tell me to be a man and suck it up. Either works. Thinking about you, obviously.

Sarah grinned, sliding her key card over the sensor and letting herself into her office. She set down her bag and texted back.

> Been going crazy. Seeing you again is all I can think about. It's bad. People are noticing. What time and where?

The reply was everything she'd hoped it would be.

Six. My place.

Dropping into her chair, she grinned at the ceiling.

～⁓～

Max had a few menus out on the counter when the doorbell rang. He'd showered and shaved after his shift, changing into a pair of cargo shorts and the blue T-shirt his sister said was a good color for him. Walking to the entry, he smoothed the top of his hair, wishing for once that he was capable of cleaning up like Sean.

Jesus, what was with the nerves?

He opened the door and his throat went dry, his mind blanking of anything but the beautiful brunette with the shy smile and the stretchy, flowy dress that seemed to spill down from a pair of skinny straps all the way to her toes.

"Hi, Max," she said, twisting her fingers in front of her.

He nodded, suddenly tongue-tied like he hadn't been since *ever*.

There was a satisfying exaggeration in the rise and fall of her chest, a pinkness in her cheeks. Finally, his head engaged and he regained his ability to form words. "Sarah, you look gorgeous. Come on in."

He'd show her around first. Tell her about all his manly carpentry skills and feed her whatever she wanted to eat. And then for dessert, *she* was the something sweet he'd been craving since he dropped her off the other night, his dick so hard he'd thought the thing might explode before he got home. And not in a good way.

Sarah smiled and stepped into the entry.

Looking past her to the space he'd been rehabbing from the guts up, he suddenly wondered whether she'd be comfortable. The lack of traditional furniture hadn't bothered him before, even when Sean was pointing it out. It was functional in a minimalist way. But now he wished he had more for Sarah to see. More to make her—

The door hadn't even closed all the way before his back was against it, Sarah having basically launched herself at him, throwing her arms around his neck as she pushed to her toes to kiss him, bringing all his favorite curves and soft spots flush against him.

He didn't miss a beat. The second she made contact, it was like he'd been wired to react. He had his fingers in her hair, his palm cupping the back of her head. The other arm cinched tight around her waist, holding her even closer than she'd pressed herself.

"I couldn't wait," she whispered against his mouth between kisses. "This is all I've been able to think about. Getting back to you. To this."

He growled against her mouth, almost losing it when she opened beneath him, the tip of her tongue venturing past her lips to lick his in invitation. It started with a single kiss, but the days since he'd touched her, the nights of barely resisting the need to go to her—they broke him. He filled her mouth with his tongue, taking it the way he wanted her body.

Thrusting deep, he groaned as their tongues met and mated. Rolled and twined. Holding her tight, he picked her up and carried her a few steps until their positions were reversed and it was her back against the wall at the base of the stairwell. "Fuck, Sarah."

"Yes," she hissed, her fingers sliding over the brush of his hair. "You should totally do that."

Even hard enough to hammer nails, he stopped to laugh against her neck, to squeeze her in to him, because she made him feel so much more than he expected. But then her nails were scraping lightly against the back of his head, and the laughter was over. He was leaning into her, pressing closer as he gathered up her flowy dress by the fistfuls until it was piled around her waist. Until his hands were on the sweet firm curves of her ass and her shoulders were braced against the plaster.

Running his teeth along the delicate shell of her ear, he told her what to do.

"Legs around me, beautiful."

Damn, that soft mewl of appreciation when she did what he asked.

She was spread against him, nothing but her silky panties and his shorts between them. "Can you feel me, baby?" he asked, knowing the answer from the way her breath hitched and her legs tightened. Like she couldn't get him close enough.

"Yes," she breathed, meeting the rock of his hips with the press of her own. "So good."

"This is nothing," he promised, his voice already gravel rough as he rolled into her again and again. "Barely a taste, sweetheart."

Those sounds she was making, little and desperate, spurred him on. "Are you ready to feel me inside you, Sarah? Stretching those tight-as-fuck walls until you think you can't take any more?"

"Oh yes, Max," she cried, her fingers clutching at him harder, her hips rocking against his that much faster.

And yeah, he could feel how close she was, like he could feel her wetness soaking through his shorts. Nothing hotter in the world. Or at least that was what he'd thought until he started grinding in earnest and Sarah's head dropped back against the wall, her eyes locking with his as her breath held. Her lips parted, her mouth opening farther and farther until finally that suspended cry ripped free, followed immediately by another and another as she came against him.

When the last tremors subsided, he kissed her slowly, one side of her mouth and then the other. Her cheeks and her forehead. Her eyelids. Eventually, he lowered her legs, and her dress fell back into place. They stood staring at each other, their breathing strained but slowing, her fist in the front of his shirt.

Blinking up at him, she smiled. "So this is your place, huh? Nice."

———

Sarah had never been so relieved to come home to an empty apartment in all her life. Piper had another event with the radio station, so the apartment was quiet as she lay in bed, her body tender and sweetly, satisfyingly achy, thanks to Max's thorough attention.

It wasn't like she'd never gotten off before. She'd been with Cory for years, and while they'd never gotten too carried away—easy enough for him since he'd been banging anyone he felt like—she'd had his hand in her pants plenty.

Not. The. Same.

With Cory, there had been a slow build. A steady course. A spot that seemed to work and very little deviation once he'd figured out what it was going to take to get her there. In all honesty, it had felt a little like work with Cory.

With Max though—she threw her arm over her forehead, wondering how she could be getting riled up again after four mind-blowing, toe-curling, she-hoped-he'd-done-enough-with-the-insulation-because-quiet-she-was-not orgasms—it had felt like the best possible kind of play. Like a journey several hours long and full of super-fun discovery. Like every look, breath, touch, or word from Max set her on fire in some new and crazy-hot way.

It was *so good*.

Biting her lip, she scrunched up her eyes.

Their next date wasn't for a whole week. She'd never make it.

———※※※———

"When you asked if I was free after work," CJ grumbled, grunted, and then swore as he scraped his knuckles on the doorframe to the room Max had decided to make his bedroom, "I was kinda thinking you were looking for a beer or something equally Friday-night-ish. Not moving a freaking two-thousand-pound bed frame."

"Stop your bitching, and consider yourself lucky I'm still working on the second-floor rooms so it couldn't go up there."

"Yeah, yeah. Shit!"

"Watch your toes, man." Max laughed, feeling too damned good about his purchase. A cop's salary wasn't huge, but the return on investment from rehabbing houses meant he could pretty much buy what he wanted. And he'd wanted an actual bedroom.

It had been bugging him since he'd had his fingers inside Sarah's tight, wet body the other night. Making her come with his hand on his sofa and then the mattress pushed against the wall had felt like fooling around in high school. Sarah had no complaints. But he kept thinking she deserved more. Better.

So he'd gone out and ordered a few things. A bedroom set, some sheets, and a few new pillows, plus a comforter set that was pretty classy but still cool enough for dudes.

Okay, it was a lot of shit for one night. But it was Sarah's one night. The one she wouldn't get a do-over for, and she'd trusted it to him.

So yeah, he felt pretty good about it.

"Am I even going to meet this girl again?"

Max blinked.

"Don't try to bullshit me. This stuff is for Sarah. You can't seem to go more than fifteen minutes without mentioning something downright *amazing* about her, but I haven't seen her since the wedding, and as far as I can tell, she wasn't actually there with you."

Max grunted, shaking his head. "I don't talk about her that much."

The look CJ gave him suggested otherwise. "Yeah? Then how do you explain me knowing her favorite dessert is a brownie, she's got that new Samsung phone, she'd like to visit Thailand someday, and she doesn't know how to ski."

When Max just blinked at him, CJ gave an abbreviated shrug, thanks to the two-thousand-pound bed they were hefting. "I've got more if you want it."

"Not necessary." Then looking at the man he trusted with his life, Max asked, "For real? I talk about her that much?"

"Don't freak out. It's cool to see you into someone like this. But yeah, me and everyone else at the precinct are wondering when you're gonna bring her around."

"I don't know, man. We'll have to see." He wouldn't be bringing her around to anything. They only had one date left.

But he couldn't think about that now.

"You better at least have some beer in the fridge," CJ said, wiping the sweat from his brow as they got everything set up.

"Yep. Grab two, and then get your ass back in here. You're not off the hook until we figure out what the hell a sham is."

Maybe it was old-fashioned of her, but Sarah had hoped to keep the number of people in on the demise of her virginity to a minimum. Just the critical players. Max, for all the obvious reasons, and Piper, because Sarah couldn't keep anything from her. But as for the casual acquaintances and burgeoning new friendships? Sorry, but not so much. Which was why Sarah had been dodging and weaving for nearly two days, terrified if she spent more than five consecutive minutes with any one person, *they were going to know*.

Her solution: going solo. She'd wanted a new dress for her date, so she'd gone shopping. Alone. Which turned out to be a much more efficient way of getting it done. She'd hit the lingerie store and a beauty shop where she'd stocked up on an entire arsenal of products sworn to make her skin irresistible. Everywhere.

Now she was dressed in her new black cocktail dress,

wearing the sexiest lingerie the boutique had to offer and a pair of stiletto heels she'd actually purred over when she saw them in the store. Her hair was up in a loose twist with a few tendrils hanging around her face, and for jewelry she'd chosen a pair of gold chandelier earrings with a delicate chain bracelet to match.

The intercom buzzed, and the butterflies that had been gently flitting about suddenly went mosh pit. This was it. Tonight, Max wouldn't stop; he wouldn't hold back. Tonight, he'd give her everything she'd been asking for. And tomorrow…it would be over.

She hadn't been thinking about that part of their arrangement, but now—

The intercom buzzed again, and she rushed the last few steps down the hall.

"Sorry, Max, come on up."

"Is Piper there?" he asked through the small speaker.

She blinked, surprised by the question. "She's out with friends."

"So, here's the thing, Sarah. We've got reservations, and I'm a little worried if I get you alone up there, we might not make it out of that apartment again. And I really wanted to take you out someplace nice. Any chance you'll meet me downstairs?"

Her smile spread wide. "Far be it from me to get in the way of your plans."

"You are my plans."

Wow. With the power of his voice alone, the foreplay had begun.

The restaurant was gorgeous. It was an intimate little French place designed to give diners the illusion of eating under the canopy of an enormous tree. Sprawling branches strung with white lights covered the ceiling and crawled down the walls. Everywhere she looked, there were little cutouts and nooks packed with rustic kitchen staples, flickering candles, or racks of wine. It was beautiful and so incredibly romantic that she had to remind herself more than once that the devastatingly sexy man playing with her fingers across the small table wasn't hers to keep. He was doing her a favor. And like he'd promised, he was doing it very well.

"What's going on in that beautiful head of yours?" he asked, setting his glass of Bordeaux aside.

"Just thinking about everything you've done to make this night special. It's too much."

He leaned forward, the cool gray of his eyes meeting hers. "It's not too much. I told you, it's going to be my first time too. We only get this first once, and I want to make the most of it."

"You're a good guy, Max."

He shook his head. "If I were really that good, I wouldn't be plotting to make tonight so off-the-charts incredible that the next guy *doesn't stand a chance* at measuring up."

Her breath hitched while her insides clenched in anticipation as a heat only Max could inspire spread throughout her body.

Max leaned back in his chair, his eyes leaving hers to catch the waiter's attention as he signaled for the check.

They took a cab back to Max's place, riding quietly through the city streets, and when they arrived and stood together in his living room, Sarah could barely breathe.

"Nervous?" Max asked, reaching for her hand and pulling her closer, his thumbs tracing patterns across her knuckles. She was eager and excited. Aching for more of what Max had been giving her, but definitely nervous.

Her mind whirled with less-than-sexy thoughts: How long would it take? How much would it hurt? If it lasted, would she even want it to?

And then the worst thought of them all.

What would happen when it was over? How would she go from that heart-fluttery nervous anticipation every time she even thought his name to just being friends?

"A little," she admitted quietly. "But not because I don't want to do this."

Max nodded, wrapping his arms around her for a moment before bowing his head to kiss her neck softly, gently, sending a wave of goose bumps cascading across her skin.

He kissed her earlobe and, voice low, confessed, "Me too."

Her eyes shot wide as Max stepped back, looking anything but nervous. Yet, she knew he wouldn't have said it if it wasn't true, at least on some level.

How did he always have just the right thing to say? Know just how to put her at ease. Casting him a flirtatious grin, she promised, "Don't worry. I'll go easy on you."

And there was that devastating grin she loved. The one almost as effective as his kisses. "Come here, Sarah."

She followed him to the room off the living room where he'd had his office stuff the last time she'd been there. Only today, what she found beyond the french doors stopped her heart. She looked back into the living room, and in the place where his mattress and the milk crates with his clothes had been in the far corner was his desk and more milk crates with files and books.

She looked back at him. "You did all this for me?"

"You like it?" he asked, shoving his hands deep in his trouser pockets, so his broad shoulders pulled forward, somehow making him look all the bigger. All the sexier.

"I do. But…" She hesitated. He'd lived in the building for six months. Sean had been relentless in giving Max crap about never buying furniture. And now tonight, he'd brought her to this beautiful, private space complete with matching nightstands on either side of the raised bed and an area rug on the floor. "I love it."

He pulled her the rest of the way into the room where the lights were set at dim. The only response he gave her was the press of his lips to hers and the slow sway of his body as he held her against him. Her arms linked around his neck, and for a moment, her eyes pricked with the threat of tears.

"Thank you, Max."

He shook his head, looking down at her with dark eyes. "Thank you, baby."

And then he was kissing her again, still slowly, but this time with the hunger that had been building with every date. She opened beneath him, welcoming the first thrust of his tongue with a trembling moan. And like that, her body was alive, on fire.

Ready.

Her fingers clutched at the back of his neck as she pressed into him, wanting to feel all of him. Max groaned into her mouth, his hands coasting over the curve of her ass and down to the backs of her thighs. Between her legs.

"Max." She shuddered as he brought them even closer and she felt the hard bulge of his shaft between them.

"You are so damned beautiful," he groaned against

her neck. "I didn't know if I'd be able to make it through dinner without pulling you out of there and bringing you home. But now, baby, I need to see you again. All of you."

It had been one of those lines Max wouldn't cross during their dates. Even when he'd had his fingers deep inside her, their clothes had stayed on. When she'd asked him about it after, his answer had been that he was just a man and even his restraint had limits.

But tonight that restraint was cast aside.

She nodded and he took her by the shoulders, gently turning her so she faced away from him. The barest hint of stubble scraped the spot where her shoulder and neck met, followed by the lightest suction. Her belly tensed as liquid heat spilled through her center. Drawing the zipper down her back, inch after inch, he followed the path of newly exposed skin with soft kisses that ended low on her spine, just above the racy panties she'd bought for him.

Brushing his thumb over the scalloped edge, he growled, "Turn around for me, baby."

Hands going to the narrow straps of her dress, she did as he asked. Max knelt before her, his eyes hooded, his hands resting lightly on the fabric at her hips. "Show me."

Slipping the straps from her shoulders, she let the dress pool around her feet so she was standing there in her heels and scantily cut bra and panties. Max's eyes burned a path up her body and back down.

"My every fantasy." Hands moving back to her hips, he pressed his mouth low against her stomach, licking the spot and then sucking just hard enough to pull at that achy place deep inside. Kissing lower still, he mouthed the front of her panties and then licked the silky panel between her legs.

His breath was warm against the place that was already wet. His tongue, a decadent stroke that nearly buckled her knees. Then he was standing, working the buttons of his shirt free before shouldering out of it.

Her mouth watered at the sight of all that bare skin and hard muscle. Because Max was the most beautiful man she'd ever seen. And in that moment, he was making her feel like the most treasured, valued woman in all eternity.

His motions were quick and efficient as he freed the tongue of his belt and undid his fly. "On the bed, Sarah."

She could hear the urgency in his voice, the restraint, and it only added fuel to her fire. Shucking his pants but not his boxer briefs, he stepped over to the bed, stopping in front of her where she'd sat at the edge.

The black fabric of his shorts was stretched over his thick shaft, tempting her in a way she'd never been tempted before. Reaching for him, she smoothed her hand over his covered length, gently squeezing. Max's breath left him in a hiss as he jerked under her touch. She licked her lips, wanting more. Fingers creeping past the elastic, she freed him, pushing the briefs down his thighs.

Her breath was coming fast, her heart racing as she stared at his engorged length. She'd known he was big. Had felt him beneath his clothes before. Noticed and contemplated the difference between him and Cory.

The *significant* difference.

Max stood in front of her, every muscle in his body tensed, but the only contact he made was the gentle brush of his hand over her hair to where it was pinned in place. Slowly, he removed the pins one after another as she ran her fingers over the taut skin, wrapping her hand around him and—

"Enough, baby," he said, pulling back from her grasp. "It's too good."

Retrieving a condom she hadn't noticed before, he opened the package and rolled the protection on. Her heart skipped. Was this it?

He knelt in front of her again, pulling her knees forward so they bracketed his ribs and he could kiss her, tease her with slow thrusts of his tongue that had her insides clenching and her hips shifting as she tried to get closer to him. She needed contact.

Max undid her bra and helped her out of it, breaking from their kiss to look at her breasts. Thumbing her tight nipples, he rumbled, "So many temptations, where to kiss first?"

"Anywhere," she whispered, feeling like she was on fire.

He shook his head, giving her another of those devastating grins. "Everywhere."

His mouth sought her breast, his tongue circling the nipple before drawing hard against it. Crying out, she arched into him, moving forward until she was practically straddling him where he knelt. He shifted his attention to her other breast, giving her his teeth and tongue as his strong hands squeezed and kneaded her ass, spreading that delicious sensation of sensual possession throughout her body.

"More," Max panted against her soft flesh, burning a path of devouring kisses down her stomach. Lower. Hooking his fingers into the sides of her panties, he edged out from between her legs so he could pull the garment down. "I need to taste you."

Then, eyes locked with hers, he slowly, deliberately palmed her knees and pressed them open. She trembled—from the vulnerability of her position, from knowing that any second those dark-gray eyes would drop, and he would be looking at her *there*. From wanting him to.

Shouldering his way between her legs, he slid his hands beneath her, and cupping her bottom, he lifted her to his mouth.

"Max!" she gasped as he licked through her sex. His fingers flexed against her, and his eyes closed in what might have been pain, but when they reopened, she saw pure, unadulterated pleasure in them. He tasted her again, sinking into it like he'd never get enough. Her back arched, and she cried out at the sudden sensation rocketing through her. Eyes closed, she writhed beneath a kiss so all-consuming she could barely catalog what was happening, except that it was the best thing anyone had ever done to her.

His tongue dipped inside, stroking in and out as she gasped his name and clutched at his hair. Arching her hips, she begged for more and cried out when he replaced his tongue with one finger and then two. He played with her, running circles around that throbbing bundle of nerves with the tip of his tongue and then giving her the flat of it. Sucking her. Pumping his thick fingers in and out. Two became three, and *oh*, sensation was building fast within her. Hot and sweet, it was so much and not enough and—

"Please," she begged, her hips rocking to meet each

thrust and lick. Need laced tighter and tighter. "Please... I need... Yes, please... Max..."

Stroking her with a beckoning curl of his fingers, he hit a spot she'd heard rumors about but hadn't, until that moment, been sure actually existed. Everything stopped, her entire being refocusing on that singular spot that sent lightning forking through her body.

Shocked, she looked down to where Max was staring up at her from between her legs. Her chest hurt; her body trembled.

Reaching for him, she brushed her fingertips against the short strands of his hair. He climbed up her body, one arm sliding under her to pull her higher up the bed. And then he was braced above her, her knees at either side of his hips, her fingers light against his chest and face. She blinked up into Max's waiting, patient, heated eyes.

"I think my next breath depends on you," she whispered, a calm coming over her even with her body tensed on the edge of release.

Supporting himself on one arm, Max brushed her bottom lip with his thumb and then positioned himself so he was at her opening. The thick head nudged against that place of give where she was wet and slick and so very sensitive. He waited a beat, maybe giving her a chance to change her mind or maybe just to collect himself, but then he pushed inside, penetrating her a bare inch before easing back out. The stretch was greater than it had been with his fingers, but it was good. The kind of good that had her heels sliding up the backs of his thighs and her fingers splaying over his perfect butt, urging him back for more.

He sank again, an inch and then an inch more.

Repeating the process again and again. Each penetration ratcheting up the tension within her. She'd been so close before, but this wet friction was so much more, so completely different. Like nothing else. No one else. Just Max.

Another stroke, not quite as shallow as the one before, and she could feel herself nearing the edge. Her inner muscles clenched and pulsed around him. And then he was there, the head of his cock at that point of resistance within her.

He held where he was, letting her feel the acute strain of pressure through one breath.

Their eyes met, and he reached between them, pressing his thumb against her with the perfect amount of pressure, the perfect pace—and suddenly she was hurdling back to that place she'd been so close to before. Another shallow stroke, coupled with the steady rub of his thumb, and Max above her, his brow dotted with sweat, his eyes burning into her, and she could feel herself ready to fall.

"Come for me, Sarah."

Starbursts exploded behind her eyes and she shattered, crying out as she came apart in a gripping wave of ecstasy so intense it nearly swamped the accompanying single short stab of pain. Her eyes shot open, her breath stalling in her lungs as Max took her completely, filling her in a way she couldn't have imagined. Buried deep within her, he waited out the pleasure crashing and surging around him, until it eased to a gentle lap.

She'd had no idea.

Smiling up at him, she was overwhelmed by emotion. She wanted to say things she shouldn't. Things that were outside their arrangement. Things that were true nonetheless.

Max returned her smile, staring down at her, the restraint still evident in his features. "So fucking beautiful," he whispered.

Her knees slid farther up his ribs, and he caught her by the back of the thigh, holding her as his hips pumped slowly, in and out.

"So good," she gasped, her hands going to his hair, to his face. His mouth and jaw. Max was staring down at her, watching her every response. Reacting to it. Ramping up her pleasure faster than she could believe. He shifted again, rocking forward so the contact increased with every stroke, the sensation amplified with every thrust.

It was impossible that anything could feel like this. That any man could—

Suddenly, a laugh escaped her lips and she slapped her hands over her mouth, her eyes going wide as Max stopped, a crooked smile on his face. "Laughing?"

She shook her head, horrified and yet delighted at the same time. "Now I get why they wrote your name on the bathroom wall."

That cocky smile cranked up a notch, and oh, what it did to her. "Yeah?"

Another slow thrust had her toes curling.

"Oh yeah. Reputation totally deserved," she gasped when he did it again. "I'm impressed."

"Glad to hear it." And again. "So, baby, you ready to find out whether you like *hard and fast*?"

Chapter 14

HOURS LATER, MAX COULDN'T REMEMBER EVER experiencing a comfort so great as holding Sarah in his arms while she slept. There was only one problem. She wouldn't be sleeping in them the next day. Or the day after that.

Not unless he asked her the question he'd been thinking about since the night he proposed this arrangement of theirs. Would she give him the rest of her time in Chicago? It wasn't what they'd talked about or agreed upon. Only now everything felt different.

They'd had their one night, and selfish fuck that he was, he wanted more.

Only he didn't want to take a moment that had been damn near perfect and ruin it by asking her for something she might not want to give. Christ, he didn't want to take away anything from what they'd just shared.

She stirred in his arms, blinked a few times and then peered up at him with an adorable, bleary-eyed look. Sighing, she snuggled closer, her fingers trailing not so subtly down his abdomen.

He grinned when she poked at his dick and gave it a squeeze.

He was hard. Had been for probably an hour.

"Help you with something, ma'am?" he asked, not bothering to hide the smirk in his voice.

"Yes, well, since I enjoyed this beginner class so

thoroughly, I was wondering if maybe an *advanced* class might be available?" she asked, pressing her breasts into him now.

And there it was. The perfect opening.

Rolling her to her back, he pushed his thigh between her legs and pulled her arms overhead, trapping her wrists in the loose hold of one hand. Her eyes widened, and she went a little breathy.

Someone was definitely ready for the advanced class. "We've got a variety of options you might be interested in," he said, using his lips to toy with her nipple before giving it the smallest nip.

"Max!"

"There's an *accelerated* program that begins in the next five minutes and ends about fifteen hours from now."

"Fifteen hours," she said, and he hoped like hell that was a pinch of disappointment he detected. "Sounds intense."

"I won't lie to you. It's pretty rigorous." He brushed his thumb across her cheek and manned up. "But if you were interested, there's another class, a *deeper*, more *extensive* study that's only completed when your instructor drops you at the airport at the end of the term."

Sarah was quiet, and Max wondered if he'd just royally screwed up something perfectly sweet. But then she was pulling her hands free and linking her arms around his neck. "Are you sure, Max?" she asked quietly, hopefully.

He nodded. "Baby, never been more."

A welcome wave of cool air poured over him as Max stepped into the bustling diner. They always attracted a degree of attention when dressed in uniform. Some good—like the little kid whose eyes had gone saucer-wide with hero worship the minute he'd seen them. Some less than good. It went with the job.

Seated in a booth by the windows, Carl waved Max and CJ over with a beaming smile that only seemed to get bigger through the years.

"'Bout time you boys showed up. Stop for a nap on your way over?" he ribbed, pushing the menus across the scarred tabletop.

"Can't rush the hero work, Pops," CJ replied as they joined him.

Max dropped into the booth beside him. "Especially not with this marshmallow dragging behind." Then grinning across at Carl, he added, "Foot chase this morning, and your boy here could barely keep up. Dropped to his knees right in the alley, wheezing, 'Go on without me!'"

Not exactly how it had gone down, but Max was going to tell it that way. This was payback his partner had coming in spades.

"Fucker," CJ muttered affectionately from behind his menu. "I woulda had that guy myself if it wasn't for the cat. Mangy beast came out of nowhere."

Max snorted into his hand, looking across at Carl, who was shaking his head, mouth pulled to one side. "You know I'm gonna be hearing about my boy letting a little pussy get in the way of a bust through retirement, right?"

Probably more like a week or two, but yeah, Carl could count on it. There wasn't a whole hell of a lot to ride him over, now that he'd been on desk duty a few years.

"No worries," Max gloated. "I got the guy."

"Seriously, Pops, that kid could have scored a track

scholarship if he'd stayed in school rather than dealing outside one. Fuckin' waste."

Then CJ was elbowing Max, nodding across to where his dad was smoothing his hair as his favorite waitress came up to take their order. Linda was the reason they'd been Wednesday regulars for three years running, and Max had a feeling one day he was going to walk in and find Linda on Carl's lap, a diamond on her finger. He couldn't wait. For now though all she got was their order, and then it was back to shooting the shit.

Carl wanted to know if CJ was any closer to giving him a grandkid and whether Max had seen the sale Home Depot was running on the band saw he'd been looking at. They exchanged shop gossip over BLTs and turkey clubs, and when a call came over the radio, Max and CJ exchanged knowing looks. It was an all-too-familiar address, close to where they were.

Max threw down enough to cover the lunch, and Carl told them to be safe, watching them with pride in his eyes as they left.

"Always," CJ promised as Max nodded.

Max's father had been kicked off the force when Max was just a kid. Vick had been a shitty cop and an even shittier dad. But while he'd still been working his beat, Carl had been his partner. And after, the saving grace in Max's life. It was like the man had seen what Max was up against at home and one day just consciously decided he wasn't going to leave Max alone in it.

From time to time, he'd show up at Max's games. Catch him after school and take him out for a haircut or a burger and ask about classes. Really ask—like wanting to know whether Max had been able to get the extra credit on the project he'd been working on the last time they went out. If he'd beat that Meg girl out for the top grade in trig. If he'd ever gotten around to asking her out. How things were at home.

Carl had introduced Max to community service, showing him ways even a teen could get involved and make a difference.

He'd been the man to instill a sense of right and wrong in Max, a sense of pride and worth. And it had been Carl's footsteps Max had been following when he joined the force. And now, even at thirty years old, making Carl proud still meant a hell of a lot to him.

That was what Max was thinking about when they arrived at an apartment he'd visited too many times before. Neighbors had called it in again, and as he and CJ hoofed it up those last steps, he could hear the violence within. Sounds that echoed back to his youth.

"You wanna go?" a voice thundered from beyond the door. "Go! Get your shit, and get your worthless ass out of here. Think anyone's going to want you now?"

Another crash, and this time the voice that cried out was small and weak.

Christ, the kid.

CJ's eyes cut to Max's, and with a nod, they moved in. It happened fast, the way it was supposed to. A flurry of controlled actions, over within seconds, all parties separated and Max radioing for an ambulance for the mother who looked like her wrist might be broken and the five-year-old girl with the big, blue eyes who reminded him too much of Molly and had a bloody gash running down the side of her face.

He'd been here before.

The first time, the mom hadn't wanted to press charges. She'd said she was fine, that nothing physical had happened. Max fucking knew she was lying, but there wasn't any evidence he could see. The second time, she'd stood there with a black eye and the skin across the bridge of her nose split, swearing up and down it had been an accident. The matching swollen split knuckle across the dad's right hand suggested otherwise, and despite her pleas, Max had taken the guy in. But it didn't stick, and now here this asshole was again, giving him the whole "Come on, I didn't mean it" bullshit, while blood ran down his kid's face, thanks to the bottle he'd launched across the room. *Because he hadn't even noticed her standing there*.

This time the wife was pressing charges.

This time it was going to stick.

This time, Max walked out of there knowing this kid wasn't coming back.

Jesus, how could people do this shit to each other?

―――――※※※―――――

Sarah was staring at her phone, chewing her lip in indecision. She wanted to see Max. See everyone. But she probably had a conservative two hours left before she'd get through her notes and could close out this project. She loved closing out projects.

She was going to call. It wouldn't be a big deal. She'd just meet Max at the bar with everyone else…an hour or so late. And then she'd still have the night with him.

Why was she even debating about this?

She pulled up her contacts, ready to get it over with, when she heard a knock at her office door.

"Max?" she gasped, pushing up from her desk. "I was just going to call you. What are you doing here?"

Looking freshly scrubbed and, based on the time, having probably come straight from the precinct locker room, he shrugged and stepped into her office. "I know I'm early, and I don't want to get in your way, but I thought I'd just hang out and wait for you to finish. Then we could leave together." He pressed a kiss to her lips and then glanced down at her desk before giving her a sheepish grin. Or at least as sheepish as a tough guy like Max could offer. "But I can take off if you're swamped. No problem."

Swamped? Absolutely. And if he really didn't mind? She glanced up at him, and the words on the tip of her tongue fell away.

"Are you okay?" she asked instead, resting her palm against the center of his chest.

He nodded, but she could see the lines of strain in his face and his eyes.

Something wasn't right. "Is it CJ? Max—"

"No, babe. Everyone is fine. Just one of those days that gets to you, you know. On the scale, it wasn't even that bad, just…"

"Just one of those days," she said, taking his hand and leading him to the couch. He sat down, and though they were in her office, she didn't hesitate when he pulled her into his lap and tucked her head against his chest.

"I'll let you work. Just give me one minute like this, and then you can get back to it."

Linking her arms around his neck, she pressed her brow to his. "I was about done anyway. How about one minute now, and then we get out of here. Go back to your place and take a few hours like this. The whole night if you want it."

His fingers tightened in her hair and he nodded, not saying a word.

———

A week later, Sarah was grabbing her purse, just heading out to lunch with Maria and a few other girls from work who were all clamoring to go back to the little Italian place with the waiter who looked like Tom Hardy. Exactly like Tom Hardy, complete with lips that were "just freaking begging for a nibble," according to Roxi from shipping. And while Tom Hardy was no Max Brandt, Sarah definitely wanted a chance to judge for herself. But then her phone rang and it was Sean, apologizing for getting in the way of the look-alike celebrity stalk and asking if she could meet him for lunch instead. It was about work.

Sending off a regret-filled text for the girls and a dictate to go ahead without her, she took the stairs down to the restaurant, where Sean was already waiting. Once they were seated by the bank of windows overlooking the lakefront, Sean asked for a bottle of pinot to be brought over.

"Wine okay with you?" He checked more as an afterthought, but she knew he would cancel the order if she said no.

Sarah laughed, raising her brow. "Really?"

Sean gave her his charming, professional smile—the one that was remarkably different from what he'd been flashing when he called Brody a chode slurper for nailing a bull's-eye the Wednesday before. Sean asked a few questions about events for the following week, talked a bit about numbers, and then leaned back in his chair when Joy stopped back at the table with the wine. When he and Sarah both had a glass in hand, Sean cocked his jaw to the side and gave her an assessing look.

"What?" she asked, forcing herself not to fidget.

"I need a favor."

Lifting her glass to her lips, she took a hearty swallow, nodding at him once she set the glass back on the table. "Go."

Whatever it was, she could handle it. If the job in Manhattan had fallen through, she would be fine. Even though it was the job she'd been after for three years and she'd wanted it bad enough to take on this interim position. It was going to be fine. If she lost the job, then maybe—

"The project Kim is wrapping up in Manhattan is delayed, and we're asking if you'd be able to give us another three weeks to let her close it before moving over."

The breath she'd been holding was starting to hurt, but no way was she going to let on how deeply this subject affected her, so she released it slowly rather than in a desperate gasp. They still wanted her. Even better, this meant three more weeks with Max!

Wait. Even better? Where had that come from? This was the job she'd been waiting for. There was nothing better than knowing it was still hers. The bit about having more time in Max's arms and bed and with his group of friends—well, that was definitely a bonus. Just not better.

"That means you want me to keep filling in here?" she asked to clarify the point.

"We'll be back to full staff by then." Lifting the menu she was sure he knew by heart, Sean gave it a single glance before setting it aside. "But you've been doing a remarkable job with the projection work I've been giving you. I could still use a hand."

That caught her attention. The project she'd been helping Sean with the past few weeks had been satisfying with a capital *S*. It was the kind of work she only hoped they would give her in New York—after another year or two. If she was looking at more of the same now, then count her in. She'd let them push Manhattan back as long as they wanted.

Sean continued. "That said, we fully recognize we've inconvenienced you enough already by asking you to accommodate our schedule with the transition from San Francisco to Manhattan, so if you'd like to get on with your relocation plans as scheduled, it's entirely up to you."

"No, no. Three weeks is fine. I'm happy to stay," she assured him with an eager rush.

Sean raised a brow. "I'm serious, Sarah. No hard feelings. No impact on your coming position. If you left on schedule, they'd have something to keep you busy."

"I'm good!" Sweeping up her glass, she reached across to clink his. "I'll stay."

Looking as satisfied as she felt, Sean grinned. "Glad to hear it."

Six hours later, Sarah was practically skipping up the walk to Max's place. She couldn't wait to tell him. He'd known how exciting it was for her to work on that piece of the marketing strategy. He'd even taken her out to celebrate. And this would be even better, because instead of leaving in just over three weeks, she'd have more than six.

Max swung open the door before she had a chance to knock, and she launched herself into his arms, kissing him over and over because *she got to keep him for another three weeks!*

Laughing at the barrage of kisses, Max caught her by the back of the head and then, holding her still, took control. He gave her his tongue, licking and thrusting deep, until she was moaning and wrapping her legs around him.

The world was spinning, and she never wanted the ride to stop. The door closed and then she was braced against it, with Max hard between her legs.

"You're so fucking hot," he growled, rolling his hips exactly right. "Tell me what I did to earn this kind of hello. I'll do it every time I see you."

So many more times!

"I've got the best news, Max." Draping her arms over his shoulders, she ran her fingers through his hair. "Turns out I won't be leaving at the end of August like I thought."

That sexy, possessive look blinked clear, and then Max had her on her feet as he jerked back.

"Whoa, Sarah, wait. What are you talking about?" he asked, alarm she didn't understand filling his eyes.

Then it hit her. *The phrasing.*

He thought—

Oh man.

Raising a hand, she shook her head. "Settle down, slugger. You don't need to freak out," she said, laughing, because the poor guy looked like he'd just stepped on a land mine and was waiting for it to detonate. "There's a delay in New York, and Sean asked if I'd be willing to spend the extra weeks here."

That still, breath-held tension dissipated, and Max palmed the back of his head. "Wow, I thought you were saying—" He didn't bother to finish his sentence. They both knew what he was thinking. A smile spread across his face as he pulled her in tight. "So I'll get to keep you a few more weeks, huh?"

Wow, she liked the sound of that. Still pressing her hand to that sexy spot at the center of his chest, she met his eyes so he'd know she meant what she was about to say. "Only if you want to. I mean, just because I'm here doesn't mean *this* has to be a part of it."

"Oh, I want it," he promised, his hand sliding over her ass and curving between her legs. "I want every extra second I can get with you. You sure you still want me?"

To a moderately disturbing degree. "I do. Especially if it means I get three more weeks of the *advanced* class."

Max's eyes darkened, his voice going rough. "What exactly are you planning to learn in the advanced class, Sarah?"

She pushed to her toes and linked her arms around Max's neck, pulling him down to her as she murmured her answer in his ear.

His body tensed as an agonized groan rumbled from deep in his chest. And then he was moving in a blur. Her legs were caught up at either side of his hips, his hands gripping the backs of her thighs in a rough hold that was *definitely* doing it for her, while his mouth devoured hers. She'd take that as an addition to the curriculum.

———

It was one of those perfect days. Sunshiny and warm, with just enough breeze to keep the air from feeling hot. The sky was cartoon blue with a few puffy clouds scattered across it. And to top it off, Max had Sarah wrapped tight around him, her arms locked across his chest, her thighs spread at his hips, and the throaty rumble of his bike between their legs as he rode up Peterson on the Northwest Side.

Max hung a right, digging the way Sarah clung to him as he took the turn. A few blocks up, he cut the engine and waited for her to crawl off the bike before rocking it up on its stand and stowing their helmets.

"I'll never get used to that." She laughed breathlessly from the parkway where she stood finger-combing her dark hair back into a low ponytail, while watching him with a wide smile on her face.

He was pretty sure he'd never get used to the way that smile hit him dead center every time.

As soon as the thought hit him, he realized how true it was. She'd be gone in a matter of weeks. A fact he kept trying to ignore, but couldn't quite manage. He'd give anything to go back to when she wasn't leaving for another month and it still felt like he had forever with her. Now there was a ticking clock between them, and Max was doing his damnedest not to let that dark cloud on the horizon ruin the rest of their time together.

He grinned back at her. "I hope you don't. For that smile, you can come back to Chicago, and I'll give you a ride anytime you want."

"I'll remember that," she said, looking away before

he could read anything from her. Like whether the thought of coming back might hold some appeal, or if she simply hadn't wanted him to see her certainty that it would never happen.

Reaching for her hand, he started walking toward the gate at the side of the house. "Thanks for coming with me today."

"You sure Ernie won't mind?"

Max threaded his fingers with hers, tugging her closer for a quick kiss. "He'll be stoked. The guys at the precinct have been giving me grief for weeks about wanting to meet you." Especially CJ, who'd helped him move in the living room set that Sarah had spent an entire day helping Max pick out the week before. "Don't be surprised if they won't leave you alone."

"Consider me warned," she said with an easy laugh.

He was breaking another long-standing rule: *no dates at "family" parties*. But damn, if it didn't feel good to have her at his side. He hadn't even thought about bringing her until CJ asked if she'd be there. At which point Max realized that while he'd never brought a date before, all the other guys had. Sure, they were usually wives or girlfriends of some significance, but hell, so was Sarah.

She meant something to him, and while he had her, he was proud to show her off.

The music was cranked as he held the gate open and followed Sarah around the side of the bungalow to where a dozen cops were sitting in mismatched lawn chairs, their significant others clustered together at a picnic table in the back corner.

Leading Sarah over to where Ernie was manning the

barbecue, a can of MGD in one hand and tongs in the other, Max joked, "All this for me? Damn, man, I'm flattered."

"Brandt, you made it." His buddy greeted him with a grin that only got wider as he looked Sarah up and down. "And you gotta be Sarah. We were starting to think you were a figment of this guy's imagination. What the hell's a gorgeous girl like you doing with this bag of nuts?"

Sarah was waving him off, a pretty blush in her cheeks. "Oh no. You've got it all wrong. I just met this guy. He agreed not to give me a ticket if I'd come with him."

Christ. Add Ernie to the list of guys to fall for Sarah Cole.

Ernie snapped his tongs in the air, so all the guys looked over at them. "First one of you to get Brandt out of the way gets the next brat. I got dibs on his girl."

Laughter and good-natured ribbing sounded all around them, while Max shook his head and pulled Sarah into his hold. They joked around some more, grabbed a couple of drinks, and then settled in to chat with Ernie and a couple of the guys.

"This is a gorgeous yard," Sarah gushed as she took in her surroundings. "Max said you built the pergola yourself. I'm impressed."

And if Ernie hadn't been gone for her already, that would have done it. The guy started talking about the landscaping, which had been a bitch of a job. Max knew firsthand because of the couple of weekends he'd helped. Sarah listened like she'd never heard anything more fascinating in her life, oohing and aahing at all the right times. Asking questions that invited Ernie to tell her more about what was obviously a topic close to his heart. Anyone else, and Max's BS meter would be spiking, but Sarah had always been interested in hearing what made other people happy. She was just that kind of sweet and special.

And he had less than a month left with her.

Shit.

Pretty soon, the guys were all clustering around, introducing their better halves and falling for the woman Max didn't know how he was going to let go.

"Come on, this girl!" Mick boomed in his thick Chicago accent, tears of laughter leaking from his eyes. "Max, you gotta put a ring on that, and I mean like yesterday. Otherwise, some other lucky schmo is gonna snap her up."

Max coughed into his free hand.

"Jeez, Mick, easy," Jimmy cut in, walking up in a pair of faded cargos with beer cans sweating through both side pockets. "You're gonna scare her off. We gotta woo her some."

Sarah was laughing, her hand at her throat, her eyes bright. Beautiful.

"Sorry to break your hearts," Max warned, knowing what he was about to say wouldn't do any good. These guys had known her for five minutes, and they were already goners. *Welcome to the club, boys*. "But don't get too used to Sarah being around. She's only in town for another couple of weeks before she's moving to New York for a badass job in Wyse's top-earning hotel."

"Nah, nah. We just need to give your girl some more information to work with. Make sure she knows that beneath this crude exterior, our boy Brandt's got some quality shit going on."

Sarah was trying to keep a straight face, but Max was cringing.

"We gotta get her on the hook."

"I think Carl's a step ahead of you on that count." Sarah pinned Mick with an amused look, recounting Carl's tall tales from that first night. Yeah, Max remembered. The guys were hooting it up, rolling with Carl's lies. But Max tensed, knowing it was too much to hope that steel-trap mind of hers would have forgotten what else Carl had said. "And then there was the whole taking a bullet thing," she added, shaking her head with laughter—until the other guys cut off abruptly.

Her head came up with a snap as she looked from one to the other before turning those big, brown eyes on Max, the question unmistakable within them.

Before he could answer, Jimmy stated solemnly, "Yeah, our Max here's a real hero. That's no joke." While Mick added, "He did good that day. Made the whole city proud."

The fingers woven with his tightened, Sarah's eyes taking on a glossy sheen as they lowered, slowly scanning Max's body like she was looking for the blood soaking through his clothes. "That scar on your thigh. It wasn't a camping accident."

No. But it had been easier for him to tell people that.

"It was a long time ago, Sarah," Max stated firmly, catching her chin with the crook of his finger and bringing her gaze back to his. "It wasn't serious."

The guys turned away from them then, suddenly fascinated by the char marks on their brats. They had wives and girlfriends who worried, but this was the first for Max. He'd never had to have "the talk" before.

His dad had been a cop, so he and Molly had grown up understanding how it worked. The same with Joan. But Sarah—hell, she was smart enough to know the risks he faced on a daily basis. Still, there was a reality to what he did for a living that she'd just had brought home.

Max led Sarah past the pergola and around the far side of the house where there was a strip of grass maybe three feet wide. Tears shimmered in her eyes as she shook her head.

"I know you're fine," she whispered, her voice thick. "I can see with my own two eyes you're okay, but the thought of a bullet—" Her voice broke off, and she looked into his eyes as if willing him to hear what she was saying, to understand what it meant to her. "I know how dangerous your job can be. How important it is, and that's why you're willing to risk yourself every time you go out there. But—you were sh-shot, Max. You c-could have been killed."

"But I wasn't," he said gently, firmly. "Baby, I'm right here." Then pulling her to his chest, he wrapped his arms around her back and held her close. He could say that all he was doing was trying to offer her some comfort, but there was more to it. He was trying to get control of his own heart, of his own voice. Because seeing this woman look at him like that—like the idea of him being hurt, no matter how long ago, nearly broke her—it affected him. More than he was ready for.

"Don't cry," he pleaded, feeling her back shudder within his arms, her worry soaking into his shirt. Her tears were gutting him. Making him wonder how he was ever going to let her go.

Sarah sniffed once more, then quickly straightened.

"I'm sorry. I shouldn't have gotten so emotional, Max. It took me by surprise, and the thought of anything happening to you—" She broke off again, but she was already pulling herself together. Peering up at him with watery eyes, she sighed. "I hope I didn't embarrass you in front of your friends."

He brushed at her tears with his thumb. Then ducking down, Max kissed her. Tasting the salty emotion on her lips, he pulled her close again. "Never, baby."

—∿∿∿—

Hours later, they left the party, Sarah sharing tight hugs with the girls she'd talked to, promising to send Vin's wife, Peg, a recipe and Nora, one of the two female officers at the party, a snapshot from Times Square when she arrived in New York. At first it had seemed strange when she realized the only plus-ones at the party were filed under "significant other." Emphasis on *significant*. Most were wives, and the couple of girlfriends in the mix had been with their guys for years. And then there was her.

The summer affair with an expiration date right around the corner.

As they cut through the city streets, Sarah's head resting against Max's back, her arms holding him tight, she tried not to think what it would be like to have all those people as *her* friends. To know she'd see them in a few weeks. To be around to congratulate Darcy when Mick gave her the ring she'd accidentally found the week before. To see Clara's baby when it was born. To have Max making her feel beautiful and special for more than just a few weeks. To be there every night and know he'd made it home safe.

She sighed, calling up thoughts of New York. Waiting for that soul-deep churn of anticipation. The anticipation was still there, yes, but it wasn't powerful enough to distract her from the ache of good-bye.

Chapter 15

SARAH HAD NEVER BEEN TOO TROUBLED BY NIGHTMARES. She'd had bad dreams before, ones she'd wished she could forget, sure. The stress-spurred, irrational variety that reared their ugly heads from time to time over the years: a ghoul chasing her through quicksand that was about to seep into a laptop with the only copy of her final paper stored on the hard drive, a presentation to deliver and the horrifying realization that all the data had changed overnight and nothing she'd prepared was current, Cory walking into her office and informing her he was her new boss and she'd accidentally married him after all.

That business where her brain screwed with her during off hours usually sent her pulse racing, and when she woke, it was typically with a gasp as she bolted upright in her bed.

That kind of traditional bad dream she could take, because when it was over, she'd run her fingers over the cool sheets, grounding herself in the comfort of what was real and the knowledge that what wasn't was already fading from her mind.

What she'd woken from this morning had been nothing like that. To begin with, there'd been no silent scream or full-body lunge thrusting her into a waking state. She'd been still, quiet, blissfully drifting beneath the warm breeze as Max dropped a circle of kisses around the full swell of her belly. Their fingers had been threaded together, and when he smiled up at her, she'd known with soul-deep certainty that somehow she'd found everything that mattered. That she had as much happiness as one life could provide.

Then she'd blinked. Just opened her eyes into the darkness of predawn, not understanding where the sunny afternoon had gone, why the sheers weren't billowing into the room. Her smile fell away as the soft sheets grounded her in a reality she found no relief in. Her hand moved to the flat of her stomach and she felt gutted, the sense of loss greater than anything she could remember.

Because in this reality, the Max sleeping with his arm thrown over her and his head in her hair didn't love her. They hadn't been married for three years and weren't counting the days until the miracle growing inside her was finally in their arms. The house that had been filled with light and love and laughter was a mostly empty shell Max owned alone and looked forward to moving on from.

None of it was real.

She tried to close her eyes, hoping she'd drift back into the world she'd just lost, because more than anything, she wanted that perfect peace back, if only for another ten minutes. She wanted Max to murmur in her ear that she was his. That he loved her. Only there was no going back. She was awake. And this wasn't forever.

Silently, she pulled back the sheet and padded into the kitchen, where she stood at the sink with a glass of water and waited for her brain to rewire itself. For reality to become the relief, because *this*, what she actually *had* right now, was exactly what she wanted. The perfect job lined up in a city she'd been salivating over for years, and a stint with a sexy, generous, highly skilled bad boy warming her bed in the meantime. There were no complications. No questions. No letdowns or betrayals or expectations for anything beyond what they had that very minute. It was perfect and safe, and it was *supposed* to make her feel like she had in that dream.

A floorboard creaked behind her, and then Max was there, his strong arms wrapping around her.

"You okay, baby?" he asked, his voice rough from sleep. Comforting.

Setting the glass on the counter, she turned to him and pressed her face against the warm skin of his chest. "Just a nightmare."

He stroked her hair and held her closer. Rested his chin on the top of her head so they fit together like two pieces of a puzzle. "Mmm, come back to bed. Whatever it was isn't real."

She swallowed past the knot in her throat. "I know."

It wasn't real. Even if she suddenly wanted it to be.

Max took her back to bed, tucked her into the warmth of his body, and held her close and tight as she waited for sleep to return. Only instead of falling back into that taboo dream world, she lay there thinking about how Max's arms felt around her. How she'd started anticipating seeing him at the end of the day, wanting to share the details of the hours they'd spent apart, knowing he'd laugh about the prank housekeeping had pulled.

She thought about how she'd gotten so used to seeing him in the morning. How he'd rub his big hand over his head, trying to wake up as he poured coffee and asked her what her day looked like. How sometimes, for no reason at all, he pulled her in for a hug and just held her close. How he made her feel wanted. How he made her feel wonderful. She thought about how she couldn't help wondering what it would be like to wake up with this man every day and feel *loved*.

This wasn't working.

"Sorry, Max," she whispered, inching out of his hold. "Think I'm just awake now."

"Want me to get up with you?" He was already pushing the covers aside, completely willing to get up with her at four fourteen. Definitely not helping the cause. "We could walk the lakefront or grab some breakfast."

"No, no. Just rest." She pressed him back with a hand at his shoulder. "We'll get something when you're up." And until then, she'd work. Spend some time doing what she loved to do best. Reminding herself why she loved it.

Only the work didn't help. In fact, it might have actually made the situation worse. Sarah spent the next three hours failing to accomplish anything, and worse yet, every time she'd had to forcibly drag her thoughts away from the bedroom down the hall, she'd *resented* it.

Which. Was. Insane.

The dream stuck with her all day. The emotions it stirred stayed fresh and sharp in her mind. By evening, she was about ready to jump out of her skin. A part of her—the rational, reasonable part—knew the answer was getting out of there. Getting some distance and maybe a little perspective. But the other part of her wouldn't hear of it, choosing instead to stay close to Max, because soon enough she wouldn't be able to.

"What are you thinking for dinner?" he asked that

evening, one muscular arm braced against the doorframe to the kitchen. He was wearing a Red Hot Chili Peppers T-shirt that, thanks to his stance, didn't quite reach the worn jeans hanging criminally low on his hips. It was calendar-quality stuff.

But was she thinking about dropping to her knees and worshipping that insanely hot inch of bared skin the way it deserved? No. She was thinking she felt every kind of screwed up and that nothing would be better than walking up to Max and sliding her arms around his ribs while she buried her face against his chest and just breathed him in.

He looked like sex on a stick. And she wanted *a hug*.

"Sarah?" he asked when she didn't answer him. Then he was walking over to her, giving her exactly what she wanted—the hug. The comfort. The support. The exact opposite of what she needed, which was a less-perfect man. Someone it wouldn't kill her to walk away from.

"You seem tense. What's going on?" Rubbing his big hands over her arms, Max dropped a kiss at the crook of her neck. "Talk to me."

What was going on was that she'd had a glimpse into a life she'd never let herself consider. A life she couldn't have and wasn't supposed to want. Because this thing with Max was about sex. Fine, more than sex, but absolutely unequivocally *less* than what was suddenly slithering through her mind.

Maybe that was the problem. The solution? Heck, she didn't know. Maybe what she needed was to take away some of the tenderness and focus on what had brought them together in the first place. She needed to put this relationship back where it belonged—on sexy ground.

Turning to him, she reached for the back of his neck and tugged him down to her. "I don't want to talk."

Max's mouth met hers in a soft press, tender and sweet, his arms circling her back and holding her close. It was the kind of embrace that had caused the temporary short circuit in her brain, and she didn't want any part of it.

Pulling back, she nipped at his mouth and then kissed him again, harder. Max's brows drew together, his eyes going dark.

"That's what you want?" he asked, his voice dangerously low.

No. It wasn't what she wanted, but tonight it was what she needed. Max had promised to show her everything he knew about sex, and what she needed to learn now was how to get her emotions out of it. How to make it about her body and not her heart.

Pressing her hands against his chest, she gave him a shove, one that didn't move him an inch until he willingly stepped back. Sarah whipped her shirt overhead and tossed it on the floor, refusing to meet Max's searching eyes.

She didn't want him to see what she wasn't ready to acknowledge herself. The emotions she'd somehow let out of the box from eight years ago. The ones Max had *warned* her about that day in front of the Science Building, when he'd caught her watching him too intently. She'd been standing there wondering how things could be so easy and right between them, how she could be feeling everything she was feeling, if there wasn't something more than friendship at play.

But when she'd asked him, Max's answer had come in no uncertain terms.

No.

He hadn't wanted those feelings then, and they weren't fair now. The arrangement between them had been clearly defined, and falling in love wasn't part of it.

Something she'd do well to remember.

Slipping her thumbs into the waist of her cropped jeans, she flipped the button and lowered the zipper. Her hips shifted from side to side, as she eased the jeans past her thighs to where they dropped to the floor.

Stepping free of the denim, she asked, "What are you waiting for?"

The question seemed to snap Max into action. Suddenly he was stripping with an economy of motion that had her mouth watering and the heat churning low in her center. His shirt landed beside hers, his jeans, belt, and boxer briefs a few feet away. Then he was advancing on her, naked and beautiful, those heavy muscles flexing with each step. Her breath hitched as he caught her around the waist and hauled her up against him. She wrapped her legs around him and shoved her fingers into his hair, holding on as his mouth slammed down on hers.

His tongue was thrusting deep, his hold on her ass just this side of rough as he held her, rocking her over his shaft. Her back met the wall, and mmm, it felt so good. She wanted him inside her, hammering against that spot that made her mindless. She wanted him slamming into her so hard he drove the tenderness away.

She could do this.

She could keep her heart out of it.

But then Max released her mouth, his breath coming hot and ragged against her jaw and throat. "Fuck, Sarah, what are you doing to me?"

And she felt that pang deep in her chest. That twist and churn deep inside.

She couldn't let him talk to her, not when they were like this. Even knowing not to read anything into his words, just the gravelly sound of his voice was too much for her.

"Don't make me wait," she panted, squeezing him closer with her legs and using her forearms on his big shoulders as leverage to move against him.

Pushing off the wall with Sarah wrapped tight around him, Max turned toward the bedroom—toward the bed he'd bought so her first time wouldn't be on a mattress on the floor or in a hotel room. Because he wanted it to be special for her.

Shaking her head, she nipped his jaw. "Not the bed."

Those heated eyes met hers. He was looking too close.

"I don't want soft tonight." She couldn't take it.

"No?"

She shook her head and levered herself against him again, her eyes drifting closed at the wet friction from Max's thick cock sliding between the spread of her sex.

A second later, her bottom met the solid top of his kitchen table.

Releasing her hold from around his neck, she planted her hands behind her.

Legs spread, heart pounding, she waited for him to retrieve the condom from his discarded wallet. He rolled it on, but instead of driving into her the way she'd expected, he dropped to his knees.

Eyes gone wide, she tried to scramble back. "No, that's not—"

But then Max had her by the backs of the knees and was towing her to the table's edge. "Don't worry," he said from where he was licking his lips between her legs. "I'm not going to be gentle."

Sarah about combusted on the spot, because that was just the kind of promise she needed.

His mouth covered her sex, greedy and hot. He sucked and licked, sucked harder and bit softly, but not too softly. His thumbs were at either side of her sex, holding her open, as he devoured her with hungry intent. It was too much, too intense, exactly what she needed.

With his mouth covering that dangerous bundle of nerves that seemed to be connected to every far corner of her body, he gave her another breath-stealing suck that took her to the edge and launched her over.

"Max!"

She was still coming hard, as he stood and leaned over her. Gripping her hip, he thrust full length, filling her with everything she could take. She gasped, her breath punching out as he pushed in. Sensation rushed through her, flooding her senses and short-circuiting her resolve. Her inner walls pulsed around his slow retreat. He thrust again, giving her even more, pushing into her so hard and deep she swore she could feel him everywhere.

"Again," she begged, caught in the dark intensity of his eyes. "Like that."

This was what she needed. Physical. Release.

Another slow withdrawal pulled and teased every tender nerve. Another measured pause. "So beautiful, baby." Another driving thrust left her filled to overflowing with the man who was making her want more than she could have.

She could feel him everywhere—in the pressure where he met that deepest spot within her, in the decadent stretch from taking him, and the almost painfully hard beating of her heart. Each ragged breath reminded her of just how badly she wanted him.

He dragged his length from inside her, easing that too-intense pressure by teasing her with the slightest push and pull, until she begged him, "Max!"

Shoving deep, he grunted as his groin trapped that pulsing sweet spot between them. Her inner channel spasmed, wrenching tight around him. "Like that, baby?"

So much.

"More," she whispered desperately. Because she couldn't fight what was happening. She wanted to feel him everywhere. She wanted to ache from him for days.

He was thrusting in earnest now, making her clench and shake, giving her everything she'd asked for and more. "Too gentle for you?"

She was so wet. So slick. So full. "*No.*"

"You sure?" His voice was like the most seductive threat. A sensual warning. He angled his head next to her ear. "*Or do you want me to fuck you harder?*"

She clenched around him, the spasm almost brutal in its intensity. Crying out, she nodded desperately, begged almost incoherently until she managed the necessary words. "Do it. Harder."

The sound that ripped from Max's chest was the sexiest she'd ever heard, and then he was shafting ruthlessly inside her, again and again, catapulting her over the edge once more. Watching her as she fell and then catching her with the gentle rock of his hips.

"Jesus, Sarah, it's never like this for me." Pressing

his forehead against hers, Max held her tight. "How the hell am I going to let you go?"

She closed her eyes against his words, but they were already too deep inside her. For the first time in a long time, the goal she'd set her sights on was out of reach. Beyond her ability. Because this wasn't just a physical encounter, and that flimsy defense she'd tried to erect around her heart wasn't holding.

She loved him. And there was no coming back from that.

―⁓―

"Where's Sarah?" Brody asked as Max walked into the bar Wednesday night.

As questions went, this one ranked benign at best, but still it rubbed in a way Max wasn't exactly thrilled about. Mostly because he kept thinking it himself. Why wasn't she there? The answer was simple.

"Back at Piper's place tonight." The bar was more crowded than it usually was on Wednesday, and he had to speak up to be heard as they walked back to the table.

"Shoulda brought Piper too. Bit of a firecracker, that one." Brody rolled three darts between his palms, a wicked glint in his eyes. "She could give our girl Molly a run for her money."

Max glanced up and saw his little sister with her hands wrapped around Sean's neck, fake strangling him as the guy made a show of squinting up his eyes and sticking his tongue out. "Yeah, she could. But Piper's not even there. Sarah's parents live back in North Carolina, and they just got home from a cruise. She wanted to call and figured her mom might keep her on the line a few hours talking about the trip and catching up."

She could have done it from his place and been there when he got home. He'd have been happy to stick around and work upstairs—give her space for her call, then order in some dinner after. But she'd passed.

Totally fine. Not a problem.

Only the tightening of the muscles across his shoulders not only called him a liar, but made him feel like a jackass too. Because seriously, he didn't own her. It was good she had a life outside him. He loved how independent she was. Besides, they were still a few weeks from when she'd leave for New York. He just couldn't help thinking about each passing day taking them closer to when he wouldn't be able to see her at all.

It sucked, and he felt like a pussy. Especially since Sarah wasn't taking her impending departure quite the same way. Up until Saturday, he'd thought they might be in the same bittersweet boat—both wanting everything they could have until good-bye finally came. But then, he didn't know.

Jase and Emily were standing across the table from Sean and Molly, their fingers caught in a loose hold that caused a pang in his chest. Yeah, total pussy.

"Hey, guys, Emily."

"How's it going, man?" Jase asked, stepping closer to his wife to make room for Brody and Max. "Big day of bringing down the bad guys?"

"Nah, word's out that I'm on the street." Max nodded for Brody to throw first. "We're expecting the criminal element to lay down their arms and get in line."

Sean let out a short laugh, then straightened, his expression blanking as he went for his phone.

Molly sat back, brow raised. "Five bucks it's his dad."

"Nobody's taking that bet," Brody said, setting the darts down rather than starting the game.

Sean shot them an apologetic look and signaled to give him five. No one minded. The hotel was more than his job, and Sean Wyse II was more than just his dad.

"You have a chance to look at that order we talked about last night?" Molly asked, turning to Brody when Sean headed toward the front door.

He pulled a face and shook his head. "Sorry, Mol. Run in back with me now, and we'll take care of it." Then because it was Brody, and the guy couldn't help but be the hostess with the mostest, he leaned back over the table. "Want me to have Jill bring you guys anything?"

"I'm good," Max answered as Jase and Emily declined in kind. Then Em got a call too, and like that, it was just Max and Jase.

Jase picked up the darts and gave Max a wicked look. "Hope you've got some tissues."

Grinning, Max stood and crossed his arms. They were pretty evenly matched but seldom went head-to-head. "Sorry, man, you'll just have to use your sleeve."

They threw a few rounds, volleying trash talk because it didn't get any better than that. Then Jase stepped up to the line and tossed. "How long's Sarah got left in Chicago?"

Max rolled his shoulder. "Not long enough."

Jase's head came up with a start.

"What? I'm into her," Max said, defending himself and wondering what was so surprising. "It's fucking good between us."

Jase patted down the air. "No, I can see that. Just didn't expect you to see it too. I'm happy for you, Max. She's a great girl, and seeing you guys together is awesome. You thinking about trying the long-distance thing when she goes?"

This time it was Max going traffic stop with his hand in the air. "No. Not a chance. That shit never works, and from the few tries I've seen my friends make, it pretty much blows until it's over. I'll take having all of her now and a clean break when she leaves. I mean, if you think about it, it's actually pretty sweet. We both know the score. There's a ticking clock on this relationship, which means no one has to hold back or be careful or whatever."

It made sense to Max. So he wasn't sure what was with Jase standing there, looking at him with his head cocked to the side. "What do you mean no one has to hold back?"

Yeah, right. Jase might have it bad for Emily, but before they got together, the guy cycled through girlfriends like Max went through breakfast cereal. He might not *want* to remember the *before* time, but Max was betting he did.

"Come on, man. You know how it is when you've got to gauge everything you do to make sure no one gets the wrong idea. Like sleeping over. I never did it, because wrapping my arms around the warm body across the bed might have given the girl ideas, even though I'd gone out of my way to be clear she shouldn't get them. Going out more than once or twice. Or seeing the same girl two nights in a row. You can't do that and expect them not to wonder if maybe you've started to reconsider."

"Yeah, yeah," Jase answered, but clearly there was

still something on his mind. "So all those things you never let yourself do with the other girls. You're doing them with Sarah?"

That was the best part. Max leaned in to his buddy. "She sleeps over damn near every night, man. My pillow smells like her shampoo. And I cook with her, Jase. I actually cook *for* her."

Jase's chin snapped back. "With what? You have a single frying pan and a pot. What'd you make her, an egg and some ramen?"

Asshole. "For your information, I bought myself a bunch of kitchen shit from that store where Brody made you get yours. Set of pans. Couple good knives. And I'm confident enough with my manhood to tell you I even have a set of those 'nested' bowls. The little baby one is so small that Sarah picked it up and kissed it." At Jase's look, he grinned. "I know. But why not? Couple more things to move, and it's nice while I've got Sarah here. Hell, maybe I'll cook for you guys sometime. But I've only got two kitchen chairs, so someone's going to have to use the lawn chair."

Nodding, Jase walked back to the table and reached for his beer. "And you're sure Sarah isn't getting the wrong idea? Because just listening to you, gotta say, I kinda am."

"Not a chance." Max glanced around the bar, making sure the rest of the guys were still otherwise occupied. "She's all about New York. I mean, we're having fun. A hell of a lot of it. But she makes *me* look clingy."

He probably should have waited until Jase put the beer down, because now the guy was coughing up foam.

"Shut up," Jase croaked, grimacing as he rubbed his chest.

"I'm serious. I keep thinking we've only got so much time left, so all I want to do is make the most of it together—which I will deny saying if you breathe a fucking word of this to anyone." Jase was waving him on, the understanding between them clear. "But just this week, it's like half the time she's got this little furrow between her eyes. I ask what's wrong, and she says she's thinking about work. She's mentally moving forward, even though I want to keep her here with me until I actually have to let her go, you know?"

He thought about Saturday morning and how she'd woken up with that nightmare and all he'd wanted was to hold her. Like somehow the power of his arms alone would be enough to banish whatever unwelcome thoughts had crawled into her consciousness. Nice thought, but Sarah had turned to work instead.

"You think maybe she's just, I don't know, giving the brakes a tap because she knows the relationship has to end? Like maybe better to slow down before that happens?"

Max rubbed the back of his neck, thinking about what it was like when they were together. When he was inside her. The way their eyes locked and that connection lit up. "Nah. No way. It's just how she is. And I shouldn't be whining about it, because it's part of what makes her so fucking perfect."

He knew exactly where he stood with her. He knew what her priorities were. Her plans. Which meant there wouldn't be any excuse for getting in her way.

Chapter 16

SARAH STOOD IN FRONT OF THE WALL OF GLASS ACROSS from the mezzanine-level Wyse coffee shop overlooking the lake, her untouched coffee cooling in her hands. It had been a week since she realized she loved Max, and the feeling wasn't going away. No matter how hard she tried to put the distance back between them, she just couldn't make it happen. If anything, she was sinking deeper every day.

This morning, she'd fled from Max's bed at the crack of dawn after realizing tears were leaking from the corners of her eyes as she thought about saying good-bye. He hadn't seen her cry, but she hadn't been willing to risk him noticing if she stayed, so despite it being Saturday, she'd gone to work to try to clear her head. So much for that. She'd already been there an hour and a half, and that deep churn of nerves in her stomach still hadn't settled. She'd tried to talk herself down, tell herself that, in the scheme of things, falling in love didn't really change anything. She'd known her emotions were getting away from her. She'd been ready for the inevitable hurt when she left.

Sure, having gone and fallen in love with a man she was leaving in two weeks' time hadn't been part of the plan, and it upped the expected ache on an exponential level. But she'd recover. And until she left, she'd hold this epic lapse in judgment close to her chest. Quietly.

Tenderly. Gratefully even. Yes, it was going to hurt. But a part of her had believed she'd never feel this way again, and even knowing how much harder it was going to be to say good-bye, it was good to know she'd been wrong. *That she could still love*.

"Looks like some deep thoughts going on there, Sarah."

She glanced over to find Sean had walked up beside her. Smiling, she turned to him. "Just realizing it might be harder to say good-bye to Chicago than I was expecting."

Sean nodded, pushing his hands deep into his suit pockets. He squinted out to the lake for a moment before meeting her eyes with a serious look. "Sarah, I know you've been looking forward to New York, and I've been laying it on pretty thick about trying to score you for Wyse Chicago. But I'm not just screwing around, and I'm not talking about you staying on in some position that doesn't challenge you or compete with the offer you have from Manhattan."

They'd been through this before, but this morning Sean's tone was devoid of all teasing. Today he sounded serious. And today? Sarah crossed her arms and rubbed her fingertips over the back of her thumb. Maybe she was ready to hear what he had to say. "Okay, you have my attention."

A smile tugged at Sean's mouth, and he cut her a conspiratorial look. "You sure you want to hear? It's gonna mess up all your plans."

"You wish." She doubted it could, but what was the harm in listening? If nothing else, maybe it would distract her for a while. Keep her mind from drifting back to Max and the way he smelled and tasted and made her feel alive. Yes, she definitely needed the distraction. "But by all means, give it your best shot."

Satisfaction lit his face. "Let's go to my office."

She nodded and walked with him to the bank of elevators. It was still early, but in the hotel industry, there were always people around. And while the Chicago staff was incredible, more like family than coworkers, certain conversations were best held behind closed doors.

Sean glanced at his watch. "Pretty early to be at work on a Saturday, Sarah. Especially since you don't work weekends. Everything okay with you and Max?"

Her stomach bottomed out, but before she could find the words, Sean held up a staying hand. "Scratch that. I don't want to know, because I'd like there to be no confusion about the context of this conversation."

Her brows rose in question.

"I'm talking to you as *my* friend and as *your* employer. Clear?"

The elevator doors glided open, and they stepped inside. "Clear."

Sean punched in his floor, and when the doors closed, he turned to face her straight on, his expression as serious as she'd ever seen. "Forget about the guy you're dating."

"You're shitting me," Piper gasped, holding a pillow over her head like some ginormous hat. It was almost noon, and she'd texted Sarah thirty minutes before, begging her to bring a sandwich to counteract her night of excess.

Ready for a break and hungry herself, Sarah had stopped on the way home, only to discover Piper was still in bed and hadn't realized she wasn't actually in the apartment.

Now they were sitting on Piper's bed, a couple of Potbelly subs laid out between them.

Sarah nodded, taking a sip of her drink. "It was really cool. For all the pushing about the job thing, he didn't want me to make my decision based on a guy—even if it happened to be one of his best friends. Or maybe especially because of that, since he knows Max so well."

"Wait." The pillow came down, and the light in Piper's eyes faded just a little. "He wasn't hitting on you?"

Sarah's eyes bugged. "Sean? No way. Piper, this is about *work*. Focus."

"It would be easier to focus if this was another install-ment in your sexual chronicles." At Sarah's glare, Piper heaved a sigh and picked up a chip. "Fine, I'm listening. Sort of."

"Piper, all these side projects he's been giving me. The work with sales and marketing, the projection project, everything I've been telling you about this last month and a half—"

Piper froze mid-chew, a guilty look on her face. "Full disclosure here…when you talk about work, I some-times zone out."

Sarah pinched her lips between her teeth, but now that she thought about it, she remembered her friend warning her it might happen. "Okay, nutshell version: the work he's been giving me is awesome, above my pay-grade stuff, dream-job stuff."

"That's good."

Sarah laughed. "Yeah, it is. Because Sean just offered me *that* job."

Now she had Piper's attention. "Here in Chicago?" At her nod, Piper sat straighter and pushed her lunch aside. "But you were dying to move to New York, Sarah. It's all you've talked about for more than a year."

Sarah shifted. "I know. And it's a huge decision. But what he's offering—"

"Is Max figuring into the equation? Because, Sarah, I know he's great, but think about last time. The trade-off you made."

"I remember." She'd given up the position she'd accepted to follow Cory to San Francisco because that was where *he'd* been offered a job. There'd been less discussion than there should have been, most of it revolving around the idea that they wanted kids, a couple of them at least and early. Cory wanted her to stay home, and she'd agreed, so his career needed to be the priority.

That choice had haunted her for years, driving her priorities, her choices. Her commitments.

Even after he'd been out of her life for good, Cory had continued to impact it. Sometimes in a good way— after all, having something to prove had more than paid off for her—but also in not-so-good ways. She'd completely closed herself off from life outside work. From relationships. From anything that felt like there was even the smallest risk to her heart or her plans.

Cory had made her afraid. And she'd lived that way for years. Until Max had shown her how to be brave again, and how good it felt to connect with someone else.

She wanted to tell Piper that Max wasn't figuring in the equation, but she couldn't.

When her only response was silence, Piper offered Sarah her last potato chip.

Yeah, that about summed it up.

—∿∿—

Trim work was a bitch, but damn, when those mitered edges lined up just right and all the rough cutouts around the windows and doorway were finished, it transformed the space. Max rocked back on his heels and blew out a low whistle. This room was going to sell the place.

Pulling his phone from his jeans, he walked over to his window seat and looked down at the street below. It was Monday night, and the neighborhood was coming alive with couples walking hand in hand, lights blinking on, and the occasional squeal of some delighted kid seeing a parent come home. This would be a nice house for a family one day.

Sarah answered on the second ring. "I know I said seven, but I just got the Madison numbers and I kind of hate to put it down when I've got everything fresh in my head."

Max chuckled into the phone. "Don't sweat it. Any idea what you're looking at for timing?" It was weird calling her like that, when he wasn't sure he'd ever called a woman trying to gauge how soon he'd get to see her. Wondering if she might make it sooner than that if he talked dirty in her ear. He could try, but Sarah took her job as seriously as he took his, and having her name tied to the projects Sean was giving her was putting a grin on his girl's face that Max wouldn't want to see come off. So maybe no dirty talk, at least not now.

A slow breath sounded through the line, and Max stood a little straighter, listened a little closer. "Everything okay?"

"It is," she answered quickly, only to leave a pause after. "It's just I don't know what to tell you for timing. Mind if we take the night off so I can make some more progress with this stuff? I'm getting so much done, and I hate to—"

"Hey, it's fine. No problem," he assured her. He could hear the tension in her voice and didn't want to be the reason behind it. Yeah, he was going to miss her— but hell, it was just one night. And okay, she'd been busy with Piper on Saturday and most of Sunday, but he'd seen her for a few hours the night before. He'd gotten to fall asleep with her in his arms, which was one of his favorite things. And he'd see her the next day. So no big deal. "Have fun, and, baby?"

"Yeah?" she asked softly.

"Don't work too hard."

Jesus, who was he with this stuff?

"I won't," she said, and he could hear the smile in her voice. "Thanks for understanding."

"You bet, beautiful." Max thumbed off the phone and headed downstairs. Dinner for one coming up.

Traffic in the city was nuts with the rain, and Sarah's cab had been moving at a snail's pace for the last five minutes. It was Wednesday night, and the guys—minus Sean, plus Emily—were playing darts. An easy group activity where the deep-eye staring would be at a minimum and the openings for heart-to-heart discussions about the future of her and Max's relationship would be zero. Darts with the guys would be safe. A relief considering what a complete chicken she'd been the last few days.

Ever since Sean put the offer out there, Sarah had been a wreck. Heck, even before the offer, she'd been losing it. But since this new job opportunity presented itself, Sarah had been straight-up avoiding Max. She couldn't relax. She had to tell him about the offer.

She would.

She just wanted to figure out her own feelings first. So far, she hadn't.

But Max wasn't dumb, and while he'd been willing to let her canceled plans and excuses go for now, he wouldn't forever.

The cab stopped in front of Belfast, and Sarah paid with her credit card before climbing out into the drizzle. Warm light was spilling out from the entry, the sound of laughter and cheers greeting her when a girl ran in ahead of her. This was ridiculous. She wanted to see Max, wanted to feel his arms around her.

Time to bite the bullet.

Inside, everyone was already gathered at their table. Brody had Molly in some sort of headlock, and she was trying to bite his arm. Jase and Emily were seated across the table, laughing shoulder to shoulder. And Max—her heart did that little tumbling thing, because Max looked up, his eyes locking on hers as that sexy smile spread across his face. She was smiling too as he closed the distance between them with long strides, taking her in his arms and tipping her head back for a kiss that was every kind of happy to see her. This was the kiss she'd fallen in love with. The one that made her knees weak and her heart ache with everything she was feeling.

His mouth still fused with hers, Max lifted her so her toes hung inches off the ground and, with his arms locked around her waist, walked them back to the table. They were greeted by gagging sounds, courtesy of Molly; Brody offering up a cheer that spread like wildfire and had half the bar clapping like Max had just pulled Sarah from a fire; and Jase and Emily getting that look in their eyes that typically preceded them disappearing for a while.

"What?" Max demanded, a giant grin on his face as he pulled her in closer still. "I can't give my girlfriend a kiss after not seeing her for a few days?"

Girlfriend. Max hadn't called her that before, and while it wasn't any profession of love everlasting, the needy part of Sarah's heart clung to it, snuggling it close just the same.

"A kiss? Sure." Molly laughed, shaking her head, her eyes all bugged out. "But that? Come on, Max, there are kids around."

There weren't any kids around. It was a bar. But still, Max looked duly chagrined, which had Sarah reaching for the front of his button-down and pulling him back for one more quick kiss. "I'll take a hello like that any day of the week."

"Yeah?" Max grinned, his brow pressed to hers, deep-eye staring a go.

And it felt so right. Even with Molly muttering an affectionate "Gross" from across the table, and Brody asking Jase and Emily where they were going. Sarah wanted to melt into this moment forever.

They needed to talk.

⁓

Three nights later, she still hadn't done it.

The mattress dipped as Max returned, sliding under the cool sheet and pulling Sarah into the heat of his naked body. Her heart ached with how right it felt to lie there like that with him, while her belly tensed, thinking about the conversation to come. Maybe. If she decided New York was what she wanted, she didn't need to tell Max anything. But if she kept thinking about Chicago the way she was—because it was a really, *really* good offer—they had to talk. And that talk was going to break all their rules.

God, she just wanted this to last. But with her flight only a week away, time was running out and—

"Hey, what's that look about?" Max asked, brushing a bit of hair from her brow and tucking it behind her ear in one of those tender caresses that left her feeling beautiful and cared for and all too vulnerable. It was only eight, so there was still light enough from outside for Sarah to read the caring in Max's eyes. "Talk to me, Sarah. Something's been going on with you, and it's killing me that you won't tell me what it is. Is this about you leaving?"

And like that, her time was up. No more avoidance.

"Remember when I told you I was going to be staying these extra weeks?" she asked, working her hand free so she could stroke the hard line of Max's jaw.

The corner of his mouth hitched up. "Yeah, I do. Don't suppose Sean's found a way to get me another reprieve before you have to go?"

"Would you like that?" she asked quietly, afraid if she spoke any louder, her voice would reveal more than she wanted.

"Another couple of weeks of this?" Max looked at

her like she was crazy to even ask. "You know I would. Why? What's going on?"

She smiled weakly. "When I first brought it up, you seemed...maybe a little wary."

A beat passed with Max just looking at her. Then propping himself up on one arm, he shook his head. "Sarah, I didn't know you were still thinking about that. Hell, that you'd been thinking about it at all. Baby, I'm sorry. I guess it just took me by surprise for a minute before I understood what you were talking about. I didn't mean to hurt your feelings."

He looked so genuine staring down at her, but he'd always cared about her. The affection had never been in question.

"I wasn't hurt," she assured him. "At the time, I would have freaked if you'd started asking me about changing my plans or suggesting we try to make a future together."

He'd heard it. Max was too sharp not to. That tricky qualifier, *at the time*. "Okay, so why are you bringing it up now?"

Because she loved him. Because she was staring at two paths ahead of her. And even though all she wanted was to spend the next few months going on the way they had—laughing and lazing their free time away together, letting the course of things naturally play out so she didn't have to push this thing between them—the terms of their mutually agreed upon fling were about to expire. And she owed Sean an answer in two days.

She didn't want Max to play into the equation, but he was already there. This sexy, six-foot question mark that made her believe in the possibility of something bigger, maybe even more important than her career. Only she couldn't say any of that, not now. "Because it feels like something's changed with us. And I'm wondering if it's just me, or if you feel it too."

Brows drawn forward, Max licked his bottom lip. "Of course I feel it too. There's a lot between us. But, baby, that doesn't change anything except how I'm going to look back on this. You've got a plan. A good one. And as good as *this* has been, I couldn't live with myself if I let *us* get in the way of your career."

The sentiment meant so much to her, but still she couldn't help wishing that Max wasn't quite so support-ive. That he was maybe just a little conflicted about what to do where they were concerned. That he struggled, in some small way, with the possessive impulse to selfishly hold on to her, no matter what the cost.

She sat up and, tucking her knees beneath her, pulled the edge of the sheet to her breasts. "I appreciate that, because my career is very important to me." For the lon-gest time, it had been the only priority in her life. Now though… "But what if there were options other than New York?" Holding up her hand, she shook her head and tried again. "No, forget that. What if New York had never been on the table, and I was just *here*. Would you still want an end date for this thing between us—or would you want to see where things went?"

Max sat, shifting so his back was against the head-board, concern in his eyes. "Without New York, we never would have started this. So why even—"

"But say we did," she urged, hating the pleading in her voice, but not being able to stop it.

"Sarah, what's going on? Is there a problem with the

job? Do you want me to talk to Sean? They moved you out here, have your things in storage. I can't believe they'd pull the rug out—"

She cut him off. "The New York position is still available."

The relief was there in his eyes, as obvious as the nose on her face. But still, she had to tell him what she was thinking. She had to put herself out there one more time. "This thing between us, Max, it feels right to me. Like it could be more than either one of us was thinking."

"Sarah…" he began with a slow shake of his head.

She knew what was happening. Once again, she was offering Max more than he wanted to take—and suddenly more than anything, she wanted to cover her ears and hum, anything to pretend his next words weren't coming. But whether she wanted to hear them or not, she needed to. Max wasn't like Cory. He wouldn't lie to her or play her or try to snow her into a relationship with rules she didn't understand.

The muscle in his jaw jumped once, twice. "Being with you is more intense than anything I've known in years. But we both went into this knowing it wasn't going to be forever. It was just going to be the good time we had together during an intermission in your life."

She nodded, turning to the window so he wouldn't see what that summary did to her. Blinking against the push of tears that weren't fair, she nodded.

Smoothing the backs of his fingers over her shoulder and down her arm, he spoke quietly. "Look, I get it. When things are good like this, it's easy to wonder what it would be like to have more. But Sarah, you've got plans. A job you told me yourself you'd been working toward for years. I don't want to be the guy who gets in the way of that. I just want to be the one making you remember your time in Chicago with a smile. We have a week left, baby. Let's make the most of it."

That would be the rational thing. The smart thing. But somehow, Sarah had stopped thinking with her head, and her heart knew what he was suggesting was beyond her.

Throat thick, she peered up at him. "Max, I'm sorry, but I don't think I can do that."

He looked like she'd slapped him, and she felt all the worse for it.

"Of course you can. Why would you even say that?"

She wanted to laugh, because he looked like the idea of missing out on one minute together would break him. Yet he was holding fast to the security of her leaving.

As if sensing a dead end, Max shook his head and then smoothed his features. That flash of concern and urgent tone were gone. A calm he'd probably perfected on the force was now in play. "Okay, Sarah, I get what's happening. We got in a little deep, but it's not a big deal. We just—"

"No." Pushing off the bed, she pulled the sheet around her, leaving Max with the comforter—not that he wanted it. The moment he saw her move, he was up too, sweeping his jeans off the floor and shoving one leg in and then the other, his eyes locked with hers the whole time.

"You're not even interested in hearing what I have to say?" he challenged.

What could he possibly say? "Max, I'm not just in a little deep. *I'm in love with you.*"

He straightened, seemingly stunned by the words she couldn't believe were a surprise to him.

"No." Running a hand over the top of his head, he stared past her. "You only think you are."

She ignored that.

"I didn't mean for it to happen. At first, I didn't even see it coming. And then when I realized my emotions were becoming invested in a way I hadn't expected, I tried to pull back. I tried to put some distance—"

His eyes closed, pained lines creasing his brow. "But I didn't let you. Because I thought, *What the hell, she's leaving, so why not go all in?*"

He was counting on her leaving. That was why it had felt so free. So safe. So easy. Because the boundaries were built around her flight to New York.

Now she knew. Max was just having fun. The way they'd both agreed to.

"Max, I'm sorry I stepped outside the lines on this. I'll get over it. But I need some time."

"You're leaving in a week. I know things are different than we thought, but Sarah, we could still be together." He let out a frustrated breath. "I don't want to give you up."

"I'm sorry," she answered, meaning it with all her heart. "But you have to."

"Why?"

Because she'd learned her lesson, and she wasn't going to let her feelings for a man cost her another job she truly wanted. She'd asked Max to take New York out of the equation and tell her what he wanted, but it was only when he'd taken himself out of the equation that she'd been able to see the truth of what *she wanted*.

"I'm not leaving Chicago."

Chapter 17

THERE'D BEEN A HANDFUL OF MOMENTS IN MAX'S LIFE where choosing the right thing meant certain pain. Two of those moments involved Sarah Cole offering him more than he could take. The third was stepping in front of a tweaked-out junkie when he'd had a gun aimed at his own kid. Max had known the guy was going to fire, but there was no way he was going to let him hurt that boy any more than he already had.

The first time with Sarah, he'd been twenty-one, and he'd barely been able to walk away. He'd wanted her so much. He'd been watching those full lips since the first night he'd gotten them to curve for him. And those eyes, he'd been half hard every time she cut him a look that said she thought he was bad…and she liked it, but had sense enough to know better.

He could remember the ache and effort it had cost him for nearly two months—working every excuse he could come up with to see her, while making sure the walls that kept them from becoming more than friends remained sturdy. Because it wouldn't be just some hookup with Sarah, and that scared the hell out of him. He'd been avoiding relationships as far back as he could remember—through high school when he started seeing signs of the kind of drama he got at home. Flaring tempers. Betrayals. Words turned into weapons. No thanks.

Same through college. He was a one-night, keep-it-casual guy, and until Sarah, that had been all he wanted it to be. Hell, even with Sarah's smile and laugh ending his nights for those last two months of school, he hadn't wanted more. Which was why he'd made damn sure he held back through every lingering glance, every weighted pause, every moment of that *thing* pulsing in the air between them. Until she'd done the unthinkable.

It was his final night on Safewalk, and Christ, he'd wanted it to last. Wanted to walk the long way back to Sarah's dorm, maybe just sit and talk a while, before he had to say good-bye. She had another year, and he was starting work in two days and the police academy in the fall. Tomorrow, everything ended, but he'd thought he still had the night. Only, the minute they'd stepped out of the library doors, the sky that had been threatening rain all damned day finally opened up and poured. Sarah had taken one stunned look at him, laughed, and dashed into the night.

They'd made it halfway to her dorm when she'd suddenly stopped. She was breathless. Fucking beautiful with her hair streaming back from her face, her lashes clumped together in wet points, tipped with raindrops.

"What are you doing?" he asked, laughing and trying to hold his hands above her face as a shield.

Shaking her head, she looked up at him, and suddenly everything stopped. Not the rain or the cars or the waves crashing against the breakwater beyond the quad, but everything that mattered. Like his heart and his thoughts and time.

"Sarah?"

She caught him by the shirt, there in the middle of campus. The only warning of what was coming, her breathy "I can't help it" the second before she'd pushed to her toes. He'd met her halfway. Something in his wiring must have taken over before he could think of all the reasons why he needed to stop, and on instinct he'd sought out her mouth. That first kiss was like lightning over the lake—a white-hot crack that split him down the center, searing at first contact and then rolling through him, deeper and deeper, shaking up everything in its path.

She wasn't supposed to kiss him. And this was why.

A car alarm blared in the distance, breaking the spell, but only long enough for him to register where they were and why no matter how badly he wanted to drown in her kiss right there in the rain, he couldn't risk what would happen if he didn't get them somewhere private and fast.

They ran back to her dorm, her hand in his as he pulled her along until they reached her room and she dragged him inside. Dripping wet, he wrapped his arms around her, falling back into the kiss he'd been telling himself for months he couldn't have. Growling softly into her ear, he asked, "What are you doing, Sarah?"

"Giving in" was her breathless answer before pulling at his shoulders, his arms, his hair like she couldn't get him close enough. Which worked for him, because damn, the feel of her body beneath his hands was heaven.

He'd fought this so long, but right then he realized it had been a losing battle from the start. He just hadn't wanted to admit how far gone he was. How this girl had changed the way he thought about what came next and what they could be together. She'd been saving herself for love, and despite both of them knowing she deserved better, she was giving hers to him.

He kissed her again, pulling back to ask, "Sarah, baby, are you sure?"

She had to be, because in that moment, Max realized he was hers. He had been from the night they met. He'd tried to deny it. Fight it. Make damn sure she didn't get any ideas about it. But here he was, fucking floored by the revelation that he loved this girl.

Sarah nodded even as she pulled his mouth back to hers, opening to his kiss and moaning around the thrust of his tongue.

Jesus, he had to slow down, because she hadn't done this before and he wasn't sure they were going to do it tonight. But when they did, whenever she was ready, he was going to make it the best fucking first time on the books. Not because of his ego, but because he needed her to have it. If she was going to give him something as precious as that too-sweet heart of hers, then he was going to prove he was worthy.

"I'm sure." And Christ, the way she was looking at him. "Max, I know I said I was waiting for love, but I don't want to anymore. I just want this. I want you. I swear it doesn't have to be anything but tonight."

Her words filtered through the haze of his brain, and Max froze, one hand on the perfect curve of her ass, the other cradling the back of her head. He pulled back, searching her eyes. Because that wasn't what she was supposed to say.

"You don't want more than tonight?" he asked, hoping like hell his voice hadn't cracked.

"I know a relationship between us would be… No, I

don't. For once, I just want to cut loose and have some fun. Stop feeling like I'm taking everything too seriously and missing out on half of what life has to offer. For once, maybe I don't want to do the right thing."

The right thing. Shit.

There it was. If he'd been on the fence, those three words were all it took to knock him off, landing him securely in this area he knew too well. The land of rules.

And the most important one: if you know without question what the right thing is, do it.

"Sarah, sweetheart, we've got to stop."

She hadn't fallen in love with him. But one day she'd fall in love with someone…and when she did, what she'd held on to would mean something to the both of them. It would be special and lasting and… Fuck, he wanted to put his fist through the guy who finally earned her heart.

She shook her head, a look of panic filling her eyes. Then she was trying to pull him closer, and when he braced his arm against the wall over her head to keep her from doing it, she hooked her fingers into the belt loops of his jeans. Oh man, he liked that a lot.

But it didn't change what he had to do. "Sarah, I can't be a part of something you're going to regret. Not when it's this big."

She looked up at him with those soulful eyes he'd been falling for without even realizing it. "I won't regret it."

"I think you will. When the right guy shows up, Sarah, you're going to wish you had this to give to him. You gotta know that I care about you way too much to let you make that mistake."

He could see the hurt in her eyes, on her face, and in the subtle droop of her shoulders, and he fucking hated that he'd been the one to put it there.

Still, he'd done the right thing. By the time she locked her door behind him, she'd been thanking him for being the one to think straight. Agreeing with him that as much fun as it might be between them, it would be a mistake and one she couldn't take back. She'd felt okay about the way the night ended.

What he was feeling was new to him, and it fucking hurt.

Fast-forward through the years, and Max was staring into Sarah's face again, that dull blade sawing into him deeper with every passing breath. Because this thing that was already more than he thought he could handle had just gotten infinitely bigger. She thought she was in love with him. Now—not eight years ago when he'd been ready to go all in. Before he'd met Joan and once again learned what a shit storm he'd stir up by trying to convince a woman on her way out to stay. Before Joan had realized what a mistake she'd made and shown Max his own mistake in return.

He should have known a girl like Sarah wouldn't be able to keep her emotions out of it. No, scratch that. He *had* known. He'd banked on it, looking forward to all the soft and sweet she had to offer, because he'd been so damn sure things between them wouldn't go too far. That this relationship would be safe for both of them. Why wouldn't it? She hadn't fallen in love with him back in school. They'd been friends, but in the end, all she'd wanted was a single night.

Turn a single night into a couple of months, and that was how it was supposed to have gone this time too.

But he should have known. He'd seen it before, the way sex could skew a person's perspective, heighten emotions, and make someone see things that weren't really there. Yeah, Sarah thought she was in love with him, but given enough time, she'd realize she wasn't. That if she'd done what she'd planned to do from the start—date around, get more experience—she'd recognize what she'd known that last night in school. He wasn't the man she wanted forever.

He groaned, pinching the bridge of his nose.

"Sarah, let's back this up some."

She was pulling on her clothes, not looking at him anymore. "To where? The part where I fall in love with you, or the part where I decide to stay in Chicago?"

To the part where maybe there was a chance she could still do something about it. "Let's start with Chicago. Does Sean know what you're thinking yet? I mean, I know he's always talking about wanting to steal you away from Manhattan, but are you sure he's not just being charming?"

What if she tried to get out of the New York position and Sean didn't have anything for her in Chicago that could compete? What if she was throwing away an opportunity she'd been working forever for, because of him? Jesus, let it not be too late.

Sarah's eyes closed, her hands dropping to her sides. And when she answered, her words were heavy with disappointment. "Some people mean the things they say, Max."

Ouch. But considering the number of times he'd told

her he didn't want to let her go, and that now they were having this conversation, yeah, he had it coming. The thing was, he'd meant what he'd said. It was going to be hard to say good-bye to her, and he hadn't known how he was going to do it—but tough or not, he *was* going to do it. "You talked to him?"

"Yes. He came to me with an offer over the weekend. I'll be based out of Chicago and work with the sales and marketing teams for the Midwest. I still have my choice of position, the one in New York or here in Chicago. No negative ramifications either way." She met his eyes. "Just so we're clear, the Chicago post pays better, means more responsibility, and offers the kind of challenge I thrive on. This job will make my career."

Damn. He shouldn't have been surprised with the way Sean had been ogling her work ethic all summer. "Sarah, that's terrific. I didn't mean to imply— Look, I didn't know this option was even on the table. And I didn't want you making any decisions based on me." He rubbed his head, looking at the floor. "And you didn't. Which is good."

She nodded, staring down at her thumb. "Which leaves you and me, together in Chicago. Indefinitely instead of for the next few days." She sat at the edge of his bed and peered up at him with sad eyes. "So now do you see why, as good as this feels with us, it's time for it to be over?"

"Yeah, baby, I see." It was going to have to end eventually. As much as he didn't want to let her go, it would be better this way.

Max drove her home, neither of them talking much. What else was there to say? They would still be friends, but she needed some time first. Some space. A few weeks. He wished things were different, but it was what it was, so he parked on the street and walked her up to her door, where he kissed her good-bye for now. Just a single lingering press of lips that hurt his chest to no end. There were tears in her eyes when she gave his hand a gentle squeeze and then slipped into her apartment alone.

Shoving through the Belfast door, Max was confronted with the glaringly warm and inviting atmosphere, the upbeat music, and too many happy people for the way he was feeling. He should have stayed home, but after he'd dropped Sarah back at her apartment, he'd gotten restless. Itchy and uncomfortable.

A short cab ride over—because he'd fully intended to knock enough back that driving would be a no-go—and he was there. But Belfast wasn't going to work either.

Too many friendly faces. Girls he'd had some fun with a time or two perking up at the sight of him walking through the door.

Not gonna happen.

He turned around and walked back out, making it about three steps into the night before Brody was there, pulling him around by the arm. "Hey, man, what gives?"

Max looked his buddy over. The burly guy had that wild mane pulled back with an elastic, so there was no missing the concern written all over his face.

"You're alone?" Brody asked, checking his phone like maybe there'd be an answer in the form of a group alert from Molly. "Thought you were hanging out with Sarah tonight."

Max scrubbed his hands through his hair, pacing a few steps forward and back. "She's staying in Chicago. And wipe that smile from your face, Brod, because that's the death knell to me and her you're hearing."

Brody had the good sense to school his features before shoving those meaty paws of his deep in his pockets. "Why? I mean, you two seemed good together. I have a hard time seeing her making any ultimatums or springing a bunch of demands about the relationship on you."

"No, it wasn't anything like that. It was me. I let things go too far, said some things I shouldn't have." Max groaned, that raw spot in his chest aching. "Why the hell couldn't I leave well enough alone?"

Brody sighed. "Come on, man. Chin up. Maybe it doesn't have to be the end."

That was where he was wrong. "When a woman tells you she loves you, and you tell her she shouldn't, it kind of has to be the end."

"Shit."

"Yep."

Brody stepped aside for a couple of girls headed into Belfast, and Max leaned back against the building. It was still relatively early, but he was beat. "I'm into her. You know that. And if it was just a matter of her scoring an extra month in Chicago before she had to blow out of here, I'd be fucking ecstatic. Because yeah, I want more of her, *a little more time*. Not forever."

"You mean you don't want to give up your freedom," Brody added pointedly.

Max shrugged a shoulder. It wasn't as simple as that. With Sarah, the explanation didn't feel right. Like it was more about *her* freedom. And he knew better than to try to lock her into something she'd only offered because she wasn't experienced enough to realize she was reading more into her feelings than was actually there.

Brody gave Max a hearty clap on the back. Fuck, the guy was strong. "How about we go inside and I get you drunk."

It was what he'd come for, but still Max found himself looking down the street toward home. He could call Sarah and try to talk to her. Tell her he was sorry, and—

What? No. He'd already said enough.

Brody still had a solid grip on Max's shoulder. After a beat, Max nodded. "Yeah, sounds like a plan."

For a second, Max thought he saw disappointment register in the big guy's eyes, but maybe it was just a combination of the passing headlights and Max's own BS. Because then Brody looked fine, his grizzly-bear smile firmly in place as he gave Max a shove toward the bar.

"Let's go get you liquored up."

"We've *got* to keep meeting like this."

Sarah's head snapped up to find Sean leaning against her office door. He was wearing a crisp gray suit with a light-blue button-down and a darker-blue tie draped around his neck. With the exception of his jacket hanging from one finger, the man looked both immaculate and as disheveled as she'd ever seen him in the office.

"Don't you ever sleep?" she demanded, frustrated by the trespass into a sanctuary she'd been certain would be safe for at least a few more hours—and by Max's guy, no less. Though that thinking was going to have to stop.

Now that Max wasn't *her guy*, Sean was going to have to be relegated back to *her boss*. And *her friend* too. No more sticking a *Max* qualifier on him every time their paths crossed.

Sean coughed out a laugh, making her do a double take. "This from the chick elbow deep in work I'd be willing to bet my left nut wasn't even part of her assigned load at *6:07 a.m. on a Sunday*?"

Yes, this guy had her number. "Sometimes work is the most comfortable place to be."

He cut her a look and muttered. "Damn, you really would have been perfect."

He thought she wasn't taking the job. "You haven't talked to Max?" she asked, again conflicted about this one smudged line between her personal and professional lives.

Frowning, Sean shook his head. "Fond as I am of the guy, I try to get through breakfast before calling him. What are you working on?"

"Sales and marketing reports from last year."

Sean's brow quirked. "Chicago's reports?"

"And Minneapolis. Madison, Cincinnati. A few others."

He dropped his jacket over a chair and stood at the side of her desk, looking down at her with a grin as he worked his tie into a practiced Windsor knot. "So you want to write up the HR announcement, or should I?"

Cocky. But he was right. "Why don't you do it. I'm kind of busy with *my new job*."

Tie neatly in place, Sean pumped his fist, indulging in a guttural "Fuck, yeah!" that Sarah couldn't help but grin over. Nice to be wanted.

Max had showered twice, flushed his system with a gallon of water, and forced a cheeseburger and fries down since crawling out of bed at noon. Now at four, he was finally ready to face the world. Or at least the guys and Molly. And Emily, who he still couldn't manage to lump in with the rest of the meatheads that made up his non-cop family.

He hadn't bothered buzzing up to let the Fosters know he was there, since the security door was propped open with a construction cone. Riding the elevator to Jase's floor, he stared at the wall ahead and tried to figure out what he was going to say about Sarah.

Just thinking about saying *It's over* out loud made his gut hurt in a way that had nothing to do with the booze from the night before.

He'd texted her the hour before because until yesterday she'd been planning to come with him, and hell, he knew it was too soon, but he asked if she was up for seeing everyone anyway. If maybe they could talk. He'd deleted the part where he told her he missed her before sending it, because he really didn't want to be *that guy*. She texted back, because she was Sarah and she probably didn't want to be *that girl* who refused to acknowledge someone just because he was the dick who'd turned down the most precious gift she had to offer.

Her answer was what he'd expected. She didn't think it was a good idea.

No surprise, but for all Max's experience with women, he had no fucking clue what to do next except wait it out. Everything would be better once they could get back to being friends after a few weeks' time. Until then, he'd have some explaining to do.

Sean was on the phone down the hall. Giving him a quick wave, Max let himself into Jase's place and took a hit of the garlic-and-onion-laced air. Damn, Brody was cooking. Sarah would have loved this. Everyone was in the kitchen—Brody standing over the range, bitching about Jase's kitchen equipment while Emily studied Brody's culinary techniques and Jase leaned against a counter, studying his wife.

Molly grabbed a beer from the fridge, nodding at him with a warm smile. "Hey, Max, just catching everyone up. The roommate has vacated the premises."

"No shit?" he asked, going in to ruffle her hair, because apparently he'd never grow out of annoying her, and that screwed-up smile-scowl of hers was the only thing that might ease the sucky feeling he'd had for the past twenty hours. "I didn't know she'd decided to move."

Spooning up a small taste from the pan, Emily shook her head. "She's gone? What's that for notice?"

His little sister shrugged, cranking the top off her beer and then taking a long swallow. "Yeah, well, she told me yesterday. I guess she and the boyfriend got swept up in their *passion* and decided they couldn't bear being apart. Few hours later, the boyfriend was there with three of his friends, loading all her crap into his cousin's pickup."

"What about rent?" Max asked, his thoughts going to Sarah. Molly needed the money, which was why she hadn't been too picky about who she let move in with her. He'd tried to convince her it would be worth the short-term loss in shared rent to hold out for the right roommate, but she never wanted to wait.

Only now Sarah was staying in Chicago, and Piper's roommate was going to be back in October sometime—

"Looks like the transition's going to be pretty seamless," Molly replied, cutting off that train of thought. "The boyfriend has a buddy who happens to be looking for a place. Something about relationship trouble. He needs a room, and I've got one. So he's moving in Wednesday when he gets his stuff back."

The hair on the back of his neck stood up, and Max exchanged a look with Brody. "You've never even met the guy?"

"I met him this morning for a few minutes. He seems okay. Besides, it's not like we'll be hanging out all the time," Molly said. Taking a swig of her beer, she propped a hip against the counter across from them. "I don't need a buddy, Max. I just need someone to cover rent. And this guy's willing to do it, so I'm good." Then craning her neck to look past him, she asked, "When's Sarah coming?"

It said a lot that Max was disappointed to see the end of a conversation about some unknown entity shacking up at his sister's place. But damn, at least it had distracted him from thinking about Sarah for a little while.

"She couldn't make it tonight," he dodged as Brody went all deep focus on sautéing. Obviously he knew the score but wasn't going to be the one to spill about the breakup.

Which left Jase, Molly, and Emily waiting on his answer. Two out of three sported DNA that ensured they were hardwired against letting him off with a cursory shrug and grunt. Max was looking at a *bare-all* situation. Shit.

"Yeah, what's she up to?" Molly shot him a little-sister look and added, "Hot date?"

The bands of muscles across his chest constricted. "She wasn't really feeling up to it."

Jase nodded and reached for a pretzel.

Damn, he loved that guy.

Sean sailed in all smiles, snagging a baby carrot from the platter on the counter. "Sorry 'bout that. When Dad calls… You know how it goes. What'd I miss?"

Lifeline! Max was a breath away from throwing Molly under the bus by sharing her new roommate status with Sean—who was guaranteed to get all over her about it—when Emily proved why she couldn't score one-of-the-guys status.

"Sarah isn't coming? Is she sick?" she asked, genuine concern in her voice.

"Who, Sarah?" Sean shook his head. "She's not sick. At least she wasn't when I left her at seven this morning. Sure, she looked a little sleepy." Popping the carrot into his mouth, he grinned. "Don't think she got quite enough sleep last night."

Max didn't move. He didn't breathe. He was vaguely aware of the clatter of kitchen tongs hitting a pot, and all eyes shifting from Sean to Max.

Jesus Christ. He turned to Sean. "She was working at *seven*?"

A nod. "No idea when she actually got in, but she was there when I showed up at six." He shrugged. "She's got a lot going on with work right now." Then seeming to think better, he gave Max a pointed look while holding up a warning finger. "But before you get any ideas about putting the beatdown on me, I told her to go home. Not my fault she wouldn't listen."

Rubbing at the ache in the center of his chest, Max wanted to puke thinking about that early retreat to work, wondering how long she'd been there before Sean arrived. If her fallback in times of stress had helped any.

Sean had said that Sarah looked tired. Did that mean her eyes were red? Had she been crying?

Christ, he wanted to call her. Go over there and put his arms around her. But even he had enough cognitive brain function to recognize that he'd be doing it for himself. She'd asked him for time.

Max couldn't give Sarah what she thought she wanted, but he could at least give her this.

"Max, man, you all right?" Jase asked, suddenly standing in front of him, concern furrowing his brow. "Everything okay with you guys?"

Ahh shit.

Chapter 18

THE DAY WAS DRAGGING ON FOREVER, WHICH MADE THE week since Max had dropped her at her door the longest in history. Piper had kicked around with Sarah for a few hours earlier in the afternoon, but once she skipped out for a pottery class, thirty minutes in the apartment alone was all Sarah managed before the walls began pressing in and thoughts of Max squeezed her too tight.

Hoping to leave that sense of claustrophobic wrongness behind, she opted for a walk on the lakefront.

The evening air was cooling fast, a blanket of cloud cover pulling low across the sky. She made it to the lake before the first drops fell. It was just a sprinkle, and each small splash against her cheeks and brow felt refreshing. The smart thing would have been to head back, but she hadn't exactly been making the best decisions regarding *when to say when*. Why start now?

She kept walking, taking the winding paths through the parks and beyond the harbors. Past the beaches and breakwaters.

She thought about Max. The way it had felt being in his arms. In his bed. In his lap when he'd been playing with her hair while they shared a beer and talked late into the night.

If only she'd been able to adhere to the rules, they might be together now. Even with her staying in

Chicago, if she could have kept the relationship casual, there would have been no reason to end things.

She sighed, knowing the truth. That it only would have prolonged the inevitable. Eventually, fighting her feelings would have proven too much, and she'd have given in to her heart. Max was the kind of man she'd never been able to resist, but who had *always* been able to resist her.

Her throat ached, bruised from too many days of fighting her heartbreak. And failing.

When the first tears breached her lids, mingling with the wetness on her cheeks, she stopped walking and just stood where she was, looking out over the turbulent waters of Lake Michigan.

What was it that made her such an easy pass?

Her phone chirped with a message. Wiping her eyes, she laughed, that broken feeling easing at the sight of Molly's text.

> UR wk of sulky alone time is up. Be @ UR place in 15. No arguments. U can dump my brother. But if U want to brkup w me, U have 2 do it face 2 face. Expect ugly tears. PS don't break my heart ;-p

Sarah stared at her phone a second longer, then starting to walk, she texted back.

> I have a bottle of wine and a bag of frozen pot stickers. Better give me 30.

Molly was waiting in the sheltered doorway when Sarah made it back to her building.

"You're freaking nuts," Molly announced, waving a hand at where rain streamed from Sarah's hair and down her face to the water sloshing out of her shoes with every step. "I like it though. That's my kind of crazy you're rocking."

The laugh that slipped free felt good, and Sarah just shrugged. "I needed some fresh air, you know?"

"More than you'd believe. But before we get into that, are we good?" Molly asked, a tragic look on her face, but that same glint of amusement in her eyes that made Sarah love being around her. "I mean Max is a ween, obviously, but whatever happens with you guys, he wouldn't want us to stop being friends. That said, who cares what he wants? I want to know about you and me. Like how hard I'm going to have to fight for this *bramance*, because I kinda think we have a good thing going here. I mean, do I need to make some grand gesture to win you back? Storm out into that rain and kiss you full on the mouth, *Notebook*-style? Or are we good?"

Sarah laughed and, feet squishing with every step, walked up to Molly, whose eyes had gone saucer wide. "Oh shit. You're going to hug me now."

And that was just what Sarah did, giggling as Molly squealed and shivered in her wet hold, trying to get away and threatening everything from murder to food poisoning before Sarah finally released her and unlocked the door. "We're good. Come on up."

⁓

Max swallowed the last of his burger and stacked his napkins and silverware on the empty plate for Molly who was working that night.

"Thanks, Max," she said, circling the table to clear. "You sure you don't want a beer or something?"

"I'm good. Playing with power tools later, so no booze for me." He needed the activity to wear him down and keep his focus off the brunette he couldn't see.

"Good plan." Then looking across to Emily, Molly asked, "Are we meeting at your place tomorrow?"

Emily swirled a fry through her ketchup, making the pattern of…a heart? "We were, but Jase and I are going out west to see his parents in the morning. Not sure we'll be back early enough. Lena said you and Sarah should just go over to her place, and if I'm running late, I'll catch you at the bookstore."

He wasn't going to ask, didn't need to know. But *fuuuck*, it was driving him nuts that apparently everyone got to hang out with Sarah except for him.

One more week. That was when their agreed-upon space cushion got popped and they could get back to being friends the way they were supposed to be. He could wait. He could be cool.

"So what are you girls up to tomorrow?" Damn, maybe being cool was still a little beyond his ability.

Emily had turned her plate and shoulder-bumped her husband, who was looking down at the ketchup heart like she'd just delivered him a Maserati. She turned back to Max. "One of our favorite authors is going to be over at this little indie shop. She's doing a reading and then signing books after."

Molly reached for Emily's plate, but Jase held her off until he'd snapped a picture with his phone. Jesus.

"Nice. Have a good time." He totally sounded like he meant it and not like some jealous, petty wuss who wanted in on what seemed like the most boring way to kill an afternoon ever.

Pushing back from the table, Max tossed a couple of bills down to cover his meal and Molly's tip. "My new counters aren't going to install themselves. I'm outta here. Have a good night, guys. Emily."

"Later, Bro," Molly offered with a jut of her chin before weaving her way back toward the kitchen.

Emily cast Jase a wink and he stood, telling Max to hold up. They walked to the front, stopping at the bar to bump knuckles with Brody before heading out into the cool September night.

"How's it going?" Jase asked, walking a ways down from the door.

"Good, man. The place is really coming together. Getting started on the downstairs bathroom next."

Jase held up a hand. "Sarah. I'm talking about things ending with Sarah. It's been a couple of weeks, and you seem pretty chill about it being over."

Yeah, that was what he'd been going for. His friends and nosy little sister didn't need to know that he'd resigned himself to never sleeping again, or that he basically had a highlights reel of all things Sarah playing nonstop through his mind. Better to keep that shit to himself so it wasn't weird once he got her back as his friend. "It is what it is. You know me. I don't get too attached."

Not to most girls anyway.

With this one, he wasn't entirely sure he'd ever completely let her go.

Jase looked down the street and let out a long breath. "Yeah, except what I meant was you seem pretty chill, until you don't. Like when the girls mentioned going to that book thing with her. Suddenly you didn't look very chill at all."

Being a guy most people found hard to read, and generally intimidating enough that they might not even want to try, Max sometimes forgot just how easy it was for his buddies to see right through him. Letting out a slow breath, he admitted, "I miss her."

"I remember that feeling. Sucks, huh?" Before Jase and Emily had gotten it right, the guy had about gone out of his mind when they'd broken up. It had been ugly on an epic scale. Way worse than how Max was handling his shit. Which made sense, because Jase and Emily were meant for forever and Max and Sarah were meant to be something else.

"You guys seemed good together," Jase added. "On a lot of levels. You talking to her at all?"

Max grimaced. "No. I got another week still."

When Jase didn't say anything, Max looked up and found his buddy staring at him with a perplexed expression on his face. "A week for what?" Jase asked.

"She said she needed space before she could do the friends thing. She said a few weeks. A few equals three. It's been two."

"And then you're just going to check in and see how she's feeling? See if she's interested in trying to hang out as friends again?"

Max wasn't nuts about the tentative way Jase was suggesting it. "Trust me, it's going to be fine."

"Uh-huh. And you're going to be okay with being just friends too?"

"Yeah, man." The attraction had been there back in school, and they'd managed friends just fine.

"So no problem, you know, not putting your hands all over her when you see her, leaving her mouth alone, and by that I mean not staring at it like a starving man would a gyro from that place down by Cubby Bear?"

Max shifted, thoughts of Sarah's mouth flooding his mind.

"Being cool when she starts to date the next guy," Jase went on. "You're thinking all that isn't going to be a problem."

Fuck yeah, it was going to be a problem. But Max wanted her too much to let something like his inner caveman get in the way of Sarah having the kind of life she wanted. He'd be happy to have her in his life the only way he really could.

"No. No problem at all."

A slap on his shoulder was Jase's only response. They both knew he was lying. So what? He was doing the right thing.

—*w*—

Saturdays sucked. Flopping back in bed, Sarah stared out at the early-morning light hitting the building next door and tossed her comforter off with a sigh. Sure, she was lucky enough to have made friends who were awesome at reminding her there were a million things in her new city to fill her time, but even if she'd managed to book every minute of every day, it wouldn't have been enough to fill that aching, empty place inside her. The place that seemed to get that much bigger every time she thought of Max.

The reading the weekend before had been fantastic. Watching Molly go all fangirl on the author, asking her to sign the page where her favorite scene started and then pulling out a book that looked like she'd read it maybe six or seven hundred times was unforgettable. Especially because this author wrote scorching-hot romance, and they all knew exactly which scene that dog-eared page marked.

She'd wanted to tell Max about the way his sister's hands had shaken, and how for the first time since she'd met her, Molly had been at a total loss for words, barely able to speak. She'd wanted to feel that gruff laugh rumble from his chest while he was holding her close. And then she'd wanted to find a quiet place and whisper in his ear all the crazy-hot things that scene described. She wanted Max to make her feel the way he had until that last day together.

She wanted Max. End of story.

Why wasn't it getting easier? And why was Sean such a raging hemorrhoid, banning her from the office or even logging into her hotel files on the weekends? So she'd been spending a few dozen extra hours there each week. Big freaking deal.

Not that working would have really helped. For the first time in her life, her work woobie wasn't capable of soothing away her problems. The fact that she was still feeling the loss of her relationship with Max as acutely three weeks post-breakup as she had that first night was a problem.

Her phone vibrated on the nightstand.

It was Max. She sat up straighter, her heart doing a little stutter step as she read his text. He was downstairs but didn't want to wake Piper by buzzing up. And he wanted to talk.

Five minutes later, Sarah had brushed her teeth and hair and thrown on a pair of jeans and a chunky sweater. She'd wiped away the evidence of the tears that had sprung to her eyes and the surge of emotion at seeing his message. If there was any red left, she'd blame it on having just rolled out of bed. No reason to clarify that she'd already been awake for hours.

The morning air was fresh and cool, the sky a brilliant blue. The trees had turned, and everywhere she looked, bits of russet, burgundy, and gold were catching in the breeze and tumbling down the otherwise quiet sidewalks. It was a beautiful start to the day. Max was waiting beside his bike in an open, black leather jacket and broken-in jeans. One hand was stuffed in his pocket, the other pulling off his aviators and giving her an unobstructed view of those gorgeous gray eyes she was terrified she'd never get over.

He looked too good.

"Hey, Sarah, thanks for coming down," he said without making a move toward her. Which was probably the appropriate thing to do, even if her body was begging her to step into his. "Any chance we could go grab some breakfast and talk?"

Her stomach churned and she wrapped an arm around it, trying to steady herself. Trying not to get her hopes up that he was there with a change of heart. But all she could hear was the single thought bouncing around her head over and over.

Please.

She looked at the bike behind him and the two helmets resting on the seat. It was almost as tempting as the man himself, but without knowing what Max wanted to talk about, wrapping herself around him probably wasn't the best idea.

"Why don't we head down to Southport for a coffee. I wouldn't mind a walk."

Max nodded, his eyes intent, his smile genuine. "Damn, it's good to see you, Sarah."

Her throat felt thick, and for a moment she wasn't sure she'd be able to hold it together. Because yes, it was so good to see him too.

They walked quietly at first, Max asking her about the new job and whether she'd started looking at apartments. She told him about the handful of places she'd looked at the week before with Julia who worked in sales, and how Emily had a friend who was moving at the end of the month, and she planned to go check the place out on Monday. Sarah asked about the progress on the brownstone. Their answers were brief. Polite. Strained in a way conversation between them had never been.

Max cleared his throat, looking down at her from the opposite side of the sidewalk. "Gotta admit I've actually gotten a ton finished on the place. But mostly because I didn't have anything I wanted to do more." He stopped walking and brushed a bit of flyaway hair from her face. That touch. So small, but it was the spark that started a chain reaction throughout her body. "I've missed you, Sarah."

Her heart hurt from thumping so hard, from the swell of emotion rising up inside her. "I've missed you too."

The thin curve of Max's mouth widened into a full smile. Reaching for her, he pulled her toward him, and this time Sarah couldn't contain the small gasp of relief as his arms closed around her. It felt so right. "I hate not being able to see you," he growled, his cheek pressed into her hair. "How about we agree not to let anything like this get in the way of us being friends again, huh?"

Friends.

Sarah blinked. She tried to swallow, but her throat was suddenly too tight. Slowly, her hands came up between them, breaking his hold, and she stepped back. Eyes on the concrete beneath her feet, she quietly stated what she only wished was a question: "Your feelings haven't changed since the last time we talked."

Neither of them moved, but she could feel the growing distance in that space between them.

"Sarah, I meant what I said." When she still hadn't looked at him, he caught her chin with the crook of his finger and brought her gaze to his. "The time we spent together was incredible, and I'd never want to take it back. But going forward, we're meant to be friends."

The handsome face so close to hers blurred as tears pushed to her lids. The last clear image she had was Max's expression of shock. Like he couldn't understand how what he'd said might still be difficult for her.

"I don't think I can do this," she whispered brokenly as she closed her eyes and the first tears fell.

"What?" One word, harshly issued.

How could he not understand? *How could he not feel the same way?*

"Max, when you showed up this morning, I thought maybe things had changed. That you realized you wanted *us.*"

His measured breath brought her eyes up, the unease written in the lines of his face breaking her heart.

"I'm sorry. I wanted to see you. As friends. I didn't mean to—"

"I know you didn't. You wouldn't," she said, cutting him off and digging deep to regain her composure. "But I just don't think I'm ready to spend time with you like this."

His arms crossed, a furrow digging deep between his brows. "But it's been three weeks."

Her chin pulled back. "I said I needed some time."

"You said *a few weeks*. Sarah, we're going to be friends. Those complications we gave up trying to dodge three months ago have bred like bunnies. We've got too many people in common to think anything else is an option. We're going to see each other."

"I'm not talking about social situations, Max. I'm talking about you and me alone. Talking and walking. Your arms around me. The way you look at me, and how it makes me feel. I get that there's a disconnect somewhere in there. That your intent doesn't match my expectations, and it isn't your fault, but it still hurts. *I love you*. And I'm glad that you're able to move past everything so easily, but I can't—"

"Easily? Are you kidding me, Sarah? I've been counting down the days, waiting to see you again. It's been killing me to be cut off from one of my best friends."

"*Best friends?*" she coughed out incredulously. "We've only been together a few months, how can you say that—?" She left the rest of her question unsaid... *and not love me*.

The firm, unyielding stance was gone, and Max was all motion, pacing the three-foot square of concrete beneath his feet, his hands fisting, arms crossing and uncrossing.

"Because it's different with you, Sarah. It *always* has been. From fucking day one, and you know it."

"It *is* different with you, and yes I do feel it. Because I love you!"

He was shaking his head, the muscle in his jaw working overtime. "*You only think you do*. Because you don't have enough experience to see how sex muddies the emotional waters. It can make people think they feel more than is actually there."

Throwing her hands up, she challenged, "Speaking from experience, Max?"

He scowled at her, though how this man could possibly think he had the right to be angry *with her*, she couldn't fathom. "You know it doesn't work like that with me. But with other people, especially women, sometimes they just think—"

"Save it." Sometimes people fell in love. Even when they weren't supposed to. And she didn't need Max Brandt telling her she hadn't just because it would be more convenient for him. "Look, I'm not really up for coffee anymore, but you should go and get one." That way she could walk home without him and be inside her apartment before he got back to pick up his bike. The only thing this conversation was accomplishing was hurting her and pissing them both off.

"Sarah," he said, reaching for her again, but she pulled away.

"I'm sorry, Max. But you and I don't see eye to eye on this, and there isn't one damn thing you can say to convince me my feelings aren't real."

He looked desperate, and then he just stopped. His expression cleared, and he nodded like he'd finally figured this mess out. "You need to date someone else."

Her breath froze in her lungs, and her aching heart skittered to an uneasy stop. No way was she hearing him right. "W-what?"

"You think this is real, but once you give yourself a chance to be with someone else, you'll realize I was right. Sex has a way of skewing things. You planned on this from the start, right?"

What? She'd had a plan, yes. But that was before she realized she knew exactly what she wanted and she didn't need to waste her time with men who would never measure up. Only now—

"You wanted more experience, Sarah. To do your research. Figure out what you really want, all that. And when you do, you're going to see you don't really want me the way you think you do. You just need some perspective."

She was blinking too fast now, the short draws of breath she managed not nearly enough. "You want me to sleep with someone else."

"I want you to stick to your plans." Max was still talking. She could hear the low rumble of his voice, but as she turned and walked away, the only words she could hear were the ones that had nearly broken her four years before.

"Sarah, I get it. You're pissed," Cory said, pacing in front of the chair where she sat in the apartment she'd helped him pick out but that would never be theirs together. "It was a shitty thing for me to do. You caught me. I'm sorry."

"Sorry, but only because I caught you." Not for what he'd done. Not for betraying her or holding her to a standard he hadn't applied to himself. "How could you? You were the one who wanted to wait until we were married. You. I offered myself to you, and you turned me down. Why?" Damn it, she didn't want to cry. She didn't want to care enough for tears. She'd already given him too much.

His jaw cocked to the side as he gave her an assessing look. After a moment, he seemed to relent. "Because I liked the idea of having a virgin for a wife. Because you're precious to me. I love you."

Love. It wasn't supposed to feel this way, so one-sided. Where had she gone wrong? When?

"This is over, Cory. I'm leaving."

"Sarah, come on," he said, his tone gentle, his eyes pleading. His lies were so practiced she would never have been able to see through them if she hadn't walked in on him herself. He reached for her hand, but she pulled away, his touch making her sick. "Don't talk like that. Think about what you'd be throwing away here. Think about what we have."

"What we have is a lie, Cory. If I could never think about it again, it would be too soon."

"Okay, I deserve that. But we can work this out."

It was like she hadn't known this man she'd been about to pledge her life to at all. How could she have been so blind?

"Fine. To show you how much I love you, how much it means to me that we have this life we've been planning, I'll let you even the score. Get some payback to take the sting out."

She shook her head, at a loss for words. Payback? Sting?

"We don't cancel the wedding. But I'll give you a free pass between now and then. That's how much I love you. That's the kind of sacrifice I'm willing to make for our future."

Sarah's knuckles had whitened where she'd gripped the arms of her chair, trying to hold on in a world that suddenly seemed to have flipped on its side.

Cory was waiting, an expectant look in his murky brown eyes.

"A free pass?" It couldn't be what she thought.

"Yeah, well, within reason. I think it's only fair you use protection."

She was going to be sick. She was going to—

She started to laugh. "That's how much you love me?" she demanded. "Enough that you're willing to let me go screw a few randoms to even the score between us?" To throw away the thing he'd made her feel was so special. So precious to him. To them.

Never in her life had she felt less special. Less valued. Less respected.

And never would she feel that way again.

Chapter 19

MAX HAD BEEN SITTING AT THE KITCHEN TABLE SINCE THE new bathroom fixtures were delivered shortly after three, and before that, hell, he didn't even know what he'd done. Nothing but think about Sarah and how differently he'd thought the day would go. He'd been so sure that after three grueling weeks without her, they'd be able to fall into the kind of friendship he didn't have to worry about giving up. How stupid could he be?

That was what the looks Jase had been giving him were about. Now he got it.

Trying to throw himself into his work on the house, he'd gotten as far as cutting the packaging open before shoving the box back with a growl. He hadn't moved since. It was hard to muster much enthusiasm about a few hunks of metal with Sarah's tears burned into his mind.

Christ, the look in her eyes when she'd asked him if he wanted her to sleep with another guy. The betrayal and hurt spilling down her cheeks were almost worse than knowing that while, *fuck no*, he didn't want another guy to so much as hold her hand, let alone take her to bed, that was exactly what he'd been telling her to do. And whether it had been her original plan or not, whether it was the right thing—he'd hurt her deeply by suggesting it.

His gut knotted, and he thought for the thousandth

time about calling. Texting. Making sure she was okay. But he already knew the answer to that question. She wasn't. And it was because of him.

Slowly, he registered the knocking coming from the front door. His legs felt like lead as he forced one in front of the other until he was staring at his little sister on the other side of the glass.

He let her in and started back for the living room, where he dropped onto the couch. "What's up, Molly?"

"Wow, Max, you look really bad," she said hesitantly, following him in and parking in the new oversize chair he liked to sit in with Sarah on his lap. "Is this because of Sarah?"

"Things didn't go the way I'd been expecting this morning."

"But you guys broke up three weeks ago. You've pretty much looked fine until now. I mean a little grumpier, a little more quiet volcano-ish, but overall no train-wrecky, about-to-break-down-and-ugly-cry like this business." She sat forward. "Seriously, I don't think I can handle you ugly crying on me after the day I've had."

He heaved a sigh and shook his head.

"Feeling kind of beat down?" she asked, and while her voice was gentle, Max caught something harder in those bright-blue eyes staring back at him. Something not quite right.

"Yeah," he answered tentatively. "You could say that."

Molly was out of her chair in a flash, her finger pointing in his face. "Good, you pathetic oaf. Because let me tell you, Big Brother, *now you've done it*!"

Jesus, he didn't need this today. "I don't have it in me to play word wars with you, Mol. What have I done?"

Her brow rose. "Okay, so let me spell it out for you. Sarah asked me to set her up on a date."

It was like he'd taken a battering ram to the gut. Sucking a breath through gritted teeth, he forced his eyes open. "That's good. She needs to move on."

"Yeah." Molly's lips pursed as she eyed him. "I guess she does then."

Max swallowed. Nodded. She was still looking at him like she was waiting for him to say something else. "Just make sure you pick a good guy. She deserves one."

"Yeah, I would, Max," she said, picking at her thumbnail. "But she told me she wasn't looking for a *good guy*."

His head snapped up. "What?"

"Yeah, apparently, all she wants is *a guy*. Good enough for *one date*." Molly started walking for the door. "As it happens, I know one. They're going out tonight."

"Damn, girl, you are smokin'!" Piper exclaimed from the bathroom doorway as Sarah applied the finishing touches to her makeup. A layer of lash-thickening mascara, and she was ready. Or as ready as she could be for a date she'd rashly demanded and now just wished she could cancel.

She glanced down at her knee-high leather boots, camel wool skirt, and thin, fitted cashmere V-neck. It was definitely date appropriate. "Not too much?"

"No way. It's perfect."

Sarah took a steadying breath, wishing there was more to do to get ready. She didn't want time to think about how she'd found yet another man to love, only to discover how ready and willing he was to share her with someone else. At least with Cory, he'd cared enough to want her to come back to him after.

She had no business going out like this. Not when it was taking everything she had to keep the tears in check.

Her roommate cocked her head and gave Sarah a sympathetic look. "It's just a date, Sarah. A couple of hours of company, right?"

"I know. I just—" She sighed, wrestling with the emotions trying to push to the surface. "I don't know what I'm doing going out with this guy."

It wasn't like with Cory when she'd left and all she'd wanted was to prove she was done letting him hold her back. She'd thrown herself into her career with everything she'd been saving up for him. She'd come out with her head held high and a career that had fast-tracked her to working directly with the top players in the Wyse chain of hotels. She'd done all right.

But this?

The intercom buzzed, and Piper straightened. "You're going to prove that you aren't waiting around for some guy who doesn't deserve you. I'll get the door."

Sarah smiled weakly and returned to her room to get her purse.

"Um, Sarah?" Piper called from down the hall, her voice strained. "Could you come out here, please?"

That made her wonder who Molly had set her up with.

Forcing her feet to move, Sarah stopped when she got to the front door. Piper was holding it three-quarters of the way closed, like she was not about to let this guy in.

What the heck?

Peeking around her friend, Sarah gasped. "Max?"

He was wearing the same clothes she'd admired on him that morning, only somehow he seemed to be filling them out differently now. The leather seemed to stretch around his biceps and across the hard muscles of his chest and shoulders.

"What the hell are you doing, Sarah?" he demanded, bristling with aggression.

Piper looked to Sarah. "Want me to stay?"

She shook her head. "No, go on. I'll walk Max out and see you later."

Turning to Max, she crossed her arms. "What are you doing here?"

"Telling you not to be stupid because you're mad at me."

Her brows rose slowly, her temper *not so slowly*. "Excuse me?" she snapped, and Max closed his eyes.

After a deep breath, his hands came up between them. "You don't even know this guy. It's not safe."

"Your sister does. She's known him for years. But even if she didn't, it's none of your business, Max. So again, what are you doing here? You could have texted. You could have called. You could have had enough respect for me after this morning to let me have one damn day."

Max blinked, and for a second she wondered if that look was the realization that, yeah, he could have done any of those other things, but until that moment, they hadn't even crossed his mind.

What the hell?

"It's time for you to go," she stated, walking past him and pulling the door closed behind her. Starting down the stairs, she refused to look back. "I have a date."

"You're *mad at me*," he said, following. But even a few steps behind, she could *feel* his presence there in the needy prickle of her skin wanting him closer. "What kind of date is it going to be when the only reason you're on it is because of another guy?"

Sarah pushed out the front door to the street, letting it swing shut without holding it. And then he had her by the arm, his hold gentle but firm. She whirled around to face him.

"What kind of date?" she repeated. "It's just a *first date*, Max." He winced, and she knew he was thinking about their first date and the schedule of intimacy he'd put together for them. Then his eyes hardened and he opened his mouth like he thought he had the right to say anything at all. Screw him. "You know what though, Max? I'm sort of sick of playing by a set of rules designed for someone else's benefit. I think I'll just do whatever the hell I want from here on out. And don't worry. I'll be sure to let you know how that works for me."

A guy rounded the corner behind Max, and she recognized him from the pictures Molly had sent to her phone.

She jerked her arm back and glared at Max. "My date's here."

Max looked down at the hand he'd been holding her with and then over his shoulder to where Dave Rayes was closing the distance between them. The other man's eyes shifted between she and Max, studying the exchange.

"Sarah?" he asked, coming up to them with a smile that didn't quite meet his eyes.

Max's hand fisted, and her heart skipped. But he kept it down by his side.

"Hi, Dave. Nice to meet you." Then because Max

was just standing there, she turned to him with a firm "*Good-bye*, Max."

Dave's jaw cocked to the side. And when the tension seemed beyond unbearable, his smile spread wide and he held out his hand. "You ready to go, Sarah?"

She was ready to go upstairs and hide, and have a good cry and maybe an entire straight-from-the-pan batch of brownies. But no way was she skipping out on this date because of Max. Even if he was the only reason she'd arranged it.

Taking Dave's hand, she answered, "Yeah, that sounds great."

Dave was parked around the corner, and when they got to his car, he held the door open for her before letting himself in. Once the engine started, he turned in his seat, slinging his arm over the back. "So I'm guessing that was the reason you were looking for a few hours of distraction."

Sarah let out a quiet laugh. "Pretty much." She met his eyes. "I'm sorry. I didn't know he'd be there. If you'd rather not go out—"

Dave laughed and shook his head. "Not a chance. You aren't the only one in the mood for some company. So what are you thinking? Movie, dinner, drinks? Any combination of the above?"

"Movie? You have one in mind?" she asked, curious what he'd say.

"Truth? I've been dying to see the new Marvel flick. Total sucker for the superheroes." Then he cut her a sidelong look. "But only if you're not a talker while it rolls. Sorry, but from the first preview to the last credit, I'm all about the show. Talking is for after."

Sarah laughed and relaxed in her seat. "A movie sounds great. With an option for drinks and discussion to follow."

He flashed her a crooked grin and pulled out onto the road.

———

Four and a half hours later, Dave parked in front of Sarah's building.

"Thanks so much for tonight," she said, a lightness in her heart she'd desperately needed. The movie had been a perfect distraction, and the chitchat over drinks after a great way to make a new friend. Which was all either of them was interested in. Dave had ended a relationship a month ago and wasn't looking for anything more than a break from contemplating his broken heart. Same as her. It had been perfect, right up until Sarah saw the man standing sentinel at her apartment door.

Her breath leaked out as everything she wanted and couldn't have rushed to the forefront of her mind..

"Umm, is that the same guy from earlier?" Dave asked, cocking a brow at her. "You want me take care of him for you?"

"No, I've got this," she said, turning back to him, an idea coming to her. "But maybe there is one little thing you could do for me."

Max hadn't moved from his spot by the wall, but his stare hadn't left the car once since it pulled up. She was sure he'd catalogued the make and model, along with the plates.

Dave opened her door for her and took her hand to help her out. They walked halfway to her door and stopped, at which point, she turned, grasped him by both sides of his face, and pulled him in for a firm kiss. She could feel his smile against her lips as she counted down from seven, which was the duration he'd suggested in the car. When they broke apart, he cast her a quick wink and walked leisurely back to the driver's side. She turned and walked up to the entry where Max was standing, his fists balled at his sides, the muscle in his jaw jumping with satisfying regularity.

If he didn't love her, then what the hell was he doing there, looking like he'd just suffered a fate worse than death?

Unlocking the security door, she stepped inside. "Night, Max."

Max stood by the upstairs bay window, every damn muscle in his body on lockdown. Barely able to move his jaw, he demanded through the line, "What else did she say?"

His sister was raking him over the coals after waiting half the morning to call him back. Yeah, it was none of his fucking business how Sarah's night had been, but that didn't change the fact that if he didn't find out in the next five seconds, he was going to lose his shit.

"Your phone is making funny sounds, Max," Molly answered casually, like she didn't know that every second she delayed was killing him. "It sounds creaky."

"Molly." He was giving her his most intimidating voice. She wasn't impressed.

After yawning in his ear, she finally relented. "She

said it was a second date, Max. Pretty much what she'd expected, whatever that means."

Max tried to swallow, but his throat was Sahara dry. He knew exactly what that meant, having basically written the book on what Sarah's second dates should look like. Why the fuck had he done that?

"Max? Yo—ill—re—"

He looked down at his phone and found it broken in his hand. Shit.

By the time Max had gotten it replaced and his backup info transferred, it was afternoon. He was throwing his leg over his bike outside the store, thinking about taking the afternoon to ride, when the message app started blowing up, one alert coming through after another in rapid succession.

A single string of text flashed past, tearing his world down around him.

Get to the hospital.

Chapter 20

CJ WAS STANDING AT THE NURSES' STATION WHEN MAX arrived, out of breath, a cold sweat coating his skin. "What happened?" he asked, the words scraping like gravel through his throat.

Red-rimmed eyes met his, and Max felt the floor drop out from under him. Gripping CJ's arm, he listened as his partner told him what he knew.

"...changing the oil...chest pain...neighbor found him...paramedics...heart attack...resting now..."

Jesus. Max could barely breathe. Carl was as close to a father as he had, and he wasn't ready to lose him. He also wasn't going to intrude when Carl's flesh-and-blood son was there. So instead of begging for a chance to speak to the man who'd been all the things his own father hadn't, Max asked if there was anything he could do to help CJ.

"You can go in and talk to him some. He was worried about you."

Max laughed, but the sound felt rusty leaving his chest. "Thank you, man."

When Max walked into the room, he couldn't believe how small Carl looked in his bed. He'd always been such a huge presence that seeing him like this, looking so vulnerable, was tough. The last thing the guy needed was Max breaking down in tears at his bedside though, even if that was what Max felt like doing.

So he kept it simple. "You scared the fuck out of me, Carl."

The older man looked up, his eyes glassy and swollen, but bright with recognition. Carl waved him closer, and Max pulled a chair beside the bed.

"No worries, kid. I'm not going anywhere. Least not until I see both of my boys settled."

Max ducked his head, knowing his eyes were dangerously close to watering up.

When he had his shit together, he pushed a grin onto his face. "You got a hell of a wait ahead of you then."

"Yeah." Carl nodded solemnly. "CJ said you and Sarah ended things. Too bad. I was thinking there was something special about her."

Hearing Carl talking about her after his heart attack was like having a dull blade twist through Max's gut. "She is special. But I think we'd be better as friends. If we can ever get back there."

"Friends? What the hell is that?" Carl scoffed, then started to wheeze and motioned for the pink plastic cup of water on the bedside tray. Max held the cup so the straw went to the older man's lips. After a sip, Carl leaned back like that had taken everything he had out of him. "Kid, you're doing it wrong if she wants to be friends. Talk to CJ. He'll straighten you out."

Max coughed into his hand as Carl winked, then closed his eyes, sinking deeper into his pillow. Max watched the rise and fall of his chest, thinking maybe he'd fallen asleep. But then, Carl sort of smiled. "Saw you together once. Didn't think it was friendship back then, or now."

Max's brow furrowed. "What's that? Back when? At

the bachelor party?" Yeah, he hadn't exactly been thinking about being friends that night.

There was a small shake of Carl's head, and then his
eyes squinted open. "At school. You only had a few
weeks left. I was still working up north and had a break,
so I pulled into campus thinking I'd catch you after that
Safewalk program you started. Grab a burger. They told
me you worked the last shift at the library and I headed
over, but you were walking with this pretty little brunette, and, kid, it didn't take more than two seconds to
realize what was going on there. You were in deep."

He hadn't realized Carl had ever seen them together.
Almost no one had.

"Why didn't you say anything?" Max asked.

"Figured you'd tell me when you were ready. Didn't
figure it would take until you met Joan, but you're a
stubborn sort." At Max's curious expression, Carl went
on. "You told me she reminded you of this girl you'd
waited too long with back in school. That you hadn't
even realized what the girl meant to you until it was
too late. *Sarah*. And damn, kid, just the way you'd said
her name."

Max's chest was tight, that ache he'd finally shoved
aside coming back.

"That was then, Carl. Things are different this time."

"Why, because she loves you? If you ask me, it's not
as different as you think."

Why did he feel like Carl was ripping him open by
talking about this stuff? Why did he want it to be true?
When it didn't matter anymore, because now Max
knew better.

"It's different because when it comes to all this

relationship stuff, Sarah's barely even dipped her toes in the pool. Carl, she had one real boyfriend, and he held her back from everything. When we started dating, she was so excited about finally just being another twentysomething with a patchy dating history. She wasn't looking for forever with me." Max closed his eyes. "She wasn't even looking for more than one night, but I talked her into giving me more. And then more after that, but I only did it because I knew she was leaving. She was going to be gone, so I wouldn't be able to hold her back."

"Hold her back from what, Max? A bunch of meaningless garbage most people are only willing to wade through so they can get to the deeper good stuff?"

"From having enough experience to know what she really wants. I don't want her to settle for me just because I'm the first guy who wasn't a total fuckwad to her. I don't want her to realize down the line that she wanted something different, but now she's stuck with me for her whole life."

"Her whole life, huh?" Carl asked, a twinkle in his tired eyes. "That what she was asking you for?"

It wasn't. She'd never once even suggested it. But still—

The door opened behind him, and CJ walked in with the nurse. "Time for some tests, Pops," CJ said, giving Max's shoulder a squeeze.

The guy looked like hell, the smile he'd strong-armed onto his face painful to see. Max stood and pulled his partner into a hug. "Get some rest, both of you. I'll be back tomorrow."

Outside the hospital, Max leaned against his bike and rubbed a hand over his face. He still couldn't get a full breath, but at least he knew Carl was okay. Good enough to try to help him with his love life. The old softy was in the hospital after a life-threatening scare, and all he wanted to talk about was Sarah.

Because he loved Max enough to know what she meant to him.

Thinking about Carl's last question, Max glared down at the parking lot.

Sarah hadn't asked Max for forever. She hadn't even asked him to love her back. All she'd wanted was a chance to see where they could go.

The only thing that had kept him from taking that chance was the look on her face three months ago when she'd told him how important it was to her that she not make another mistake like Cory. That she take the time to figure out what she really wanted before signing on with anyone else.

Yeah, Sarah thought she was in love with him. Joan had thought it too. But how was Sarah going to feel when she woke up one morning and realized she'd been rash in believing Max was *the one* when he was the man who'd held her back?

Max knew how that went, and he couldn't live with seeing the resentment in Sarah's eyes. He couldn't let her grow to hate him. And so he'd said no. Because he knew that if he got as much as a taste of what it was like on the other side of those boundaries they'd built, he'd want everything. His ring on her finger. Sarah wearing his last name. All of her days and nights, sweetness and smiles, for as long as they both lived.

―⁘―

This was a mistake. Sarah knew it, but she couldn't stop her feet from moving up the walk to Max's front door. To the house she'd fallen in love with, just like she'd fallen for the man who owned it.

He must have seen her coming, because the door opened before she could knock, and then Max was there, his eyes shadowed.

"Sarah," he said, stepping out to meet her. "Are you okay?"

Mr. Protective. She almost laughed, but she could see the strain in his face. This man didn't need another thing to worry about. "I'm fine, Max," she said, holding her hands together so she didn't press them against his chest. "I heard about Carl. I know he's in the hospital, and I was worried about you."

"You and Carl both," Max replied with a gruff laugh she didn't quite follow but somehow made her feel better. Then he was rubbing his hand over his face and taking a step back. "You want to come in? Or maybe just sit out here?"

She adjusted the oversize tote on her shoulder. "Have you eaten? I brought a few things, in case you hadn't. Simple stuff, so don't get too excited, but if you're hungry?"

Max's brows furrowed in thought, and then he laughed again. "I haven't eaten since lunch yesterday. So yeah, now that you mention it, I could probably use some food."

The fact that he hadn't noticed broke her heart and made her arms hurt from not wrapping them around him. "Okay then. Let's get you some dinner."

Heading into the kitchen, she started unpacking her

bag. She had a jar of sauce from the little gourmet place down the street, fresh pasta, a clamshell of spring salad, and a loaf of ciabatta that had still been warm when she took it off the shelf.

"Sit down, and I'll get this going," she suggested, but Max was already pulling out the pots and cutting board. They fell into that too-right rhythm together, moving seamlessly around each other as the table was set, the bread sliced, and the pasta drained. She was spooning the spicy, fragrant sauce over a plate of noodles at the stove when Max's arms came around her. It felt so right, so natural, that for one perfect second she melted into the hold. But then she remembered it was neither of those things, that she was only there because the man she cared for like no other was in pain and she couldn't stay away.

"Sarah, thank you for this."

"You should probably try it before you thank me," she said, trying not to sound as stiff as she suddenly felt.

"Not for the food. For being here. I hurt you. I know you're upset. I know you're a lot of things." He swallowed and let her go. "Just, thank you."

She nodded, her chest tight as Max reached around her and took the plate from her hands. "Sit down. Let's eat."

They talked about Carl. Max had been getting updates throughout dinner, and every bit of positive news seemed to lift a weight from his shoulders. The food must have been good enough, because Max devoured two plates of it, though Sarah barely managed a few bites herself. When the meal was finished, they washed the dishes together as they'd done so many times before. After the kitchen was clean, Sarah tried to keep the heavy sighs at bay until she got home, because it was time to leave, and that was the dead last thing she wanted to do.

Looking up from her tote, she watched Max where he stood in front of the sink, staring out the back window. He was tense. It was there in the hard line of his mouth, the set of his broad shoulders and the way his knuckles had whitened where he gripped the edge of the sink. Before she'd thought better, she was beside him, her hand over his.

"Max, is there anything I can do for you?"

"You should go."

She lifted her hand like she'd been burned, but before she could step back, Max caught her, a warning in his eyes. "If you don't, I'm going to do something we'll both regret, and, Sarah, I can't stand the idea of things between us being any worse than they already are."

He was right. She should go. To stay would be a recipe for disaster. But instead of simply acknowledging the wisdom of his words and backing out of the room, she stepped closer and did what she'd wanted from the minute she'd arrived. She placed her free hand against the center of his chest and looked up into his eyes.

"What if I don't go, Max? What if maybe, just for tonight, we put everything else aside, and tomorrow we go back to being whatever we are?"

Those dark brows pulled forward, turning his gray eyes stormy. "What are you saying?" he asked, but his tightening grip as he drew her closer told her he already knew. It told her his answer.

"I'm saying, I don't want to go." She moved her hand from his chest to his cheek, where she brushed her thumb against the rough stubble. "And I don't expect it to change anything."

Turning into her touch, he closed his eyes and kissed her palm. "I don't want to hurt you."

"You won't." She was the only one responsible for the inevitable pain to come, but she couldn't stop. Didn't care.

Pulling him closer, she went to her toes and pressed a kiss to his lips.

Max's arms wound around her back, one hand moving to play with her hair while the other went lower, covering her hip. Their mouths held that lingering contact as her body melted into him. It felt so good. But not nearly as good as when his hold tightened, and his lips parted against hers.

Her arms linked around the back of his neck, and she opened beneath the kisses that quickly escalated until Max's tongue was thrusting hot between her lips, and her fingers were clenching in the fabric of his T-shirt.

"Tell me to stop, Sarah." Her back met the counter, and then Max was hard against her. "Tell me if you don't want this."

Her breath was ragged, her heart racing. "Don't stop. I want this."

A guttural sound ground against her ear, making her clench with need. She looked up into Max's gorgeous face. His eyes burned over her as their ragged breaths mingled in the scant inches between them. "Max, please," she whispered.

He searched her eyes a second longer, and then his mouth came down over hers in a savage assault of clashing tongues, teeth, and lips. Her legs wrapped around his hips as he carried her back to the room where they'd spent so many nights together.

When her feet hit the floor, it was all about getting the clothes off as quickly as possible. She ripped her shirt over her head, wrestled out of her bra, and shucked her jeans and panties all at once. Max was just as efficient in getting rid of his T-shirt and jeans. And then she was backing onto the bed as he rolled on a condom before crawling over her, the hunger and intensity in his eyes enough to set her on fire.

"Just tonight," she whispered when Max was braced above her, their eyes locked. The words were for her as much as him.

"Just tonight," he answered, pushing deep with one long stroke. "*Sarah*."

Then he was moving inside her, telling her she was beautiful, perfect. Telling her he missed her and wanted her more than he knew how to handle. Telling her more than that with his eyes and his mouth and the reverent touch of his hands.

Max had been telling her for weeks he didn't want her love, but in that moment, she knew down to her soul that he needed it.

He hadn't wanted to sleep. But after all the nights of staring at the damn ceiling, on the night when he'd wanted to be alert for every minute of Sarah filling his arms, he'd ended up unconscious. It was the best night of sleep in recent history, and he hadn't wanted to wake from the dream where a sleep-mussed Sarah was scattering soft kisses around his face, neck, and chest…until he realized it wasn't a dream at all, and suddenly his hold on his consciousness was iron tight.

"Morning, handsome," she murmured, a contented smile on her lips. "Sorry to wake you, but I have plans with your sister this morning. I have to go."

His arms tightened around her, pulling her on top of him. "Five more minutes?"

Her quiet laugh was the sweetest sound he'd ever heard. "Five minutes, five hours. Sleep as long as you like. I just didn't want to leave without saying good-bye."

"I'm glad you woke me. But I meant five more minutes with you."

She searched his eyes and then nodded. "Are you okay, Max?"

He ran his hand from her smooth hip up to where her hair fanned across her back. Playing with the soft strands while he could, he nodded. Better than he'd been since she left. "Are you?"

Her fingers stroked over his stubble. "Yeah, I think I am. I feel different today."

"Different how?" he asked, wondering how many minutes he had left on his five.

"Like I think that maybe if *friends* is still what you want, it's something I could handle." She blinked down at him, as his heart began to pound. "I've missed you, Max. And I'm not worried about my emotions getting in the way anymore."

"You're not?" he asked, his throat suddenly dry as he tried to figure out why getting the best news in the fucking world felt not quite right.

"No, I'm not." She leaned down and pressed a kiss to his mouth before crawling off him. She was standing naked next to his bed, eyeing the floor before reaching down to scoop up her panties and bra. "So see you around, *buddy*?" she asked, stepping into her panties, the white cotton bikinis looking hotter on her than anything he'd seen before. Her bra was pretty and simple too. Cotton. White. Sexy as fuck.

She turned to him as she pulled the strap over one arm, then the other, until finally her perfect breasts were contained and his head started working again.

"I mean, unless you don't think it'll work."

"Wait, what? Fuck, no. Sorry, Sarah. I mean yes. I want us to be friends." Forget that he was hard enough to drive nails through a board. He sat up against the headboard and watched as she bent again, this time giving him the hottest view of her incredible ass while she gathered her jeans and shirt.

Christ.

"Sarah, more than anything I want you to be in my life." It was the truth. Not exactly the whole convoluted, messy truth, but enough for today's purposes. "I just want you to be happy."

"Great," she said, bouncing back onto the bed for a kiss. "That was the last one. Just a little left over from last night. I'm good now." Casting him a quick wink, she crawled off the bed. "See you, Max."

"Yeah, see you, Sarah."

Max took a shower and got dressed. He ate breakfast and tried not to notice how empty his place felt without Sarah in it. He rode out to the hospital and tried to ignore that sinking feeling in the pit of his stomach every time he thought about Sarah being ready to be friends because her emotions weren't in the way anymore. He talked to Carl and CJ and a nurse he cornered and tried not to wonder where the line for friends was drawn with Sarah. At least for a while, it probably meant texting her instead of calling when he had something he wanted to share with her, like that Carl was doing well and had asked about her, along with seven other cops and significant others who'd been at the hospital that morning.

He and Sarah texted back and forth a handful of times. But the relief he'd experienced with the first few easy exchanges had worn off, leaving him with an uneasy feeling in his gut as he stared at an emoticon message with a time stamp from the hour before.

What the hell was the matter with him?

He'd gotten everything he wanted. One more night of Sarah in his bed, her confident assurance that she could handle being friends, and a smiley face on his phone.

Walking up to the second-floor room with the bay window overlooking the street, he shook out his arms. Rubbed at his chest. But damn it, his gut was screaming at him that more than ever, things were wrong. He'd felt like this before, the day when he'd faced off with that junkie with the gun. When he'd known, *known* things were about to get critical.

That lives were on the line. Futures.

He looked around the freshly finished room that was going to sell this building for him. At the pale-sage walls and the white trim, the tall ceilings and the vintage crystal light fixture. The window seat with a bird's-eye view of a neighborhood perfect for a couple. A family. A life.

Jesus. He rubbed at that aching void in his chest again.

This was his favorite room in his house, but the only

time he spent in it was calling Sarah. He hadn't filled it with so much as a comfortable chair or even a cushion for the window seat.

Why?

Because he knew it wasn't really his. Not forever.

He had a plan. It was to sell this house. And so he let it sit empty.

But he didn't have to.

He stared a minute longer and then took a deep, bracing breath.

Pulling out his phone again, he called Sean. "Hey, man, I need a favor."

Four hours later, Sean had just pulled away and Max was on his way up to the house when Molly's text came through.

> Glad 2 hear U&Sarah got UR sitch straightened out. She said she's finally ready 2 move on. Guess thats gd 4 Dave. Date 3 2nite but Sarah says she's thru counting, whatever that means :-)

The recently replaced device clattered to the walkway as Max stood, clutching at his chest and wondering what the fuck was happening beneath his ribs. If this was what Carl had experienced two days before. Excruciating pain was ripping through the center of him like someone had just sunk a hatchet in it and started to hack, followed by a shooting sensation down his arm like he'd made a fist so hard the bones within were threatening to crack.

She couldn't be going out with that other guy. *Not after last night*. Not when he'd just—

Fuck!

Maybe that was what had changed. All Sarah had needed was the right guy to compare him to, and she'd seen that Max really wasn't the man she wanted. It was what he'd wanted—if you could call hating something with everything you had, but still believing it was for the best actually *wanting it*. And now he and Sarah could move forward as friends. So instead of imagining Dave gloriously struck down by lightning, maybe Max should be thanking him for giving him exactly what he'd wanted. A way back into Sarah's life.

He tried to think about hugging Dave, but all he got was the look in Sarah's eyes when she'd showed up at his place and what it had done to his heart. Basically the exact opposite of what was happening now. Sarah had made him feel alive. She'd made him feel connected. She'd made him feel loved. And somehow, someway she'd made him feel like he could love her.

Like they could love each other.

Only now there was Dave.

Max rubbed a hand down his face, his breath coming too hard to be healthy.

Damn it, what was he supposed to do now that there was some guy out there with a solid chance of scoring a piece of Sarah's heart? He could let her go. Step aside. Be happy for her.

Or he could stop being the guy too afraid of letting her down to risk letting her in. He could stop trying to take the choice out of her hands and trust that Sarah was every bit as smart and capable as he'd been telling everyone she was, and let her decide for herself what she wanted for her life. For her future. He could stop trying to protect her, stop trying to protect himself, and finally just say what he meant.

"Fuck that. I'm fighting for her."

Chapter 21

SARAH WAS JUST GETTING OUT OF THE SHOWER WHEN THE intercom buzzed. Thirty minutes early? What if she hadn't heard the door or even been home yet? Would he have left?

Throwing a towel around her, she ran for the intercom and panted, "Come on up." She darted back to her room where she threw on the first things she could find and grabbed her purse.

A knock sounded at her door, and she rushed down the hall. "Sorry to keep you waiting," she called through the panels as she undid the locks. "But you're earl—Max?"

He stood in the doorway, one hand braced on either side of the frame, his chest rising and falling like maybe he'd run from his place over to hers.

"Max, what are you doing here? Are you okay?"

He shook his head, wild eyes raking over her before looking past her into the apartment beyond. "Is Piper here?"

"No, just me," she said, reaching out to touch his arm. "Why, what's going on?"

He swallowed and then started in. "I'm an asshole, Sarah. A complete idiot who's been fucking things up with you since the day we met." He drew a breath and took a quick glance back over his shoulder. "Can I come in?"

She nodded, too stunned by his proclamation to say anything else.

"Baby, you've got to believe me when I tell you that I've tried so damned hard to do the right thing with you. But for all the rules I make around you, I just keep getting it wrong."

"Max, what are you saying?" she asked, not knowing where this was coming from or where it was going, whether that racing in her chest should be fear-based or maybe…something else. There was too much happening in Max's eyes to read.

His hands were on her upper arms, like he thought he needed to hold her to keep her there. Which was crazy considering the way she'd grabbed his forearms and was holding him just as hard, not willing to risk letting him turn away until she understood what exactly had brought him to her door.

"I'm saying that I'm scared to death of being the reason you'll end up hating me."

She shook her head. "I don't think I could ever hate you, Max. Be mad at you? Yeah, sure. But hate you? No. You're one of the best men I know. If you're worried because you don't feel the same way about me, or want the same things I do—"

"That's not it." He looked at his hands and let out a short, humorless laugh before releasing his hold on her arms. Which meant she should probably let him go too. "I've told you a little about my family. About what it was like for Molly and me when we were kids."

It sounded like they'd grown up in a war zone. "I remember. Your parents fought a lot." His father sounded like a verbally abusive tyrant, and his mother like she should have taken her kids and gone. Sarah knew his father had died after he left school and that his mother lived somewhere on the South Side.

"My mom is miserable," Max confessed, guilt in his eyes. "But when she was younger, once in a while, you could still get her to smile. It was actually pretty great when she did. But living with my dad…" He closed his eyes, like he was seeing a past he hated to revisit. "It killed that part of her. By the time she got out, she was a drunk. Bitter. Certain that if she'd left the asshole when she was young, she could have had a whole different life."

"So why didn't she?"

Max walked over to the window and stared out. When he turned back, his eyes were haunted, filled with regret. "Because of me. Because every damned time they went at it and she screamed that was it, she'd had it and she was taking Molly and leaving—I'd beg her not to go. I'd follow her around the house, Sarah. I'd cry and promise to do anything, as long as she didn't leave."

For a moment, Sarah could only stare. The thought of this big, strong man as a vulnerable child pleading with his mother broke her heart, but not as much as the other part of what he'd said. "She was going to take Molly and *leave you*?"

"She didn't think my dad would let her take me. And then when I was older, we looked so much alike that I think she didn't want to." He cleared his throat and met her eyes. "Yeah, she wanted to take Molly for years and years, but she didn't. She stayed, for me. And Sarah, to this day, every time she looks at me, that festering resentment is right there in her eyes."

It was reprehensible. Sarah hadn't been a fan of

Max's parents from the few stories she'd heard, but after this? Now she wanted to drive over to Max's mother's place—*the one he paid for*—and just shake her. Demand to know how she could have done something like that. How she could have been so selfish. So cruel. How she couldn't have loved him enough to want to protect him!

Instead, she took a slow breath, releasing it in a steady stream while she tried to get her temper in check. "Max, I'm so sorry. I don't understand how any mother could do that to her child. Let you feel responsible for her choices. Make you feel like you weren't worth protecting in the first place. I know I said I could never hate you, but in this moment, I think I really hate your mother."

A car alarm sounded in the distance, and the heat in the apartment kicked on. Max rubbed his palm over his face and looked back at her. "I don't talk about it. It's one of those things where in my head, I know I'm not responsible for what happened, but deep in the pit of my gut…that's different. And it doesn't take a shrink with fifteen letters behind her name to figure out where some of my commitment issues stem from, you know?"

Was that what this was? Max feeling like he needed to explain why he wasn't built to love her? Why he didn't think he could?

Her spine straightened, and she walked over to stand by the window with him. "I guess I could see that."

"When we met in college, all I could think was that you were a girl who wanted something different from what I had to give. And so I tried really, really hard to make sure I didn't push for something I shouldn't take. I liked your plans, your goals. I wanted you to reach them."

Her breath caught. "Because you didn't want me to resent you if I didn't."

"Yeah."

That single word hung heavy between them. Sarah reached for his hand, waited until he was looking at her, and then smiled. "Not gonna lie, I kind of wish you'd been just a little less of a good guy about that."

Max laughed, nodding before he looked back down to the street. "Me too, Sarah. From the minute I realized it was too late to change how you saw me, I wished I could take it all back."

"What?" Her smile was gone, a strange prickling feeling replacing that bit of warmth in her chest.

"I never should have warned you off. Not that I'd have lied to you. Never. But telling you I'd be no good for you, trying to prove it with that fucked-up kiss at the party and, worst of all, letting you go that last night—those were quite probably the worst mistakes of my life."

Her breath felt funny moving in and out of her lungs, too thin when she asked, "Why?"

Max's eyes met hers, stormy and dark. "Because I was in love with you. And if I'd been less afraid of getting in the way of your plans"—he swallowed and closed his eyes like it pained him to say the words—"if I'd been willing to fight and prove to you that I could be the man you deserved, then maybe…"

"What?" she asked with a humorless laugh. "We could have saved each other a few years of mistakes apiece? No Cory, no Joan, no adult sex ed class necessary?"

"Then maybe I'd never have had to let you go. Maybe I'd have been able to convince you to stay with me, to love me too. To want more than just one night with the guy who realized too late that he was ready to give you every night he had for the rest of his life. To be a part of your dreams coming true, rather than the reason you gave them up."

She was shaking, torn between tears and laughter over the bittersweet revelation that she'd been so wrong about such a pivotal moment in her life. He'd *loved* her.

But Max wasn't through breaking her heart. "Maybe I'd have been able to make you happy, Sarah. Maybe I'd have had you in my bed every night all these years. Maybe we'd have a baby between us by now. I mean, if you wanted." He turned away and rubbed at the back of his neck. "Hell, maybe you'd have made Sean's dreams come true for the Chicago Wyse from the start."

It was too much. She couldn't take another beautiful *maybe* that might have been.

"No." She needed to set the score straight.

Max swallowed, his eyes going to the floor. Sarah stepped closer, pressing her lips to that spot at the center of his chest. "The job I had lined up in Chicago before we moved for Cory's wasn't with Wyse. So no, but just to the part about Sean. Yes to the rest. To me loving you, to a happy life together. To everything that could have been ours."

She felt the air leave his lungs in a *whoosh* and then a single shudder pass through his big body that might have been a laugh, or might not. All those maybes sounded so right it hurt her heart to know they weren't. "Where does that leave us now?"

Max's arms came around her in a hold she wished would never end. "It leaves us with me, years later, on the brink of losing you again because I've been so fucking scared that if I go after you, I might wake up one day and find the only woman I've ever really loved wishing she'd left me."

She wanted to promise him that he wouldn't. That she loved him and it was real. But she knew it couldn't come from her. So she waited.

Max cupped her face in his hands, his work-rough palms as gentle as could be. "It leaves me too in love with you and all the possibilities not to take the risk, Sarah. I love you. I've never stopped. And I'm sorry for everything I've put you through, but baby, I'm willing to fight for you now. For us. I'm willing to wait as long as it takes for you to feel like I'm the man you can count on."

Her brow crumpled in confusion. "You're going to fight for me?"

She was right here, *waiting for him*.

He nodded, letting out a tight breath. "I can't fucking stand the idea of another man putting one finger on you. And it's not because I'm some caveman who doesn't want to share—okay, part of it's a caveman thing—but it's not about keeping anyone else from having you. It's about believing deep down inside that you're *mine*, the way I'm *yours*. That *I'm* the guy who can make you happy. But, Sarah, if you feel like there's even a possibility this Dave fucker could be the man for you... Damn it, I'm not going to step aside. Screw that. But I'll fight for you. I'll show you that even though I didn't get it right before, I can make it right now."

Her fingers were balled in Max's shirt, a bubbling laugh pushing up her throat. "Max, it does crazy things to me knowing that you want to fight for me. But I haven't seen Dave since that first date. He's a nice guy, but we're definitely only friends."

Max's chin drew back, and then suddenly everything about him seemed to change. "No second date? You aren't supposed to go out for a *third* tonight?"

She looked down at the pj's and robe she'd hastily grabbed off her bedroom floor, not sure where he would have gotten that idea. "I ordered a pizza to eat alone. It's supposed to be here in the next fifteen minutes. I actually thought you were the delivery guy here early when I answered the door."

Max ducked down, his mouth capturing hers in a firm kiss she was just sinking into when he broke away.

"Molly," he growled at the ceiling. Then looking down at Sarah, he asked, "Any chance you told her about our little schedule of dates?"

Sarah bit her lip, the tender just-kissed one. "Umm, it may have come up after you and I broke up. She's a really good listener." Wincing, she asked, "So I'm guessing she used it against you?"

"Yeah," Max laughed, not looking angry at all. "You could say that."

"But it worked?" Sarah asked. "I mean, you're here. All agitated and telling me you love me. Which you can't take back, even though I don't actually have another date lined up with Dave. Because I could totally get one, but I'd rather not, if it's all the same to you."

Max wrapped his arms around her waist and pulled her close, his nose buried in her hair. "Please don't. Just tell me I haven't blown it too badly over the last month. Tell me—"

"I love you." The words came from the very heart of

her. "But here are a few things I think you should know going in."

Backing her across the living room, he stopped in front of the couch and pulled her into his lap as he sat. "I'm listening."

"Whatever choices I make, Max, they're mine. I won't hold you accountable." He was nodding like he understood, but she wasn't sure he really did. "Even when I was with Cory—"

"That douche," Max graciously supplied.

"Yes, even when I was with him, and I felt like my world was closing in on me, getting smaller all the time, I didn't actually blame Cory. Yes, he cheated on me and lied to me and everything else, but the part where my life wasn't really what I'd hoped it would be...*that part* was on me. That part I never blamed Cory for, because *I* could have changed it."

Max nodded, stroking his hand through her hair. "I never want to hold you back from anything, Sarah."

She closed her eyes, leaning into his touch. Melting into his hold. "You won't. With you, my world gets bigger with every breath. There are so many things I want to do, to see, to taste and live. But I like the idea of us doing them *together*."

"Me too." Then pulling back, he looked into her eyes. "Were you really okay with just being friends?"

She wagged her head, squinting one eye. "Full disclosure? I was about ninety-seven percent sure you were in love with me too and just needed to figure it out for yourself. You're a man worth waiting for, Max Brandt. Besides, I was banking on you being way too smart not to see the truth sooner or later."

"I know I've loved you for eight years, Sarah. That was never a question. What I needed to accept was that it wasn't a bad thing."

"It's the best thing. All I could ask for."

Pressing his forehead to hers, he grinned. "Christ, I love you." Then after a breath. "Earlier, you said Molly's antics were what got me here. And yes, it's what brought me that minute, but, Sarah, I'd already realized how wrong I'd been before her text. I was already trying to make it right."

Her brows rose in question.

"Any chance I can convince you to pack a bag and come home with me? Maybe we can talk more about it there."

The pizza arrived while she was changing and throwing a few things into an overnight bag, and then they'd headed back to his place. When they walked through the door, Sarah stopped, shooting him a curious look when she saw all the plastic, cardboard, and brown paper piled in the front hall.

He'd forgotten about that stuff.

"I ran out of here in a hurry."

One slender shoulder shrugged. "Since you were running to me, I think I can overlook it."

Damn that smile. He was going to spend the rest of his life making sure she never lost it.

"Come on upstairs."

Leading the way, she looked back over her shoulder. "Did you move the bedroom up here? Oh, I can't wait to see it."

"Not the bedroom. Not yet, but I will." He'd have the yellow room done in a few days, and if that was the one she liked, he'd move them up the minute it was ready. "It's the office, actually. With the bay window."

Her smile spread wide, as she practically skipped down the hall. "Oh, I love that room! Nice spot for your office, with that gorgeous view and…"

Her words trailed off as she opened the door and saw what he'd done. Stepping into the room, she trailed her fingers over the polished wood of the solid yet feminine desk she'd admired that day they'd spent at the furniture mart. Eyes gone wide with disbelief, she turned around twice, taking in everything from the espresso leather couch they'd sat on together to the ergonomic executive chair she'd commented she needed for her office at Wyse, the area rug with bold script that had made her smile, and the black-and-white Parisian print she hadn't said a word about but he must have known she loved.

There were tears in her eyes when they met his. "This isn't your office," she whispered.

He shook his head and took her hand. "I want you to have everything you want, Sarah. I want to make you happy. And I want you to be fulfilled in every possible way."

"*You* make me happy. You didn't need to do any of this."

Pulling her closer, he pressed his forehead to hers. "I think I did. I want you in my life, Sarah. I want you in *our* home. Because that's what you've made this place feel like to me." Then taking her shoulders in his hands, he pulled back to meet her eyes. "But if you're not ready—"

She pushed to her toes and kissed him, an eager smile curving her lips. "I'm ready."

"But if you don't like any of it—"

Her arms linked around his neck, and she kissed him again. Longer. "I love it. All of it. And I'm keeping everything. Especially you."

Max laughed, his chest aching but this time with the purest pleasure. "Sarah."

She blinked up at him. "I love you. No buts."

"That's good." He picked her up and set her on the edge of the desk so her knees hugged his hips. "Because in the name of full disclosure, you should know I'm thinking this is one of those forever kind of loves. So you should maybe get used to the idea now."

She pulled him down for the sweetest kiss of all. "I love the sound of your maybes."

Epilogue

FUCKING SHOW-OFF.

Sean stood at the front of the Wyse Hotel circle drive and watched Max rev his engine and pull his bike to a stop. The pair of shapely legs—which was a fair fucking observation, not some pervy, inappropriate last-minute play on his part—bracketing Max's shifted, and then Sarah was stepping off the bike, somehow managing that frothy pile of white dress enough to keep her decent in the process. The girl had skills.

Max climbed off the bike, and despite the guy's inexplicable refusal to tux up for the big day, the off-white suit and open shirt collar looked damned good. And Sarah, well shit, she was a knockout. Total boner material—or she would be if she wasn't marrying one of his best friends.

"Sarah, you're breathtaking. Absolutely radiant," Sean offered, the filter between his brain and mouth fully engaged on Wyse Hotel ground.

"So awesome!" Molly squealed, bouncing over to her brother and future sister-in-law. Her feet were bare, and there was a bruise the size of a quarter next to her shin. How the hell had she gotten that? Sean felt a grin tugging at the corner of his mouth. With Molly, it could be anything. Like with that shock of hair in the front. When he'd seen her at eleven the night before, it had been purple, but now it was the hottest pink he could imagine.

"The ride of my life," Sarah beamed, toeing off the clunky motorcycle boots that had served as her "something borrowed" for the ride over and exchanging them for the pair of strappy heels dangling from Molly's fingers.

"You ready to do this, Big Brother?" Molly asked, sticking her feet into her boots.

The grin said it all.

"Like eight years ago." Then checking his watch, he looked back to Sarah. "Why'd we have to get here so early again?"

Sean knew why. Molly had clued him in the night before while making that little squick face of hers. Turns out Sarah was all about giving Molly too much information so she'd stick within a set of boundaries. No one had managed that before. Any time Molly even edged into inappropriate-question territory, Sarah gave her an answer sure to scar her for life. This time, the answer had to do with how hot it made her remembering Max pulling up to CJ's wedding in a tux, and that actually *being* the bride on the back of Max's bike this time might mean a little alone time was in order before the ceremony.

Hence the additional room booked for the pre-wedding activities. Definitely information Sean didn't need about his fucking favorite employee, but since Molly had to bear it, he got to too.

Sarah tugged Max down to whisper in his ear, and Molly grimaced beside Sean.

Max's brows rose, and then his expression darkened and Molly wasn't the only one uncomfortable with the way the heat had just cranked up there on the sidewalk.

Without taking his eyes off his bride, Max tossed his bike keys to Sean. "Yeah, so we're gonna go get cleaned up some before the ceremony. See you in about an hour."

Sarah had her finger hooked into a button on Max's shirt and was walking backward, leading him into the hotel.

Damn, Max had found his perfect match in that girl.

One of these days, Sean would find his own perfect match. He'd been looking. Even thought he might have found her once or twice. But despite everything on paper being *right*—the right name, the right school, the right looks and connections—he hadn't been able to pull the trigger. Then again, after the shit storm with his family these past few months, that was probably a good thing.

He'd been looking at things…differently.

But that was an issue for another day. Today he was Max Brandt's best man, and he had one last gift for his groom.

"Hey, Mol," he said, catching her hand in his before she could dart off. "Hang back a sec."

"Yeah?" She peered up at him with those vast sky-blue eyes and that open, excellent smile.

Dropping her hand, he took a step back, giving her a jut of his chin. "You get the rent from your roommate yet?"

The big blues cut away, and her smile firmed into a flat line. "I said I was going to take care of it."

She had. Six months ago, when the dick cheese holed up in her spare room stopped paying rent on time, sometimes skipping a whole month before giving her half of what he owed. Why the fuck did she have to be so stubborn? If she'd let him, Sean would've had the rent paid in full and the guy out within a week. But no. Not little Miss Independent-to-a-Fucking-Fault.

That tightening sensation across his chest warned him he needed to rein it in. Because as pissed as he was that this bullshit was still an issue—that Molly wouldn't let him help her—going nuclear beneath the awning of his hotel wasn't the image he was pushing, and it wasn't the answer either. But he knew what was.

"You remember what I told you, Mol?"

She didn't answer, but the subtle tensing of her shoulders told him she remembered just fine.

"If *you* didn't take care of it, *I* would." He'd warned her, but she hadn't listened.

Turning on her thick black heel, that sheer creamy skirt twirling around her pretty knees, Molly glared up at him. Her arms crossed, turning her into a miniature version of her brother. Well, a miniature hot and cute and not-quite-as-tough-as-she-wished-she-was version. Not that Sean would ever tell her that.

"Don't you even think about getting Max involved in this." Molly sucked a breath through her nose and narrowed her eyes at Sean. Damn, she was fun when she was fired up. But he had to stay tough—he was fired up too. "Sean, just stay out of it. This is my problem. My apartment. My life. My situation to handle. If I wanted your interference, I'd ask for it. Understand?"

He nodded once, watching as she started inside for the wedding that would be held on the garden terrace in ninety minutes with the reception immediately following.

He understood exactly. Molly had too damned much pride, and there was no fucking way he was going to stand by and let this *wad* screw her over for even one more day. Pulling his phone from his pocket, he hit Dial and waited for the call to connect. "Yeah, go ahead and load it up. Use the keys I left on the coffee table to get in... Yep, good."

Then with a twirl of Max's keys around his finger and the perfect mix of testosterone and righteous indignation thundering through his veins, Sean hopped on Max's bike, revved the engine, and took off for Molly's place.

"Get ready to meet your new roommate, babe."

About the Author

USA Today bestselling author Mira Lyn Kelly grew up in the Chicago area and earned her degree in fine arts from Loyola University. She met the love of her life while studying abroad in Rome, Italy, only to discover he'd been living right around the corner from her back home. Having spent her twenties working and playing in the Windy City, she's now settled with her husband in central Minnesota, where their four beautiful children and one naughty dog provide an excess of action and entertainment. When she isn't reading, writing, or running the kids, she loves watching movies, blabbing with the girls, and cooking with her husband and friends.

You can find Mira at www.miralynkelly.com. If you would like to be notified about release dates for the upcoming books in this series, sign up for her newsletter at www.miralynkelly.com/newsletter.